A DEATH *of*
NO IMPORTANCE

ALSO BY MARIAH FREDERICKS

Young Adult Novels

Season of the Witch
The Girl in the Park
Crunch Time
Head Games
The True Meaning of Cleavage

A DEATH *of* NO IMPORTANCE

Mariah Fredericks

Minotaur Books
New York

A DEATH OF NO IMPORTANCE. Copyright © 2018 by Mariah Fredericks.
All rights reserved. Printed in the United States of America.
For information, address St. Martin's Press,
175 Fifth Avenue, New York, N.Y. 10010.

www.minotaurbooks.com

Designed by Devan Norman

Library of Congress Cataloging-in-Publication Data

Names: Fredericks, Mariah, author.
Title: A death of no importance / Mariah Fredericks.
Description: First edition. | New York : Minotaur Books, 2018.
Identifiers: LCCN 2017044451 | ISBN 9781250152978 (hardcover) |
    ISBN 9781250152985 (ebook)
Subjects: LCSH: Murder—Investigation—Fiction. | Upper class—Fiction. |
    GSAFD: Mystery fiction.
Classification: LCC PS3606.R435 D43 2018 | DDC 813/.6—dc23
LC record available at https://lccn.loc.gov/2017044451

Our books may be purchased in bulk for promotional, educational,
or business use. Please contact your local bookseller or the Macmillan Corporate
and Premium Sales Department at 1-800-221-7945, extension 5442, or by
email at MacmillanSpecialMarkets@macmillan.com.

First Edition: April 2018

10 9 8 7 6 5 4 3 2 1

And finally, for my father

Acknowledgments

The first thank-you goes to my agent, Victoria Skurnick, who said this book was worth finishing. I asked her to always tell me the truth—and she does, making me laugh anyway. A sharper eye and a better heart do not exist in publishing.

Deep and sincere gratitude to the women of the Queens mystery writers group: Radha Vatsal, Laura Joh Rowland, Nancy Bilyeau, Shizuka Otake, Jen Kitses, and Triss Stein. I have also been blessed by the generosity and humor of my early writing colleagues, E. R. Frank, Carolyn Mackler, Wendy Mass, and Rachel Vail.

To my editor, Elizabeth Lacks: Real editors are hard to find. You are one of them. Thank you. Also thank you to the wonderful team at St. Martin's: Martin Quinn, Sarah Schoof, Allison Ziegler, Devan Norman, India Cooper, and Laura Dragonette.

Thank you, New York Public Library—where else will someone take your questions about the number of telephones in 1910 New York seriously, even joyfully? Thank you, *New York Times*, and your astonishing archives.

Thank you to Griffin Weiss, who goes to the library and eats ice cream with me afterward. And to Josh Weiss because without him, none of this would be possible or much fun.

Among the many books consulted for this novel:

The Gangs of New York by Herbert Asbury

Serving Women: Household Service in Nineteenth-Century America by Faye E. Dudden

Gilded City: Scandal and Sensation in Turn-of-the-Century New York by M. H. Dunlop

City of Eros: New York City, Prostitution, and the Commercialization of Sex, 1790–1920 by Timothy J. Gilfoyle

When the Astors Owned New York: Blue Bloods and Grand Hotels in a Gilded Age by Justin Kaplan

Low Life: Lures and Snares of Old New York by Luc Sante

The Triangle Fire by Leon Stein

In or about December, 1910, human character changed.

—Virginia Woolf

You see? The whole damn world believes in dynamite.

—J. B. McNamara,
convicted in the 1910 bombing of
the Los Angeles Times Building

A DEATH *of*
NO IMPORTANCE

1

I will tell it. I will tell it badly, forgetting things that are important and remembering things that never happened. In that, this narrative will be no different than any other. Only the specifics of what is forgotten and remembered will distinguish it as mine.

Why tell it at all, then—a story already so well known, concerning, as it does, wealthy families, a handsome couple, and murder?

Because the story you have heard is wrong. The headlines you've seen, the editorials bemoaning the sorry state of our modern world—all sincere and well intentioned. But since they did not know the truth of the matter, all quite beside the point.

Many decades have passed. There is no one now living who experienced that particular horror—except for myself. And who am I to claim to know the truth behind what may have been the first of the many Crimes of the Century?

Nobody. Less than nobody.

I was Charlotte Benchley's maid.

But before you dismiss my tale as a gain-inspired fantasy of a woman seeking brief, cheap fame, let me say something. It is the life's work of some to pay attention to things others wish to ignore. If it is your job to make sure the silver is clean, you must have a sharp eye for tarnish. If the sheets are to be smooth and straight, you must first find the wrinkles. In the matter of the Benchleys and the Newsomes, I saw the tarnish, the wrinkles, and the dirt.

If it is your opinion that a maid does not possess the capacity to understand these things, then there is no reason to read on.

But if your view is otherwise, please, continue.

★ ★ ★

At the time of the events that so enthralled the country, I had been with the Benchleys for a year. My former employer had died, leaving the bulk of her fortune to charity—and me without a job.

It was a time for funerals. The city had only recently stopped mourning the aristocratic Mrs. Astor when it became necessary to don the crêpe for my employer, Mrs. Armslow, who was connected by birth or marriage to the finest families in the city. In England, the rakish Edward VII was ailing. Leopold of Belgium had died. Earlier that year, the Apache chief Geronimo died in a prisoner of war camp at the age of nearly ninety. According to the newspapers, he had remained "one of the lowest and most cruel savages of the American continent," merely biding his time in captivity until he could return to the warpath.

After the memorial, Mrs. Armslow's niece, Mrs. Ogden Tyler, sought me out. Coming from a less affluent wing of the family, Mrs. Tyler had a democratic streak. Laying a light, friendly hand on my arm, she said, "Now you'll think me a perfect ghoul, but I must ask: have you found a new position?"

When I shook my head, she said, "Well, here's what you must do. A dear friend of mine, a Mrs. Benchley, has just moved here from Scarsdale of all places, and she is quite desperate. Her husband invented—or is it patented?—an engine. An engine part.

Or was it something to do with rifles? At any rate, whatever it is, the government wants it. The point being: oodles of money, but not the first notion of how to live. Live properly, I mean. What to wear, who to hire, what to serve. The poor woman has two daughters, as I do, and so I thought to myself, how can I help? And the very first thing that came to my mind? Jane. Jane's so clever, I said to myself. So clever and so discreet. Dear Jane, you're just what the Benchleys need. Won't you see them?"

When I arrived at the Benchley home in May of 1910, I came with the best recommendation an employee can have: the failure of all who preceded me. The Benchleys had taken up residence in a five-story town house on Fifth Avenue. Located on Forty-ninth Street, it was perilously close to the commercial district. But Mrs. Tyler had avoided the bullying ostentation of some of the newer millionaires and steered them to a house that was reassuringly modest—by millionaire standards at least.

I was admitted to the house not by the housekeeper or the butler, but a stout woman I later discovered to be the cook. She led me up the backstairs of the house to the main hallway. As I waited, I looked down corridors and into adjoining rooms to get the measure of the house. Each room was stuffed from floor to ceiling. Persian rugs covered the floors in profusion. A frieze above the entry depicted a scene from the Bayeux Tapestry, King Harold pierced through the eye. A jumble of curios crowded every surface. Vases from China and Turkey jostled with leather-bound books and Greek statuary. A sphinx and a china pug dog peered at me from the mantel. The sitting room resembled a tent, the windows lost behind an avalanche of drapery. A museum collection of paintings and portraits hung on the walls. An English tea set rested precariously on a French ottoman. A variety of gilded mirrors reflected and extended the chaos.

The neglect hinted at by Mrs. Tyler was obvious. The mirrors were dull, the rugs stained. Dust was everywhere. Coffee cups and used ashtrays sat unattended on the mantel. The coffee drinkers were of two different temperaments: one, careless, had left the spoon in the half-filled cup; the other, fastidious, had carefully arranged the cup back in its saucer and placed the spoon beside it. The smoker, I guessed, had been a visitor. The brand of cigar was far too exotic for the Benchleys as described by Mrs. Tyler, and clearly the staff was not used to emptying ashtrays. Muddy, discarded shoes—well made, but poorly tended—lay at the fireplace and something that looked disturbingly like animal feces lurked by an armchair.

A copy of this morning's *Times* lay on a table next to a chair that was some distance from the others; from the depression in the cushion, I guessed the man of the house sat there. A bookmark was stuck three pages into a copy of *Middlemarch*. Mary Roberts Rinehart's thriller *When a Man Marries* was spread-eagled on top.

Hearing the thud of footsteps on the stairs, I stepped back into the hallway, and saw Mrs. Alfred Benchley.

Mrs. Benchley, formerly Miss Caroline Shaw, was a plump, anxious woman. Her tea gown was hopelessly old-fashioned: mustard yellow with lace panels on the collar that looked as if someone had slapped napkins on her shoulders. The dark brown sash had not been properly tied. A careless laundress had shriveled the ruffles at the sleeves. The pins in her hair had not been fixed at the right angle, and the back was in danger of collapsing. In the grandeur of the house, she seemed a country cousin visiting her city relations, who sigh and count the days until "dear Caroline's" departure.

"I do apologize," she said breathlessly. "Did someone let you in? Oh, yes, of course they did. Shall we speak in the sitting room?"

Sweeping into the sitting room, she remarked over her shoulder, "We are in a complete muddle. I know everyone says it, but it is *so*

hard to find good help. I'm told girls no longer seek domestic employment; they prefer to work in shops or those dreadful factories."

It was not the first time I had heard the complaint. Mrs. Armslow
and her acquaintances had also lamented the ungrateful refusal
of the lower classes to employ themselves meeting the needs of
their betters. Houses that used to have sixteen or more servants
now made do with twelve or even nine.

I said, "It's not every young woman who finds her purpose in
service to others."

"My friend Mrs. Tyler says wonderful things about you. She's
been so helpful getting us settled in New York. I don't know what
we'd do without her. I understand you worked for Lavinia Armslow." I nodded. "And before Mrs. Armslow?"

"Before Mrs. Armslow, I worked for my uncle, the Reverend
Prescott. He . . ."

I hesitated. My uncle ran a home for women who once sold
themselves, but wished to find different employment. Until they
could, and until those who profited from their labors got tired of
looking for them, they stayed at the refuge.

Mrs. Armslow chose to devote a small part of her vast fortune
to my uncle's cause. Once a year, she would visit in order to survey
the souls in the process of salvation. During one visit, when I was
fourteen, Mrs. Armslow questioned the wisdom of raising an im-
pressionable girl among so many fallen women and offered me a
position. My future would be secured and my morals protected.

"My uncle administers a home where fallen women who seek
a better life may stay in safety," I told Mrs. Benchley.

Mrs. Benchley nodded. "I imagine it's terribly difficult for
these women to return to any kind of respectable life. And when
you think so many were forced into it, even *kidnapped*—"

She paused, eager for colorful stories of white slavery and innocent country girls seduced into vice. I asked, "Is it you who
requires a maid, Mrs. Benchley?"

"Me?" Her mind still on prostitutes, it took Mrs. Benchley a moment. "Oh, no. I have my own dear Maude, she's been with us for ages—Matchless Maude, I call her—and the girls need someone more their own age. But they're very different girls, and finding one person to suit both has been so difficult. I had thought, *Well, we'll simply get two,* but my husband doesn't see why they can't make do with one, and when Alfred doesn't see something, it's . . ." Nervous, she rubbed one hand over the other. "So, you see . . ."

"Yes," I assured her. "Your daughters require a maid."

With a sigh, she dropped her hands to her lap. "Oh, you do understand. And you speak English. They say the Irish do, but I can never make it out. Oh—you're not Irish, are you?"

"No, ma'am, from Scotland. When I was three."

Beaming, she said, "Well, that's fine. Shall we speak with the young ladies?"

As I followed her up the stairs, she said, "We'll see Charlotte first. She made her debut a month ago. Oh, it was marvelous, hundreds of people."

One of whom was Mrs. Gibbes, a friend of Mrs. Armslow's, who described the event as "a pageant of vulgarity," although she allowed "the girl was a pretty little thing."

Mrs. Benchley said, "Again, I must credit Mrs. Tyler; she told us who the best caterers were, where to get the flowers, who we must invite, and not invite, which is apparently *just* as important."

I wondered if there had been financial remuneration for Mrs. Tyler's helpfulness. She would not be the first lady of great name but small wealth to accept a fee for such guidance.

We were interrupted by a scream from down the hall. Mrs. Benchley hurried to the next door and flung it open. Coming up behind her, I saw a beautiful, airy room that looked directly onto the avenue. In the center of the room, a lovely girl stood in her chemise, fists clenched, glaring down at a bundle of light blue cloth heaped about her ankles. A sullen older woman in an ill-fitting maid's uniform stood at a safe distance.

"Whatever's the matter, Charlotte?" asked Mrs. Benchley.

"It's . . ." She waved a dismissive hand at the maid. "She's completely hopeless. She hasn't got the first idea what to do."

Small wonder. The bundle of cloth was a hobble skirt. It had only recently become all the rage among the fashionable set. A tight, narrow column of fabric, it obliged women to take tiny, awkward steps; in the words of its creator, Paul Poiret, it "freed the bust and shackled the legs." This made it difficult to put on, as one could lose balance as the skirt clutched tighter and tighter around the body.

This, it seemed, was my cue.

"If I may," I said, stepping into the room. "Mrs. Armslow's granddaughter had a skirt similar to this." Kneeling beside Charlotte Benchley, I said to the older woman, who I guessed was the Matchless Maude, "Could you bring that chair here? Miss Benchley, if you would hold on? Thank you."

Taking the skirt carefully with the tips of my fingers, I eased it over Miss Benchley's legs. A matching jacket was added. Miss Benchley surveyed herself in the mirror as I adjusted her hair and placed the hat. In some ways, she would be a pleasure to dress. She was not above seventeen years old, blessed with a natural hourglass figure, a slender waist, and graceful arms. Her fair hair was fine, but her smile, when she bestowed it, was beguiling. She had a look favored in that day, a childish prettiness, round in the cheek and bosom, with wide, admiring eyes. A girl not quite out of the schoolroom. If she knew how to give a man a look that hinted she might know a little of what happened outside of schoolrooms, then blush straightaway when he answered her look, so much the better. Charlotte Benchley, as I discovered, knew very well how to give that look.

She had a sharp eye for her own appearance and watched everything I did. She wanted the hat just so. The ruffles of the blouse should be out, not in. At one point, I wondered if her white gloves were too bright for the suit; did Miss Benchley perhaps have a gray pair? Miss Benchley did and was satisfied with the result.

Smiling, Mrs. Benchley said to her daughter, "I think she'll do very well for you, don't you?"

She put an arm around Charlotte's shoulders, but the young woman disengaged herself, saying, "And I suppose she'll be doing very well for Louise as well."

Mrs. Benchley said, "Your father feels . . ."

Charlotte tugged angrily on her gloves. "It's absurd. He brings us here, expects us to manage, then doesn't provide the most basic . . ." She waved a hand, dismissing any answer her mother could make. Then, taking up her bag, she said, "If you don't mind, I'm late. Very nice to meet you, Miss . . . *whatever your name is.* Who knows if you shall be here when I return."

As she said this last, our eyes met and I got my first clear look at the young lady of whom so much would be written in the months to come. I decided that Mrs. Gibbes had been very wrong to dismiss Charlotte Benchley as a pretty little thing.

As we made our way down the hall, Mrs. Benchley sighed. "It's too hard, having two daughters. I don't worry about Charlotte. She may be a tiny bit stubborn about getting her own way, but very often she's right. But Louise, my eldest! If you could help me with Louise, well, you would be I can't say what, but something *like* an angel. She's a good girl. Most modern girls don't listen to their mothers, and Louise does, you know. But poor thing, she can't seem to . . ."

We were at the third door. Mrs. Benchley whispered, "Well, you'll see what I mean. Louise!" She rapped on the door.

A small voice said, "Yes?" and we went in.

My first impression of Louise Benchley was of a turtle without its shell. As we entered her room, she was sitting at her dressing table, her shoulders hunched and her long back stooped. She was too thin. Her hair was a dull blond; it hung lank on her head, as if despairing of its lack of shape. Her gray eyes were large and protruding. Her arms were long, so long she often seemed to forget she had hands at the end of them. Clearly—and unfortunately—she did listen to her mother; her dress was much in her mother's style. The shade of cherry bordered on cruel.

She leapt up as we came in, extending an uncertain hand as her mother introduced us. Her anxiety was catching, and I found myself at a loss until I noticed an array of dolls upon her bed and remarked what a lovely collection she had.

"Oh." Louise glanced around the room. Truthfully, the dolls made me uneasy. Rows and rows of little female forms with porcelain faces and stiff, tiny hands. They sat suffocated in ruffles and ribbons. Mouths too perfect and small to permit breath, let alone utterance. Their hair was beautifully set—all human hair. I could not help thinking these creatures had cannibalized real women to make themselves even more perfect.

I said, "Perhaps you'd like to tell me what you seek in a maid."

Louise looked panicked. "Oh, I don't know. Anything."

Mrs. Benchley said, "Louise—" But she was interrupted by a shriek and crash from downstairs. Hurrying toward the door, Mrs. Benchley exhorted our better acquaintance and left.

Gazing at the dolls, Louise said, "Have you met my sister?"

"Miss Charlotte. Yes, I have."

She took the hand of one of the dolls, swung it as if they were walking together. "She belonged to Charlotte. When we moved, Charlotte wanted to throw them out. Maybe it was silly, but I couldn't bear it. Something you've had always, just tossed aside. I suppose that's why I have so many." She looked up at me. "I warn you now that I am completely hopeless."

"My uncle is a reverend. He says no one is completely hopeless."

"Well, I am. At everything. Everything that matters. Except badminton." For a moment, she brightened. "I am very good at badminton."

"Loyalty and athleticism—admirable qualities," I said.

"Oh, no," said Louise. "I'm a ninny. I have been all my life. But it didn't seem to matter as much when we weren't . . . as we are now. Charlotte managed straightaway. She's so pretty, so stylish. *Brave.* When we summered at the shore, she would go rushing into the waves, while I clung to Mother and cried. And it's the same here. Everything she finds so wonderful about this life I find impossible."

I asked, "What is it you find so difficult, Miss Benchley?"

She was quiet a long while before she burst out, "Anything with people. You try so hard to be pleasant and they just look right through you. You're not clever enough, not pretty enough, not . . . well, we certainly have money, but even that's not enough. Not unless you've been here a hundred years and have one of five last names."

I thought of how Mrs. Armslow used to rail against the Astors as upstarts, and said, "You would be surprised how quickly money can grow old in this city."

"It's all supposed to be so gracious, so agreeable. But in truth, it feels almost . . . violent. Everyone wants the same thing. All the girls hoping to marry into the same fortune. Their mothers wanting to be invited here or there. Oh, Mrs. Tyler tries to be kind—but all we are to those people is one less chance for them." She looked up. "Sometimes, in those rooms, it almost feels like they want to kill you."

Trying to make light of it, I said, "Well, I have never seen anyone stabbed with a fish knife or bludgeoned with a champagne bottle."

"Perhaps not," she said vaguely.

For a moment, I inspected Louise Benchley. I had met three

of the four Benchleys, and I could vividly imagine their failings as employers. And yet I felt the irresistible pull of need, the sense that I might be useful here. For Charlotte, I could do no more than any maid. But for Louise, there could be something else.

"Come," I said, taking her face and turning it to the mirror. "Let's have this hair the envy of every debutante in New York. Let the mothers bring their knives and cudgels. We are not afraid."

"I'm afraid I am afraid," said Louise, but she was smiling.

Of course, I did not take her talk of killing seriously. At the time, I thought Louise Benchley was indulging in that fascination with death that so many who live far beyond its grip—the young, healthy, and wealthy—have.

Tragically, she was far closer to the truth than I was.

2

It occurs to me that if I am to tell other people's secrets, I should have none of my own. I was one of the multitudes, a drop in the great flood that landed on these shores at the end of the last century. My father was another, my mother was not. She lies with my infant sister somewhere in the ocean.

My father was with me off the boat, I remember that much. It seemed to me the new place was just a crowd of strangers, packed in, irritable, shoving and desperate to get somewhere else. I leaned against my father's leg as we stood in line or else sat on the floor, knees drawn up. I must have whined to be picked up, because he snapped, "Stand on your own, you're a big girl, you can."

The bench I remember feeling happy about. A spot, a space of my own, where I could sit out of the press of people. My father suddenly excited as he said, "Come on," pulling me along and quickly setting me on the wood seat.

Then he said, "Stay right here," and stepped away.

I resisted when he tried to let go of my hand. It is not something I recall by sight, but by feel. My fingers fought with his, twisting and catching. I grabbed hold of his thumb in my fist, but he pulled loose. His knuckles and nails against my palm. A fistful of wool, thick and coarse—his trousers, I suppose, or sleeve. A slight burn and my hand was empty.

Do I have a last vision of him? I can't be sure. There were so many men in short, dark coats, running, hurrying. The one I remember, who looked over his shoulder as he walked away, is that man really my father? Or have I created a moment of doubt that my father never had as he ran to start his new life?

After that, I chiefly remember shoes. Mine, unable to reach the floor. I remember thinking *Swing* and being curious that they did.

For a long time, I thought the man who carried me away from the bench was my uncle. But my uncle says it was a policeman, who found my uncle's name and address, pinned to the back of my coat.

It is not every man who will take responsibility for the child his brother has abandoned. Nor every man who decides that a refuge for prostitutes is a likely home for a child; but my uncle is like that. Once he decides the right thing to do, he does it—without the sensitivity to complexities that make most of us hesitate to do anything.

I remember some education. I learned to read, write, and add with the women who came to the refuge. At eight, I can recall trying to explain to a Russian woman why the letter *C* should sound one way in "curtain" but another in "certain." I took sewing classes with the ladies, and when I got older, practiced my hairdressing skills on them.

In the evenings, after dinner, he would read to me from the Bible. Injustice was a favored theme: "Her officials within her are like wolves tearing their prey; they shed blood and kill people to make unjust gain." Also duty: "Even a child is known by his doings, whether his work be pure, and whether it be right. The hearing ear, and the seeing eye, the Lord hath made even both of them." That passage always left me squirming.

When Mrs. Armslow made her offer of employment, he did not argue, only asked whether I would like to go. I asked what the difference would be between life at the refuge and life at Mrs. Armslow's. My uncle outlined my duties, which would be mostly cleaning at first, then said, "Of course, at Mrs. Armslow's, you will be paid."

This had not occurred to me. The notion that someone would give me money for the tasks I did every day seemed extraordinary, intoxicating. I felt my uncle must be wrong. If I could earn money . . . visions of what I might do with it, as simple as buying an apple and as wild as traveling to London, leapt into my head.

I said quickly, "Then, yes, I would like to."

"For the money?" My uncle raised an eyebrow.

I knew my uncle believed that while it was difficult to do things without money, money was not a dignified reason to do anything. But I felt something new, a stubborn sense that I no longer wanted to answer questions about what I wished to do and why—and money might mean I didn't have to.

The day I left, my uncle said, "Do not get in the habit of thinking yourself a servant. Be diligent, be honest. But"—he could not find safe words—"know that we have work for you here."

"Yes, Uncle," I said. And hugged him for the first time.

★ ★ ★

And so I began my work with the Benchleys. I took my place in a small room on the top floor of the Benchley house, along with five other staff members. The ceiling was low, the furnishings sparse, and it was often cold. Many employers felt that servants would feel more comfortable if their rooms were similar to the humble dwellings from which they came. But it was quiet, and I had it all to myself.

Being maid to Louise and Charlotte proved to be two very different tasks. At first, Charlotte put me through a series of tests. Her comb was not placed right. Her dress had a crease. The bun that crowned her chignon was sloppy. Her dressing table was not arranged as she liked it—and a million variations on that theme. But as time passed, I gained her confidence, and the tests stopped. Charlotte received many invitations and was a full job in and of herself. And I had Louise to attend as well.

Poor Louise! Louise, the non-son, the eldest but not best, the lagger behind, the not quite as anything as anyone else. She was a girl always described at a deficit with others. She was not as pretty as Charlotte, not as gracious as her mother, and nowhere near as intelligent as she should have been, given how lacking she was elsewhere. Mrs. Benchley was deeply aware of her maternal responsibilities with regard to her daughters' futures. She joined several philanthropic causes, although it was difficult for her to keep them straight. Her enthusiasms were both energetic and democratic; she took up only those things embraced by the public at large. Most of her passions were harmless, although a few of them not so, as we were to discover.

In all things, she was guided by Mrs. Tyler. Through that lady's aegis, the Benchleys were granted entry to many of the finest homes. Through artful fawning and strategic expenditure, Charlotte managed to get herself invited to the Bartletts' for golf, to the Apsleys' home in Newport, and to tennis in Central Park with the very best crowd.

These entertainments brought her into contact with all the eligible bachelors of the day. The graceful, slightly balding Edward Lauder, who was a favorite with young ladies, such a favorite it was slightly odd he had not yet married. The hearty Henry Pargeter, who swung Charlotte around the dance floor with great vigor, at times only narrowly missing other dancers. And Freddie Holbrooke, who everyone understood was to marry his cousin Edith—everyone, perhaps, except Freddie.

The arrival of the Benchley girls had caused alarm among

New York families with daughters in need of a husband. The crop of suitable young men and widowers was somewhat small that year, and Mrs. Tyler's championing of the Benchleys met with recrimination in some circles. Mrs. Gibbes reminded Mrs. Tyler that she herself had two daughters, the fascinating, dark-eyed Beatrice and her pert younger sister, Emily.

"It's all very well to feel Bea's future is secure, as she and Norrie have practically been settled since childhood," Mrs. Gibbes said at an afternoon tea. "But you've still got Emily to think of."

You will have read much about "Norrie," or Robert Norris Newsome Jr. He was young, rich, and extremely good-looking, with dark brown hair that flowed to his collar, and sparkling hazel eyes. His smile was charmingly crooked, his manner joking—or spiteful, depending on your humor. And he was the sole male heir of Robert Newsome, head of one of the oldest families in New York.

The Newsomes were regular visitors to the Armslow house, and Mrs. Armslow sometimes compared their family line with her own. The Newsomes had been among the first English settlers to displace Mrs. Armslow's Dutch ancestors. The first Newsome of note was James, a devout Protestant who built a shipping business on the slave trade. Mrs. Armslow said there was a worthless streak in the Newsomes, which seems to have started with James's son, Edward, a drunkard and spendthrift. The family wealth was all but gone when Robert Newsome Sr.'s father built it back up in coal mines. The current Robert Newsome had extended the family's interests to steel, an industry heavily reliant on coal. This ensured the Newsomes' place as one of the wealthiest families in America.

In the words of those who admired him, Norrie was always doing something "unique." These bursts of uniqueness included driving the family car into a lake, throwing up on his cousin Phoebe's slippers at a supper dance, and getting expelled from not one but three schools. It was difficult to tell if it was his wealth, name, or looks, or his general air of not giving a damn about any of it, that insulated him from the censure that would have otherwise followed. But it was devoutly hoped that Norrie would settle down once married to Beatrice Tyler.

Adding to Norrie's controversial glamour was the fact that his family had just endured a scandal that made his antics seem like boyhood pranks. But more of that later.

I first heard Norrie Newsome's name in the Benchley house when the three ladies returned from a festive July 4 party at the Adamses'. Hearing them come in, I went to be of assistance. When I arrived at Louise's room, Charlotte was gleefully reliving the night's exploits. "What a drama Eleanor Adams makes of her health! Cough, cough, cough all night long. Pity the man who marries her, unless she dies the next day. And did you see Lucinda Newsome? What a frump! I barely got a word out of her all night, and when I did, they weren't worth the effort. Droning on about 'worthy service' and wanting to be a nurse. How can she be Norrie Newsome's sister?"

At the mention of Norrie Newsome's name, Mrs. Benchley and Louise exchanged nervous glances. Then Mrs. Benchley kissed her daughters and retired to her room.

When her mother had gone, Louise had spirit enough to say, "I liked Lucinda better than I liked Norrie."

Lolling on Louise's bed, Charlotte said, "You're just being perverse because he didn't pay attention to you. Norrie likes fun, and you're not fun, Louise."

"Perhaps you paid too much attention to him," Louise mumbled as I helped her into her nightgown.

"Why shouldn't I?" Charlotte sighed. "I think I might adore Norrie Newsome."

"You can't," said Louise. "What about Beatrice?"

Charlotte waved a hand in the air. "What about her?"

"She's engaged to him. Or almost is."

"And I suppose that would worry me if I cared what Beatrice

Tyler thinks." Charlotte rolled over and looked squarely at her sister. "But I don't."

★ ★ ★

I forgot about the exchange until a week later when I was carrying a basket of laundry down for cleaning. Mrs. Benchley had taken Louise out shopping, and Charlotte was in her room.

When the doorbell rang, I waited for someone to answer it. When it rang again, I went myself. Announcing, "Benchley residence, may I help you?" I saw a dazzling young man whose identity I could not immediately place.

He said, "You can tell Charlotte I'm here," omitting the pleasantries of "please" and "Miss." That was when I recognized Norrie Newsome, whom I knew from his visits to the Armslow homes.

"If you'll wait here, sir," I said, "I'll see if she will see you."

"Mr. Robert Newsome," he said easily. "And she will."

I went upstairs to Charlotte's room and said through the door, "Mr. Newsome to see you, Miss Charlotte."

There was a sound of hurried action; then the door opened and Charlotte appeared. She was flushed, her eyes bright, her body tense.

To me, she said, "Not a word to Mother or Louise, understand?"

"Yes, miss." I was not surprised. It was irregular—in fact, vulgar—for Norrie Newsome to call on Charlotte in such a casual manner. Only if a young man knew a young lady very well could he simply stop by her home, and Charlotte and Norrie could hardly know each other that well.

Carefully composing her face into its brightest, most carefree expression, she went downstairs, crying, "Norrie, you're too sweet! Tell me we can go for a drive!"

"Car needs repairs," I heard him say. "But if you're specially nice to me, I'll take you to the Waldorf for lunch."

"Does 'specially nice' mean I pay for the lunch?" Charlotte said archly.

I raised my eyebrows at this boldness and higher still when Norrie responded, "Well, since you offered . . ."

When they had gone, I wondered why on earth Norrie New-some should pay a call on Charlotte Benchley, so recently of Scarsdale. His summer exploits had been more outrageous than ever; possibly he was no longer as welcome in some houses. I had also heard that Robert Newsome Sr. had limited Norrie's funds in an attempt to rein him in; there were rumors that his accounts were overdrawn at several restaurants and certain stores no longer extended him credit. That would partly explain Charlotte's desir-ability as a dining companion.

But his manner had been distinctly offhand, so I decided it was unlikely his intentions were serious. He might enjoy flirting with the new money, but ultimately, he would get around to mar-rying Beatrice Tyler.

3

Always, in accounts of murder, there is a scream. A cry of alarm that alerts the reader that the normal course of life has been disrupted. And so it was a scream that marked the beginning of the dark events in the Benchley house—in this case, a scream of pure joy. It was September, the first autumn day with a chill in the air, and I was just debating the storage of some of the Benchley girls' lighter dresses when I heard it. The screamer was Mrs. Benchley, who had just discovered that Charlotte was engaged to Robert Norris Newsome Jr.

As I passed the sitting room, Mrs. Benchley called out to me, "Jane, oh, Jane, come in. We have the most wonderful news!"

"Mother!" Charlotte glared.

Mrs. Benchley flapped a hand at her. "It's only Jane. We must tell Jane."

To save her mother from further scorn, I guessed, "Is . . . there good news?"

"Charlotte," said Mrs. Benchley, clapping her hands madly. "Charlotte is engaged to Norrie Newsome! But it's a great secret.

Even Mr. Benchley doesn't know yet. So you mustn't breathe a word . . ."

Secret, indeed. When society heard that Norrie Newsome had jilted Beatrice Tyler to marry Charlotte Benchley, it would do more than breathe. It would howl.

Charlotte pleaded, "Mother, you won't tell anyone else, will you?"

"No, pet, not a soul. It'll be a hush-hush secret from now on, I promise. We shan't tell another soul about it."

"About what?" Louise appeared at the door.

Her mother told her the news. And with that, the second element of murder came into play: tears.

★ ★ ★

Louise wailed on her bed while I dabbed her forehead with a damp cloth and offered sweet tea when she gave herself the hiccups. I couldn't blame her. It was not enough that Charlotte was pretty and Louise not. Or had so many suitors and Louise none. Or got three marriage proposals while Louise endured her mother's comments on spinsterhood. But that her younger sister should make such a match, it was too much to bear.

Sipping at the tea, she asked, "Did I . . . did I say I was happy for her? I think I forgot to."

"You congratulated your sister, Miss Louise." It was true, she had. Right before she burst into tears and fled up the stairs.

"Do you think I could go away, until it's all over? Disappear somewhere?"

"I don't think so."

"Maybe I'll just die," she said wistfully. "Get some awful disease and die."

"Unlikely," I said. "And thank God unlikely. Don't wish for such things."

Nonetheless, I could see her point. Every friend of Mrs. Benchley's would express sympathy over her plight: the second daughter married before the first. The girls who made up the smart set would delightedly tsk at Charlotte. Did she think it was fair to be so cruel to her poor dull, plain sister?

As I went downstairs to fetch Louise a fresh cloth and a bowl of ice, I dreaded to think what the Tylers would say. They had played a long, patient game, looking past Norrie's youthful "pranks" with expectations of revived financial fortune. Now to have him snatched by a chit who had been in New York society barely a year!

On the stairs, I overheard Mrs. Benchley say, "So lovely that Norrie proposed in the park. But it's too bad he couldn't get his grandmother's ring out of the vault in time."

"I don't mind," said Charlotte. "I want the ring Norrie wants me to have. I don't mind waiting."

"No," said Mrs. Benchley, placating. Then in a low voice, "Dearest, the Newsomes will explain to the Tylers, won't they?"

There was an uncomfortable pause.

Then Charlotte said, "I don't know. I haven't met any of his family, aside from Lucinda. His father's in Europe."

A note of anxiety entered Mrs. Benchley's voice. "But Mr. Newsome *has* given his approval?" Her daughter did not answer. "Do you mean to say Norrie hasn't told his father yet?"

"I mean to say I don't know and I don't care."

So the Newsomes did not know. That didn't bode well for Charlotte. Norrie's father might well insist on the more suitable Tyler match. And yet—Mr. Newsome was in a poor position to object to his son marrying a young lady whose family was not part of New York's fabled Four Hundred, having done something quite similar when his first wife died.

I have mentioned Caroline Astor. Toward the end of her life, the old woman took to railing against the decline of public morals, particularly among young women, "who smoke and drink and do other terrible things." When she died, her absence seemed to free New York society from its former notions of propriety. Her own son, John Jacob, all but rushed from her funeral to divorce court and then headlong into an infatuation with a teenaged girl. (Whom he would marry—and leave widowed, but that is another story.)

Still more shocking was the marriage of the venerable Robert Newsome (coal) to Rose Briggs (no discernible assets). The groom was fifty-two, the bride seventeen. Which, as many pointed out, was quite thoughtful as he had a daughter the same age, and wouldn't she get along splendidly with her new mama? When it was discovered that the two girls had actually attended the same school, and Mr. Newsome had first spoken with his bride when she served him punch at a parents' day luncheon, society was beside itself with gleeful condemnation. Mr. Newsome had escaped the tensions by taking his new wife on a tour of Europe.

The Newsome children suffered. The mere mention of her stepmother's name brought Lucinda to tears. Norrie was positively savage on the subject. At a party, someone was foolish enough to inquire after his new stepmother. His response: an impromptu performance of the wedding night. The part of his father was played by a cigar, the part of his stepmother by the blancmange.

Lingering on the second-floor landing, I heard Mrs. Benchley say with uncharacteristic firmness, "But Norrie must speak to his father. And to your father—I know we are not the Newsomes, but that doesn't mean proprieties can be ignored."

Raising her voice, Charlotte answered, "Norrie will speak to both fathers when he's ready. And until he's ready, Mother, not a *word* of this to anyone. It stays a secret. I won't have Norrie rushed."

★ ★ ★

But if a secret known to two parties is no longer a secret, then a secret known to Mrs. Benchley might just as well be printed on the front page of *The New York Times*. Whether Mrs. Benchley fretted to the cook who informed her husband who happened to be the Hollicks' chauffeur, or Louise was observed red-eyed at a party, who can say? But in a matter of weeks, the rumor began to spread that Norrie Newsome had proposed—actually proposed!—to Charlotte Benchley in Central Park, and the two were now secretly engaged.

Society was shocked, and when society is shocked, it whispers. Some did not believe the story. Why had no announcement been made? Why did Charlotte have no ring? Perhaps, opined the skeptics, Charlotte had misunderstood Norrie's attentions. Perhaps she had *intentionally* misunderstood, hoping to pressure him into matrimony.

People watched the pair carefully at any event attended by both. But Norrie's behavior toward Beatrice was as it had always been, and Charlotte gave no sign of concern. Some took this as a happy sign the rumors were false. Others sought answers.

One afternoon, Mrs. Tyler found time to visit the Benchleys at home. Coming upstairs to refresh herself, she caught me in the hallway with "Jane, I'm so pleased to see you. Walk with me a little, and tell me how you are getting on with the Benchleys."

"There have been improvements," I told her.

"I'm sure, I'm sure. You've done wonders with Louise. She was looking almost alive at Eliza Talmudge's luncheon the other day. I believe she even *spoke*."

We turned a corner, coming far enough away from the stairs for privacy. Mrs. Tyler's praise became more pointed. "The Benchleys are certainly keeping better company these days. You must know that by seeing who comes to the house."

"I rarely answer the door," I said.

Mrs. Tyler leaned in closer; we were at the secrets stage.

"Come now, Jane. You see everything, even the things you're not supposed to. You saw when my dear aunt soiled herself at lunch and took her off without fuss. You saw when that awful butler was guzzling the contents of her wine cellar. And you must have seen Norrie Newsome come to the house."

Mrs. Tyler had done me a favor; now she expected one in return. "He has been to the house," I admitted.

Mrs. Tyler's eyes darkened with anger, and I added hastily, "But I have heard nothing of a formal engagement. There is no ring, and I believe neither father has been spoken to."

Mollified, Mrs. Tyler nodded her appreciation. As she turned to go back downstairs, she paused to examine the wall. "This paper is dreadful. I must tell Caroline. Or"—she glanced at me—"perhaps I'll forget to mention it."

Two weeks later, a small item appeared in a newspaper called *Town Topics*. It would be only the first of many stories written about the Benchley/Newsome affair. And one of the very few in which all the people mentioned were still alive.

* * *

When Alice Roosevelt drank too much or visited her bookie, *Town Topics* regaled the American people about the latest doings of the president's daughter. When the Metropolitan Opera House was overrun with fleas, *Town Topics* warned its readership of the dangers of infestation. When an unnamed gentleman shaved another gentleman's legs, *Town Topics* wondered why he would wish to do so—and then extorted a tidy sum of money from the gentleman to ensure he would remain unnamed. The debutante who vomited into a potted plant, the young man who put his hand up his hostess's gown, the financier who kept a mistress tucked away in Greenwich Village . . . they could all expect to read about themselves in *Town Topics*. Not, of course, that anyone of taste would admit to reading *Town Topics*.

On the morning the engagement story broke, I was taking Charlotte's newly pressed dresses back to her room when

Mrs. Benchley rushed up to me, crying, "Jane! We are in the newspapers!"

She thrust a piece of paper into my hands. "Read it. There, read there . . ."

> Can it be true that Newsome Jr. might be following his papa down the aisle with a young lady—pardon us, *another* young lady? Rumor has it the junior miss in question is none other than Charlotte Benchley, she of recent great wealth and nonexistent pedigree. How democratic! (But how many of the swellest of the swell today were anything at all twenty years ago?)

"What if Mr. Benchley sees it?" Mrs. Benchley wailed. "Or hears of it from someone else—and I haven't told him!"

Publicity might not be a bad thing for Charlotte. Norrie would be forced to either acknowledge the engagement or break it. But Mrs. Benchley was right: this was not news Mr. Benchley would appreciate being kept from him.

With sudden inspiration, I said, "But you have not known about this, Mrs. Benchley. It's been Charlotte's secret. She didn't want to tell you until a formal arrangement was settled."

Seeing Louise hovering, I said, "In fact, the only person she told was her sister." Louise was incapable of lying. If her father demanded to know if she had prior knowledge of the engagement, she could at least be truthful.

"But how shall we behave at breakfast?" Mrs. Benchley worried. "What if, as we are sitting there, Mr. Benchley reads of this?"

"Then you will be shocked and delighted," I told her.

Breakfast at the Benchleys' was a chaotic affair. There was still no housekeeper, and they had hired and lost three kitchen maids in as many months. So I had decided to supervise the newest girl myself, as I was tired of cleaning all manner of jam, butter, and hot liquid from the Benchleys' clothes.

As usual, Mr. Benchley sat at the head of the table. In my time with the family, I had rarely seen the head of the household. He was often in Washington. At breakfast, he sat concealed by his newspaper; at dinner, focused on his meal. The talk, giggles, and snarls of his family might have taken place in Africa for all they disturbed him.

On his left, Charlotte stared into the distance. On his right, Louise sat moving her eggs around her plate. Across from her husband, Mrs. Benchley wrung her napkin under the table. When Mr. Benchley cleared his throat, the Benchley women jumped.

"Someone," he said calmly, "has blown up a building."

Cries of "What?" and "How awful!" rang out in the dining room. In the confusion, I drew near to peek at the newspaper. On the front page, a photograph of a building in flames. The headline: L.A. TIMES BUILDING BOMBED! 21 PEOPLE DEAD!

Mr. Benchley said, "The ironworkers' union has demanded the city's trades unionize. Here"—he laid the paper on the table, open to the scene of destruction—"you see the union's latest bargaining tactic."

I instructed Kathleen to refill the teapot, accompanying her to make sure it was done correctly. From the kitchen, I heard Mr. Benchley say, "Charlotte. Louise."

I heard Charlotte say, "Yes, Father?"

"Yesterday, a gentleman congratulated me on the engagement of my daughter. I said, 'Thank you, but you are mistaken.' I am curious how he came to be so misinformed."

Wanting to see the reaction, I cracked the kitchen door. Charlotte said lightly, "Norrie Newsome has asked me to marry him. I intend to accept."

On cue, Mrs. Benchley burst out with "Why, Charlotte!"

Mr. Benchley interrupted her, saying, "In that case, would you ask young Mr. Newsome to pay me a call at my office?"

"Of course, Father."

"This afternoon, if possible."

Opening his paper, he added, "One day is enough for this family's name to be in the newspapers."

4

There are women who seem to make a friend of everyone they meet. Then there are some who have only a small circle of companions. And then there are those rare truly friendless individuals.

When I was young, I thought I would be one of the last. But when I was eleven years old, I met Anna Ardito.

I was pouring a bucket of water on the refuge steps, a necessity in summer when the entryway became both bed and toilet for many. It was early in the morning, and the street was quiet. I heard a scream, so fierce that I dropped the bucket. A second scream set me running down the street.

In the middle of the alley, flanked by tenements, there was a girl being attacked by two men. One had hold of her arm, the other a fistful of her hair, which he used to yank her almost off the ground. The girl kicked wildly. One foot managed to catch him in the groin, and he dropped her. A moment later, she had buried her teeth in the other man's arm, and he let go as well.

I thought she would run, but she flung her skinny arms wide and shrieked. One man took a hesitant step toward her, but she snatched up a stone and threw it at him. The other man got a handful of horse manure in his face. They cursed at her, but they were beaten, and they knew it, so they turned and ambled back down the alley.

She was brushing the dust from her dress when I ran up to her, asking, "Are you all right? Will they be back?"

"Back?" She gave a contemptuous look behind her. "No."

"Should we go to the police?" I asked.

"No police. They are animals, yes, but they are also my brothers."

She started walking, and I fell in beside her. "Then why do they act like that?"

"They don't want me to go to work. They say only whores work in factories. I say, 'No, whores sit around all day and drink like you.' And now they made me late, so . . ."

She ran down the street and disappeared.

I was not in the habit of missing people. But over the long, steamy summer days, I found myself wandering down to the alley on the off chance I might see the girl again. One evening I caught sight of her as she propelled herself forward in a queer, jerky gait, straggly curls bouncing, skinny arms swinging.

"Hello!" I shouted.

She stopped, startled. Then she pointed in recognition.

An invitation of some kind seemed called for. The back door to the refuge was open. I asked, "Do you want to come in?"

With a short "Okay," she followed me through the back and into the kitchen. Aileen, who had been with the refuge for years, put on the kettle and let us sit on the work stools by the sink. I listened as Anna answered my questions about her life. She was a little older than I was. Her family was from Italy, and she lived with two aunts, an uncle, a lot of cousins, and her brothers.

Then she said, "What about you? No mother? No father?"

"No."

"Me neither. My aunt says, 'You need to get married.' I say,

'You need to get married.' She says, 'We been married.'" She paused. "You want to get married?"

No one had asked me that question before. I thought, *Married*, but nothing came to mind. "I can't see him," I said.

Anna grinned. "Me neither."

There were weeks she did not come by. The factory kept her for as long as fifteen hours a day. One day, she arrived when I was mending one of my uncle's shirts in the kitchen. She picked up a spool of thread with a needle stuck in it, and asked, "How much you want for this? Just the needle. I don't need the thread."

"Take it," I said.

"No, I pay you. I lost mine this afternoon, and they sent me home. Said get another by tomorrow or . . ." She shrugged.

"Don't they have needles?"

"Sure. But why use theirs when they can make us bring our own? We bring our own thread, scissors . . . even sewing machines."

But it wasn't what the women had to bring that made Anna the most angry, it was what the factory made them pay for. "Five minutes late because your kid threw up on you, you get a fine. Foreman bumps into you while you're cutting, garment rips, you get a fine. Don't pee fast enough, you get a fine. During the slow season, they take two dollars out of your pay. We pay for lockers, we pay for the chairs we sit on. The other day, I say, 'Who owns this factory? Me. You make me buy that locker, this chair, my needle— it's all mine now.'"

I laughed. "What did the foreman say?"

"He smacked me."

I stopped laughing.

That spring, the foreman refused to let a pregnant woman go to the bathroom. Anna hiked up her skirts, pulled down her pants, and peed on the floor. Then, standing on her chair, she encouraged the other women to do the same. No one else did, but they banged their chairs on the floor until the woman was allowed to pee. At the end of the day, Anna was told to leave and not come back.

The things I didn't know made her angry. That we sometimes saw things differently made her angry. Once, a woman presented herself at the refuge, saying she had killed a man who insisted on giving her protection in exchange for two-thirds of her earnings. When he tried to raise it to three-quarters, she cut his throat. She hoped my uncle would shield her from the police. My uncle said she could stay, but if the police came, he could not lie to them.

The police came. The woman was arrested. Anna was furious.

"I thought your uncle was a good man. How could he hand her over like that?"

"What was he supposed to do, break the law?"

"Of course!"

Another difference. I cried when President McKinley was assassinated—partly out of a sudden affection for the sickly Mrs. McKinley, but mainly out of fear that one shabby man could kill the president of the United States. And feel no remorse; Czolgosz had said, "I killed President McKinley because I done my duty. I didn't believe one man should have so much service, and another man should have none."

"I can't understand it," I said to Anna. "Feeling you've done something wonderful by killing someone."

There was a long, uneasy quiet. Then Anna said, "Well, you can't understand it. Good for you. I understand it fine."

I started to feel that she disliked me; she came by less and less. When Mrs. Armslow offered me a job, I told myself that Anna was simply part of everything I was meant to leave behind.

But the day before I left, she arrived with a package for me. It was heavy, wrapped in cloth. "Bread," she said. "From my aunts."

"Please thank them for me."

She nodded, then said abruptly, "A servant?"

"Should I be a bank president?"

"Sure." I laughed. "Or a teacher. Not a maid. Not . . . you. Not Jane Prescott."

Suddenly, she reached out and hugged me very hard.

"I didn't know you thought so well of me," I said, half joking.

"Not really," she said, letting go. "Look, no good-byes. I'll see you?"

"Yes," I said.

"We'll stay friends?" Now she sounded uncertain.

"Yes," I said.

And we did stay friends. We stayed friends as Anna was fired from the factory for passing out leaflets. We stayed friends as Anna went to work with the International Ladies Garment Workers. We even managed to see each other during what would become known as the Uprising of the Twenty Thousand, when the city's garment workers went on strike. These days, she teased me less about my work. But her temper still flared if we disagreed, so I tried as a rule to avoid certain subjects.

Working for the Benchleys, I had one day off a week. The day Mr. Benchley demanded to see Norrie Newsome happened to be that day, and I was having dinner with Anna. In the early evening, as I rode the elevated train downtown, the man sitting next to me was reading the newspaper. The *L.A. Times* bombing was on the front page. There was a large photograph of the fire brigade standing beside the empty shell of a brick building. A screaming headline: L.A. TIMES BUILDING BOMBED! PUBLISHER OTIS CALLS THE BOMBERS "COWARDLY MURDERERS" AND "ANARCHIC SCUM."

I suspected Anna had anarchist friends, but I had never asked whether she was an anarchist herself. Part of me thought it was better not to know.

We met, as we usually did, at Morelli's, an Italian restaurant owned by her uncle Salvatore. It was a small room with a black and white tiled floor; the tiles were chipped, and the chair legs caught as you got up or sat down. Her uncle sat silently at a back table. As I came in, he raised his fingers to say hello.

Anna greeted me by saying I looked tired.

"One day," she said as we sat down, "we'll organize the domestic workers. Now *that* would really scare them. Just think—they'd have to live like the rest of us." She grinned, tore off a piece of bread. "So, how are your Benchleys?"

"Agitated," I said. "Charlotte has made a great match—or we think she has. The young man has yet to speak to her father. Or his father."

"Who cares about fathers? She's not marrying them. So, who is this young man?"

"He is Robert Norris Newsome Jr. Norrie to his friends."

Anna frowned. "His father is Robert Newsome?"

"Yes," I said. "Robert Newsome the industrialist."

"Robert Newsome the murderer," said Anna, as if she were saying nothing more provocative than Robert Newsome the horticulturalist or Robert Newsome the wine collector.

Seeing my face, she explained, "The Newsome family owns many mines. One mine, the workers went on strike. Newsome sent in Pinkerton agents to break it up. Three men and one woman were killed. Then of course, there's Shickshinny . . ."

A waiter brought our food. Anna broke off, saying, "This is not talk for meals."

"We're not eating yet. Tell me."

Sighing, she said, "Several years ago there was an accident at the Shickshinny Mine in Pennsylvania. This mine, a lot of children worked there. Boys, nine, ten years old. They're small, right? They can get in these little spaces. There's a cave-in. The boys are trapped. Parents screaming, 'Dig them out, dig them out.' Mr. Newsome says, too risky. Could wreck the whole mine. Eight dead kids—who cares? The Shickshinny Mine disaster, you never heard of it?"

Embarrassed, I shook my head.

Pouring wine for both of us, Anna said, "You think they'll really get married?"

"I don't know. He's an unpredictable young man."

"Maybe tell her to reconsider. Although I'm sure a little thing like Shickshinny wouldn't bother Charlotte Benchley."

There was a commotion at the back of the restaurant. In a mix of Italian and English, Anna's uncle directed the newcomer to the bar. A moment later, an enormous block of ice approached our table, and the man holding it said, "Anna!"

Anna leapt to her feet to greet him. There was laughter as they realized the block of ice stood between them. When the ice had been settled behind the bar, the man returned, wiping his hands and smiling broadly.

Anna introduced him. "Josef, this is my very good friend, Jane Prescott. Jane, this is the very kind Josef Pawlicec."

The man who shook my hand was shorter than I was and seemed made up of leftover parts gathered from the shop-room floor. His brown hair rose in uneven clumps, giving his head the appearance of an old shaving brush. His potato nose had been broken, and his teeth looked like they had been pushed into his gums at odd angles with gaps in between. But his eyes were large and warm, and when he said, "Very pleased," in a heavily accented voice, there was an awkward sweetness.

"Do you work together?" I guessed.

They both hesitated. Then Anna said, "Yes," and he nodded in agreement.

He held out his hand to me. "Is nice to meet you."

When he had gone, Anna sat down again. "He's very . . ." She waved her hands in the air. "But a good man. In fact . . ."

But whatever that fact was, she decided not to share it with me, adding it to an ever-growing list of things we did not talk about. As we ate, I wondered what it was about me that made me so suspect.

That I worked for wealthy families? That my uncle was a minister? Or was it simply my character? My stupidity, I couldn't help feeling.

It was not until the end of the meal that I worked up the courage to ask Anna what she thought of the L.A. *Times* bombing.

Trying to keep my tone light, I said, "Mr. Benchley says labor was behind it."

"Of course he does. The workers are trying to unionize. The newspaper does not wish to. A faulty gas pipe causes an explosion— well, it must be those terrible unionists."

"It wasn't a faulty gas pipe," I said.

"Of course not," said Anna, sarcastically. "It was bomb-throwing anarchists."

"Who else would it be?"

"Ask the owner of the L.A. *Times*."

"Why would he blow up his own building?"

Anna threw up her hands. "So people like you will say, 'Oh, how horrible! Yes, things are bad for workers, but this is too much! We cannot listen to such people.'"

"I never said that." But I wasn't sure what I had said or meant to say. And so neither of us said anything until we had left the restaurant.

Anna said, "Do something for me."

"What?"

"Come with me to a meeting someday. Hear for yourself what we believe."

I hesitated. Anna had just admitted to me that there was a "we," a larger group that she was part of. She was trusting me, and I didn't want to discourage that.

"What if I hate it?" I asked.

"Would you hate me as well?"

"Of course not."

"Then who cares?"

I wanted to believe Anna would not care. And yet . . . "Why?"

She sighed. "Maybe I don't want you to waste your life serving the Robert Newsomes of this world. Maybe I'm a matchmaker and I want you to meet an intellectual."

"So I can waste my life serving him?"

"We believe in equality of the sexes. Maybe he serves you."

Now that we were joking, I said, "Well, maybe to meet such a man, I will come."

Anna walked me to the elevated. As I turned to go up the stairs, she asked, "Do you know what Taft said about the Pullman Strike?"

I shook my head.

"When the soldiers shot six strikers, he said, 'They've only killed six of them. Hardly enough to make an impression.'"

Kissing me good-bye, she whispered, "I wonder, how many do we have to kill? To make an impression."

★ ★ ★

A few days later, Norrie presented himself at Mr. Benchley's office. A week later, Mr. and Mrs. Newsome wrote that they would be returning home for the Newsomes' annual Christmas Eve ball and the engagement would be announced that night.

Whatever Mr. Benchley had said to Norrie, it had clearly made an impression.

★ ★ ★

I would like to tell the reader that I was filled with high purpose after hearing of the Shickshinny Mine disaster. That I found my domestic duties demeaning, and resolved to pursue a new and nobler life. Then you would be reading about an altogether more forward-thinking woman. Sadly, I am not that woman, so you will have to hear how I was preoccupied with the task of getting the Benchley women through the Newsome ball without social disaster.

All three Benchley women were in a frenzy. Each felt the need to look her best. Dresses were presented, tried, and rejected in the hundreds. Shoes and jewelry matched and unmatched. We had little over a month to prepare, and as Mr. Newsome had business concerns in Pennsylvania, the Benchleys would not meet their future relatives until the actual day of the ball. A charming note had arrived from Mrs. Newsome, regretting the lack of time for a "simple tea where we might all get to know one another." But she was sure the Benchleys understood, "as this will be my very first Newsome Christmas gathering as hostess." Charlotte received that statement with a toss of her head and a comment that the staff was doing all the actual work.

Society opinion on Mrs. Newsome was violently split. Her mother-in-law, the formidable Mrs. James Newsome, had left the country rather than associate with her. Not even the revival of the famed Newsome Christmas Eve ball had enticed her back, as she let it be known that any event hosted by "that woman" would certainly end in disaster.

The new Mrs. Newsome's supporters pointed to her tireless efforts on behalf of charity, her humility, and her touching devotion to her husband. Of course she was beautiful—"catastrophically so" in the words of one admirer—and the kind of beauty that allows a woman to break the rules is always fascinating. A besotted bartender at the St. Regis Hotel had created a drink for her, the Rose Blush, a delicate concoction of vodka, sugar, egg white, and crushed berries. To those who found the New York of Caroline Astor dull and fusty, Rose Newsome was a breath of fresh air. Who else would have the insouciance to host her first ball a mere month after returning from Europe?

Mrs. Benchley could not decide which camp she belonged to. On the one hand, she was about to be related to the lady. On the other, as a newcomer herself, she was anxious about an association with a woman many regarded as an interloper.

I did find it odd that Mrs. Newsome had not made more effort to invite the Benchley women to her home. Were the Newsomes playing for time in the hopes that Norrie's attachment would burn itself out before a formal announcement had to be made?

At a time when her guidance would have been most welcome, Mrs. Tyler was notably absent. And Mrs. Tyler was not the only one who was avoiding the Benchley home. Norrie's visits had become fewer and fewer. When he did come, the visit usually ended in an argument.

According to Bernadette, a house maid who was braver than I about listening at doors, Norrie's affections were not much in evidence. "She's doing all the talking, he just grunts. She asks him, does he like her dress today? He says it's 'quite Scarsdale.'"

Raising my eyebrows, I said, "What did Miss Charlotte say to that?"

"Not a thing. She wants to marry this boy bad, doesn't she?"

"I guess so."

"Then she asks what that stepmother of his is up to—you know, trying to make it her and him against the new wife."

"Did that work?"

"No. Right in the middle of her talking, he says he's meeting friends. She says, 'What friends?' He says, 'You don't know 'em.'"

Bernadette sipped her coffee. "Now that does make her mad, so she says, 'I know Beatrice Tyler quite well, thank you.' And he goes, 'Only because your mother paid her mother for the privilege.' Is that true?"

I shrugged as if I had no idea.

"So, anyway, she says, 'I saw you dancing with her at the

Bitterhoffs'—all night you was dancing with her.' And he says, 'So what if I was? She's a very fine dancer, and I get tired of the Scarsdale Trit Trot.'"

"Oh, dear." I cupped the mug in my palms. "What did she say to that?"

"Well, she was mad, you could tell. But she's still trying to be sweet, so she goes, 'You're upset because of those notes.'"

"What notes?" I asked.

It was Bernadette's turn to shrug. "Don't know. He just said, 'Those notes are a joke, I told you.' Then he left." Bernadette sat back in her chair. "She should throw the ring in his face, you ask me."

"She doesn't have one," I reminded her.

Then, a week before the ball, Norrie left the city.

In her room, Louise whispered, "He said he wanted to go to Philadelphia to look at his business. Charlotte said he never cared before, why now?"

"Perhaps because he is getting married," I said, trying to put the best face on it.

"Maybe." Louise leaned against the wall with her hands behind her back. "Charlotte's horribly upset about it, though."

People being upset reminded me. "Miss Louise, has your sister ever said anything about notes?" She shook her head. "Letters sent to the Newsome house?"

"No. Why?"

"Nothing. I must have . . . misunderstood."

That evening, when I went to Charlotte's room to prepare her for bed, I found her dabbing at her eyes with a cloth, a bowl of ice water nearby. Seeing me, she sniffed and said, "I hate when my eyes swell up. I look like a pig."

Charlotte was so rarely self-critical, I felt sympathetic. "I'm sure Mr. Newsome will return from Philadelphia soon."

Taking up the brush, I began pulling the pins from her hair.

"And it's a good thing, isn't it, that he wants to take on more responsibility?"

"Is that what he's doing?" she asked, looking at her reflection in the mirror. "Jane? When you worked for Mrs. Armslow . . ." She turned her head to look at me, and I had to stop brushing. "You must have seen them, Norrie and Beatrice. Together."

"A lot of people came to Mrs. Armslow's," I hedged.

She fell silent, closing her eyes as I pulled the brush through her long, light hair. There were things I knew about Norrie Newsome that I had not shared with the Benchleys. By now, I told myself, Charlotte must know what kind of man she was marrying. But seeing her distress, I felt guilty that I had not been more honest.

I said, "Miss Charlotte, if you have any misgivings, perhaps it's best to wait. You haven't known Mr. Newsome for all that long."

Her eyes opened, hard and suspicious.

"Oh, I shan't wait," she said to me. "The engagement will be announced at the Newsome ball on Christmas Eve, and I don't care who doesn't like it or what they have to say. I am marrying Norrie Newsome, and there is nothing anyone can do to stop it."

Sadly, all three of those predictions would fail to come true.

5

Now I must give my account of the events of Christmas Eve 1910.
I am not the first person involved with the case to do so. Thomas J.
Blackburn, the inspector in charge of the investigation, has written
his memoir. The sister of the person convicted of the crime told
her story. For a time, one of the Newsomes' footmen, a Daniel
O'Reilly, made his living taking groups by the house and regal-
ing them with the "dark and bloody doings" of that night. I suspect he sensationalized. For one thing, he claimed it was he who
found the body. Since I am the one who found it, I know that is
not true.

The schedule for the evening was as follows: an early, intimate dinner at the Newsome house with only the two families
attending. Then everyone would retire upstairs to change for the
ball, which was to begin at nine thirty. The engagement would
be announced at midnight with a champagne toast. Prior to this,
Norrie was supposed to present Charlotte with his grandmother's
engagement ring in the Newsome drawing room so the young

couple could have a moment of private joy before the celebrations.

In a triumph of tact, I persuaded Mrs. Benchley to forego Maude's services for the evening, on the grounds that it was too much pressure for the elderly woman. I would supervise the dressing of all three Benchley ladies, with the help of Bernadette and a new girl, Mary. Bernadette's housekeeping skills might have been lacking, but she moved quickly when she had to and could not be flustered. And Mary was a sweet girl, excited to be at such a splendid party and determined to prove herself.

Household and servants took separate cars. I had never been to the Newsomes' New York home. The mansion took up one-quarter of an entire city block. It was gray stone, four stories high, its dark shingled roof rising in spires and turrets. Staring up, I counted twenty double windows. The front courtyard was large enough to accommodate a carriage and horses. Girded by massive wrought-iron gates, it seemed a fortress, proof against whatever ills lay beyond its walls. A crowd, kept back by police, had gathered on the street to watch the glittering arrivals.

As we walked to the servants' entrance, I wondered what the house looked like to Rose Briggs when she first saw it. Did she feel she had entered a fairy tale? If so, was she Cinderella or the bride of Bluebeard? To me, there was something forbidding about a house so absolute in its power. But maybe it was just the gray December evening.

I did not see the Benchleys again until the break between dinner and the guests' arrival. Bernadette, Mary, and I waited for the Benchley ladies in a third-floor guest room. Mary was beside herself, unable to believe the splendor of the house. Had I seen? They had pine garlands, threaded with gold all throughout the place! Had I seen? The gold ballroom with four grand chandeliers? Four! Had I seen? The silver punch bowl you could bathe in! Had I seen? The marble staircase, curved and rising two floors?

Had I seen, had I seen, had I seen? Mary's excitement made the work easy, and I felt less oppressed by worry.

A very different mood took hold of the room when the Benchley ladies returned from dinner. Mrs. Benchley was talking a great deal, Charlotte barely, Louise not at all. From the tension, I guessed the dinner had not gone well.

As she was yanked out of her dress by Bernadette, Mrs. Benchley babbled to Charlotte, "Isn't she lovely? Not at all what I expected. She's very sweet with him, really."

Standing stiff as I removed her dinner dress, Charlotte said, "I don't know what you mean, Mother."

"The sister's a drab creature, isn't she? So different from Norrie. He seemed in high spirits. Talked so much during dinner." From her tone, I guessed that his conviviality was fueled by alcohol. "Nice for you, Charlotte. Not all men like to talk. I don't think I got three words from Mr. Newsome. Of course, things did get awkward with Norrie's teasing. You can't blame Mr. Newsome for losing his temper . . ."

"Mother," Louise interrupted, "do you think these earrings are right?"

"Oh, yes, dear, lovely." Then, "I mean, those notes *are* terribly frightening."

Charlotte said sharply. "Mother . . ."

"I'm sorry, Charlotte, but I think Mr. Newsome is right, Norrie shouldn't joke about the notes. When you think of what happens these days. Bombs, assassinations."

Starting, Mary said, "Bombs, ma'am?"

Pleased to have someone take an interest, Mrs. Benchley said, "Yes, the Newsomes have received these awful notes, threatening all sorts of things. Mr. Newsome says it's the work of anarchists."

"And Norrie says it's a prank."

Oblivious to the threat in her daughter's voice, Mrs. Benchley said, "The last note actually mentioned tonight's ball. Mr. Newsome wouldn't say what was in it, but I overheard him telling your father he's arranged for extra security, and I should think so."

So the notes were not love letters from Beatrice or bills from outraged vendors. The image of the *Times* building, a charred shell, came to my mind. *How many do we have to kill, to make an impression?*

Arranging Charlotte's hair, I said, "Why should anyone want to harm Mr. Newsome?"

Mrs. Benchley said, "Lucinda said it was to do with some mining accident . . ."

"*Mother.*" Now there was no mistaking Charlotte's tone, and Mrs. Benchley fell quiet. Like a scolded child, she pulled at a button until I stilled her hand under the pretense of adjusting a bracelet.

That brought the discussion to a close. As we added the last touches, I was quite satisfied. Mrs. Benchley was absolutely correct in dark green velvet. Louise's hair was high and proud. A lavender dress gave her figure elegance—at least when she remembered to hold her shoulders back—and her silver slippers demanded to dance.

Charlotte was breathtaking in a Worth gown that alternated swathes of ivory and rose. Discreet threadings of pale green silk in the skirt and her gloves enhanced the impression of a flower in bud. Her bright hair was up in a Psyche knot, to reveal the slender length of her neck, and bound by a band of cream satin, also embroidered with filaments of green, which changed her eyes to sapphire. Heartbreakingly beautiful, I thought, then wondered why I had chosen those words.

Mrs. Benchley said, "Charlotte, dear, you look pale. Take one of my Pep Pills."

I have spoken of Mrs. Benchley's enthusiasms. That month,

the Object of Desire was Dr. Forsythe's Pep Pills, which promised brighter eyes, better breath, and a general return to youth and vigor. The pills had come into fashion after being championed by Mrs. Talmudge, and Mrs. Benchley swore by them.

Charlotte snapped, "Oh, for heaven's sake, Mother, I don't need your silly pills!"

Ever the peacemaker, Louise said, "Here, Mother, give them to me. I'll see she takes one." Mrs. Benchley smiled and handed the little box to Louise, who put it in her reticule. Then they followed Charlotte out.

I stood, my mind emptied of all the tiny details that had until seconds ago filled it completely. Perhaps it was the anxiety that comes with the start of any gathering, but I could not get Mrs. Benchley's story of the notes out of my head. The words of Galatians drifted through my mind: "Whatsoever a man soweth, that shall he also reap."

But fears loomed large when you were tired. Norrie was probably right and the notes were just a prank. The whole city knew the Newsomes were giving a ball tonight. Easy enough for any disgruntled employee to make mischief.

"Miss?" I looked up to see Mary standing on tiptoe. "Miss, I was wondering . . ."

She glanced at the door. Bernadette said, "She wants to watch them come in."

Mary said, "From the balcony, no one'd see. Just to see how they look and all."

Grateful for the distraction, I said, "I think it's a fine idea, Mary. Let's go."

She gave a gasp of happiness and ran to the door. "Are you coming, Bernadette?"

"Me?" Bernadette reclined on the bed. "It's enough to dress 'em. I don't have to stand around and clap."

The second-floor landing above the entry hall was high enough that we could watch without being seen, yet see everyone who arrived. Above our heads hung the vast crystal chandelier, now revealed in all its relentless glitter. The eye was drawn to it, but it hurt the eyes, and I kept my gaze focused downward.

Mary said, "Ooh, what she's wearing! I've never seen anything like it."

I searched the crowd gathering in the foyer. It was not hard to spot Rose Newsome—for, of course, that was who Mary meant.

Rose Newsome may not have been the most beautiful woman I ever saw, but I can think of no one else to claim the title. She had black hair, as dark as in a fairy tale, her pale skin a wonderful contrast. She must have brought the dress back with her from Europe, for it was a style I had not seen before, shocking in its simplicity and boldness. It began as a column of unadorned white damask for the skirt, pale silk for the bodice. But over the bosom, there was a swathe of stark black velvet, arranged at an angle so that it extended from her shoulder like a raven's wing. At the wing's lower tip, her buoyant figure trembled dangerously high above the bodice edge. Her hair was piled loosely on her head, dark tendrils falling about her neck. Rubies glinted in her hair and at her wrists; idly, I wondered if those were the same rubies she was rumored to have received from Mr. Newsome. Yet for all her feminine abundance, there was a touch of the child in her full, expectant mouth and her wide long-lashed eyes; one could easily see how she had dazzled her husband—and every other man in the room—and still charmed so many of Mrs. Armslow's friends.

Of Mr. Newsome, I saw chiefly a bald head, broad shoulders, and an important stomach. The younger Newsomes stood aggressively apart. Norrie was resplendent in his evening dress. Lucinda looked uneasy in her ball gown, her earnest, plain face incongruous set above its satin puffs and swirls. She stayed close to her brother, I noticed, often touching his arm. Strange, I thought, in siblings so different, to see such affection.

"Who's that?" Mary perched on tiptoe to see the new arrivals.

"That," I said uneasily, "is Mrs. Tyler and her daughters, Beatrice and Emily."

I held my breath as I watched the Newsomes receive the Tylers. Everyone seemed cordial—at least from this distance. Beatrice had chosen a rather daring midnight blue gown, which set off her pallor and dark hair quite well. She did not, as far as I could see, linger overlong with Norrie, but quickly moved on to Lucinda, and the rest of the family.

Then I saw a tall young man step in behind the Tyler ladies and smiled. This was William Tyler—or, as he had been known in the family, Willy Billy Bear. When Mrs. Tyler gave birth to William, a cousin promptly dubbed him Willy Billy Bear. The name stuck. Although he had the floppy clumsiness of the very tall, William was a handsome young man with reddish brown hair and the hopeful eyes of a spaniel puppy.

The Tylers were soon swallowed up in a swell of arrivals. To Mary, I pointed out Vanderbilts and Van DeWalles, Astors and Armslows. Edward Lauder, Henry Pargeter, his cousin Edith, Eleanor Adams . . .

Mary said, "You know everyone, don't you, miss?"

Then she put a hand to her pocket, perhaps to warm it, and went pale. Pulling her hand free, she showed me a small bunch of fabric. Frantic, she whispered, "Miss Louise's gloves. She left them. These are hers, aren't they?"

They were. Obviously in the chatter about bombs and Pep Pills, we had all forgotten Louise's gloves. Louise's hands, large and strongly knuckled, were not her best feature, and she was particularly shy about them. Panic might prevent her from finding a suitable excuse to return upstairs. Someone—I—would have to go down to her.

"I'm sorry, miss," Mary wailed. "I'm so sorry."

"Don't worry, Mary. We can easily find Miss Louise and return her gloves. You go back to the room and keep Bernadette company."

"Yes, miss. Thank you, miss."

I smiled. "It's easily solved. Now stop crying, no one's died."

6

But it was not so easily solved. For one thing, it is no simple thing to remain inconspicuous in uniform when hunting for one lady in a crowd of hundreds. All the guests had arrived; everyone was gathered in the ballroom. As I approached the empty foyer, I could hear the music and happy chatter. Two footmen stood at every door. They might let me in, but given the Newsomes' concerns about security, I decided to look for another way.

If the exterior suggested an English country house, the interior was a fever dream of extravagance modeled on the palaces of Louis XIV. The homes of Mrs. Armslow were extremely fine, but she was of an older, more austere generation. Here, wealth was everywhere on display, every surface gilded, marbled, brocaded, or tasseled. It was a house built for giants, with fireplaces as tall as a man, the ceilings twenty feet high, rugs so thick they muffled every step, making you feel as if you didn't exist. The rooms were endless, and it made me dizzy to look at it all.

The kitchen offered a possible entry. Waiters would be going in and out with food, fresh bottles, and glasses. Extra hands had been hired for the occasion, so no one would be likely to challenge me if I came from that direction.

The scene in the kitchen was of a well-organized chaos. Cooks stood at the massive stoves while maids and waiters rushed about. Trays flew in and out held at the waist or high overhead. Fresh provisions were still arriving, as delivery men yelled through the door, "Ice!" "Lobster!" "Scotch!" I stood in the corner, watching for an opportunity. Then I saw a man at the delivery entrance, a large pair of iron tongs in his hands. Overwhelmed by the scene, he called weakly, "Ice, I have ice . . ." It was Anna's friend from the restaurant.

I approached him. "Mr. Pawlicec. Isn't this funny?"

Starting, he smiled his odd smile. "Miss Anna's friend. How are you?"

"Fine," I said, dodging to avoid a roast turkey. "Do you have ice to deliver?"

"Yes. I should bring . . . where?"

A few inquiries and we learned that he could bring the ice to the cellar. As he turned to go back to his truck, I said impulsively, "It was nice to see you again."

He looked at me. "You work for Robert Newsome?"

"No, for the Benchleys."

The answer seemed to cheer him, and he went to the truck for the block of ice.

Turning, I spotted a waiter headed into the ballroom with a crate of liquor. I managed to follow at a discreet distance through the crush of staff, then out the door, and down the hall that was the service way to the ballroom. We were almost at the entry when the door opened and Robert Newsome Sr. appeared. I fell back into one of the recessed doors.

He grabbed the waiter by the arm. "You know who my son is?"

Buckling slightly, the waiter nodded.

Mr. Newsome tapped the crate. "I see him with one more

drink, someone's going home empty-handed. And they had better think about a change in profession."

"Understood, sir."

I hung back until Mr. Newsome returned to his party. Setting the crate down, the waiter sat upon it and said to no one in particular, "Typical. Young master's getting soused and who's to blame? The hired help."

Worried for Charlotte, I asked, "Is Mr. Newsome . . ."

"Drunk, sozzled, loaded, yes, ma'am." He looked me up and down. "Who might you be?"

"Jane Prescott. I work for the Benchley ladies."

"One getting married? Or one looks like a Pekingese?"

Moving around him, I said, "It's Charlotte Benchley who is getting married."

"So, you got the Peke. Too bad. Can't be easy getting that gussied up."

This remark would have been obnoxious from any man, but it was particularly so from him. The waiter was unfairly good-looking, and he knew it, grinning up at me, as if to say, *Think my black hair's attractive? Have a look at my big brown eyes. My sharp black brows. The slight cleft in my chin and my strong, even white teeth.* From the way he spoke, he sounded of Irish extraction and I thought he was lucky not to be working for Mrs. Benchley.

But if he had noticed Louise, he might have some idea of where she was. "I'm trying to reach Louise Benchley now. Do you know where she is?"

"Last I remember, surrounded by well-meaning girlies, wanting to be a solace to her in this difficult time."

"Where, exactly?"

"Near a plant of some kind?"

Giving up on him, I headed toward the ballroom. To my surprise, he picked up the crate and followed. "What's it like, then, working for the Benchleys? Big wedding coming up. Louise's the older one, right? No joy for her . . ."

"Excuse me, I have to find Miss Benchley."

"Hold on a minute, I'll help you look."

"No, thank you," I said.

"Well, you can follow me in," he said, lifting the crate and stalking straight through the doors into the ballroom. When he had set the crate down, he nodded toward the curtains that covered the vast windows and said, "Plenty of places to hide around here."

Now it was a grin and hints of disappearing into the drapery for an intimate game of hide-and-seek. Giving a brief smile of thanks, I left him to search for Louise.

The drapes did make it easier to creep around the edge of the room while keeping an eye out for Louise. Mrs. Benchley was nowhere to be seen. But I saw Mr. Benchley as he endured the chatter of one of the lesser Vanderbilts.

"It's an outrage!" the lesser Vanderbilt insisted. "Bombs at the opera, the mayor shot, this newspaper business, and now death threats."

A few moments later, I saw Lucinda Newsome standing silent between Mrs. Hayes-Smith and Emily Tyler. I paused, thinking Louise might find refuge in this group. Mrs. Hayes-Smith was an earnest little woman who thought herself shy, despite the fact she monopolized every conversation. Emily was a flighty, pretty girl permanently on the verge of a giggle, and only Lucinda's deep seriousness held her at bay as Mrs. Hayes-Smith said, "But what are all these rights these suffragettes want? I'm sure I have enough to do as it is without them. And I think many women think as I do."

"Oh, I do," giggled Emily. "Absolutely."

She glanced at Lucinda, trying to engage her in the joke. Mrs. Hayes-Smith also gazed at her. Her voice shaking slightly, Lucinda said, "I'm afraid I don't agree. I think no country worthy of being thought civilized can bar half its population from taking part in political life."

"But if women are encouraged to imagine they can have rich, rewarding lives outside the home, what will it mean for families?" said Mrs. Hayes-Smith. "The family is the bedrock of our society."

But Mrs. Hayes-Smith no longer had Lucinda's attention. Something had caught her eye. I looked where she looked and saw Rose Newsome. She was managing the attentions of two eager gentlemen. One was pressing on her the drink created for her at the St. Regis Hotel, the Rose Blush. She raised a hand in polite refusal.

"If," said Lucinda Newsome loudly, "the family is the bedrock of our society, then the country is in very deep trouble indeed."

And she left Mrs. Hayes-Smith with her mouth open and Emily with her mouth covered as she tried unsuccessfully to hide her laughter. Looking around for diversion, she spotted me.

"Jane," she said, smiling, "what are you doing hiding among the plants?"

Emily Tyler was not the kind of girl to trust with news of a social gaffe. The Amusing Story of the Missing Gloves would be around the room before I could reach Louise. "I need to give Mrs. Benchley a message. Have you seen her?"

"No," said Emily. Then, unexpectedly serious, she said, "It isn't true, is it? What people are saying about Norrie and Charlotte?"

As she took a step toward me, I realized her green and gold dress was familiar to me. It was not this year's style; in fact, it was not even last year's. The lace on the bodice was stiff with overcleaning, the cuffs frayed. I knew if I glanced down, I would see the seams where the skirt had been taken up to fit Emily's shorter frame.

When she heard nothing from me, Emily said, "Well, I hope it's *not* true—for everyone's sake," and moved back into the crowd.

The mood of the party was uneasy. The news of death threats

against the family combined with the rumors of an unattractive match for Norrie had the guests on edge.

A clumsy waiter nudged a guest with a tray, and the woman screamed in fright, apparently under the impression she had felt the cold nudge of the anarchist's gun. Near an elaborate arrangement of Christmas roses, Helen Lauder lectured Mrs. Tyler, saying, "It's entirely your own fault, Florence. Allow new people in and they'll take everything. You might as well hand your silver plate over to burglars."

Then I spied Norrie weaving through a clutch of small tables. Revelers taking to the dance floor left their drinks behind, and Norrie was taking the glasses up one by one and drinking the remains. Drunkenness did not improve his appearance. His hair was disheveled, his face red. His clothes looked as if he had been wrestling in them.

I looked for Charlotte nearby, but did not see her. This was odd. But it was almost eleven; perhaps she had gone upstairs to make certain she looked her best.

I saw Rose Newsome approach. Taking the glass from Norrie's hand, she passed it to a waiter, then instructed him to clear the rest of the glasses. Then, steeling herself, she turned to her stepson, who was, I realized, older than she was.

She asked Norrie, "Where is Charlotte?"

"With her grotesque mother or gargoyle sister, I suppose."

"Hadn't you better find her?"

"I have better things to do."

Her fingers curled briefly into a fist, then relaxed. "Go to the kitchen and have some coffee." He laughed. "Do it, Norrie. You . . . you have to give the ring to Charlotte soon, and your father will want to make the announcement at midnight."

"'Your father will want to make the announcement,'" Norrie mimicked her. "He should announce his own wedding. Let everyone show their joy."

I felt sorry for Mrs. Newsome, who was no doubt torn between giving her brattish relation the slap in the face he deserved and maintaining peace.

"Think of Charlotte," she said quietly. "Isn't one broken heart enough?"

Norrie gave a derisive bark, and with sudden force, Mrs. Newsome said, "Or if you won't think of Charlotte, think of your father. You've put us in an awful position. Let's at least try to get through it with some grace. He has enough to worry about with these threats."

"Threats. I say, let 'em do it. Kill us off one by one." He made a gun of his finger and shot several guests.

Then he took aim at his stepmother. Placing the tip of his finger between her dark eyes, he murmured, "Who will be the first to go? Why, the one who doesn't belong . . ."

I stepped out from the curtain and said, "Mr. Newsome? I'm dreadfully sorry, but Miss Benchley has been asking for you."

At first Rose Newsome was startled by the interruption. Then, understanding she'd been rescued, she smiled in conspiracy. "There, you see? Poor Charlotte, I suppose she wants to dance, and she's such a charming dancer, too."

Calmly taking hold of his hand, she handed it to me. "Take him directly to Miss Benchley." Then in a lower voice, "And clean him up if you can."

"Yes, ma'am," I promised her.

Just as we were about to leave the ballroom, Lucinda appeared. Reaching out, she said, "Norrie, we *must* talk."

Norrie sighed. "Not if it's the same old song. Sorry, Lu."

Lucinda looked frustrated—more than frustrated—by my presence, but she had no choice but to let us go. At first, Norrie seemed to find it amusing to be led by the arm by a servant. Then he saw I meant to keep my promise and became difficult. He jerked his arm out of my hand several times, but he was drunk and I was determined.

Finally he hissed, "You touch me again and I'll break your jaw."

I should have been afraid; he meant it. But there was something in his weak viciousness that put me in mind of drunks I saw on the Bowery, raging at the world for their misfortune—never thinking how much misfortune they caused others. For a moment, I forgot that I was only Jane Prescott, and said, "That would be a pretty scene."

We were about to test the truth of his threat when Beatrice Tyler came up behind us. Her face was flushed and her mouth was uncertain. Composing herself, she said, "Good evening, Jane. May I borrow Mr. Newsome a moment?"

"You certainly may," said Norrie, putting his hand out to her. She did not take it. "What?" he said, turning it over. "Don't you want it?"

"Do I want it back, you mean?" asked Beatrice.

"Oh, have it for now, at least."

Beatrice gazed at him, then took Norrie's hand. As the two of them made their way to the dance floor, I saw her put her lips close to his ear. After a moment, he laughed. Charlotte had chosen her opponent unwisely. Beatrice had all her mother's wits—and twice her ruthlessness.

★ ★ ★

What to do? Norrie was not with Charlotte, he *was* with Beatrice, and it was after eleven. These three truths could result in something very ugly by midnight. As I tried to decide whether to look for Charlotte or stop Norrie from dancing with Beatrice, a voice from behind asked, "Dance?" and a strong arm spun me around.

It was the Irish waiter. Unthinking, I took two or three steps with him. Then I pushed him aside.

"Rude!" he exclaimed. "And here I am about to do you a favor."

"What favor?" I snapped.

"I've seen your little lost cow by the hors d'oeuvres. Her hooves seem a tad naked."

Louise! I started off, barely hearing the waiter's cry of "You owe me, remember that!"

Louise was indeed by the hors d'oeuvres, besieged by three gossip seekers. Her hands were behind her back, and she had that wide-eyed, trapped look I knew very well. Reaching into the circle, I said, "I'm terribly sorry, Miss Louise. Miss Charlotte says you're to come right away."

One of the bright-eyed chatterers said, "Charlotte? Where is she?"

"Where she ought to be," I said. Just then the band struck up a popular tune, and the girls were distracted by the search for dance partners.

As I pulled her through the crowd, Louise said, "Then Charlotte *is* still here?"

I stopped. "What do you mean?"

"No one can find her. Mother's frantic. I'll tell her you know where she is."

"I don't," I said. "It was an excuse. To give you these." I held out the gloves—which now seemed rather beside the point.

My mind grappled with various necessities, settling on one: *Find Charlotte.*

"Miss Louise, will you do something for me? So I can help your sister?" Louise swallowed nervously at the word "do," but nodded. "Find Norrie Newsome. He's dancing with Beatrice Tyler. Find him and dance with him."

"I'm a dreadful dancer."

"You're not—and anyway, that doesn't matter. What matters is you keep Mr. Newsome away from Miss Tyler until we can find your sister."

It was a lot to ask Louise Benchley. But, lifting her chin high, she advanced in the direction of the dance floor. Yes, without her gloves.

My first task was to make certain Charlotte was still in the house. She would never have walked home—even in extreme distress. I crossed the courtyard to the Newsome garage—a cathedral of automobiles—to find O'Hara, the Benchleys' chauffeur, fast asleep behind the wheel, an empty bottle of champagne on the floor.

Charlotte had not left the party. So why at her moment of triumph was she nowhere to be found? Heart pounding, I reviewed the possibilities. Charlotte could be hiding, provoked by some insult of Norrie's. Or Beatrice's. Who, now that I thought of it, had been looking rather triumphant when she asked to "borrow" Norrie.

It was also possible that Charlotte had already gone to the library to meet Norrie, and we were all worried over nothing.

As I walked through the small courtyard back to the main house, I caught sight of a figure in the shadows. I strained to see if it was Charlotte. No, I decided, the shape was about the right height, but distinctly masculine. Seeing me, whoever it was turned a corner and disappeared.

I hurried back through the kitchen, where people were beginning to work their way through the stacks of soiled plates and cutlery. As I reached the hall to the library, the clock began to strike midnight. I listened for the clinking of glasses and call for attention that would precede the announcement. But the music and the chatter of the party flowed on.

I came to the library doors and felt a qualm. These were not things for me to meddle with. If Charlotte were in there, impatient or distraught, she would not welcome me. If even now Norrie was presenting her with his grandmother's ring, my intrusion would be even less welcome.

I listened for voices. I heard none.

Turning the handle, I stepped inside the deeply carpeted room. A fire burned, the crackling flames providing the only light. Every significant family occasion, from christenings to wakes, was held there, witnessed by the family founder, James Newsome, who now hung framed in gold above the fireplace, stern-faced and patriarchal, clad in good, plain black cloth. It was a large space, with two entrances; one led to the kitchen, the other back to the ballroom. Rows of books sat importantly behind glass. Heavy curtains hid the windows. Shadows were everywhere. Suddenly nervous of venturing too far from the door, I called out, "Miss Charlotte?" Silence answered. But not, I thought, the silence of absence.

I was about to call Charlotte's name again when I saw it. I could not tell you why the hand lying on the floor struck me with dread. The stiffness of the fingers, the desperate stretch of the arm . . . this was not sleep. My heart, swollen and heavy with fear, thudded painfully as I stepped closer to see Norrie Newsome, heir to the Newsome fortune, lying dead under the fierce, judgmental eye of his ancestor.

★ ★ ★

Destroyed.

The word kept sounding in my head even after I had averted my eyes from the sight of Norrie Newsome's ruined face. In the firelight, one could see that a few teeth still hung, white streaked with blood, to identify the mouth. Two sockets red and raw could be discerned as eyes by position only. The nose was simply gone.

The fire in the grate cracked, throwing a flare of light onto Norrie's forehead, still high and perfect, save for the damp, dark patch at his hairline. I found myself hoping that blow had been struck first, that he had been unconscious for the rest. Stupid with shock, I kept looking at the eyes. Or what had been the eyes. Particular violence had been done to them; they were not merely crushed but . . . gouged.

I forced myself to look elsewhere, down to Norrie's shoes and back up. Silk socks, pants, even buttons, all neutral things. The hand came back into view, and my gaze jumped again. A stain. There was a pale, pasty stain on the lapel of his jacket. Sauce from dinner, I decided, and suddenly had to press the back of my fingers to my mouth and swallow something sour.

Someone must be told. There it was—the thing to do. Mr. Benchley. He would know what to do, how to inform the Newsomes, contact the police. And it had to be done soon, while the killer could still be caught . . .

A log in the fireplace popped and I cried out. My breath came fast, until it felt my lungs could not keep up. In my confusion, I felt strongly that I was not alone.

I found myself rushing to the door that led to the stairs and down to the ballroom. My teeth were chattering, and I held my jaw rigid to stop them. My heart physically ached from beating so hard. I tried to gather myself, walk calmly.

"Well, hello."

The waiter—the infernal Irish waiter. I kept walking. But he grabbed my arm.

"What's wrong?" he asked.

My answer was to try to pull free. But he held on. "You're shaking, what's happened?"

"Let me go."

"Something's happened, tell me."

"No." I struggled. "Let me go."

He might have said, "Let me help you," but I did not hear him because all of a sudden I found I could say nothing except "Let me go," over and over, my voice rising until I sounded quite hysterical. But I couldn't make myself stop. Even when he had let me go and was only patting the air in front of me, saying, "Yes, all right—"

"Jane." At the sound of Mr. Benchley's voice, I turned to see him at the top of the stairs, tall and impressive in his evening clothes. "Is this man troubling you?"

Fighting to keep my mind in order, I said, "No, Mr. Benchley."

"Go back to work," he instructed the waiter.

Glancing at me, the waiter said, "Yes, sir." He slowly started making his way toward the stairs.

"Now," said Mr. Benchley, and the waiter disappeared through the double doors.

I whispered, "Mr. Benchley, would you come with me, please?"

As if I hadn't spoken, he said, "Have you seen Miss Charlotte? No one can find her. I thought perhaps she was in the library."

"Mr. Benchley, you have to come with me," I told him. Moving a little down the hall, I gestured to the closed library door.

But Mr. Benchley was not a man to be lured. "Jane, what is this?"

"It's—" I did not want to say the words aloud, but if it was necessary to get Mr. Benchley into that room before Charlotte arrived, I would. "It's Norrie . . ."

At the mention of that name, Mr. Benchley's expression turned grim and he began striding down the hall. We were steps from the door when I heard a woman scream; we were too late. But when Mr. Benchley pushed the door open, it was not Charlotte but Rose Newsome we saw kneeling helpless by the body. The other door to the library stood open, casting an ugly yellow light into the dark room.

"Stay away," she screamed toward the door. "Stay away, my darling, please! You mustn't come in." Looking to us, her eyes wild, she whispered, "His father can't see him like this, please, keep him away until—"

But the yellow light was cut as Mr. Newsome appeared at the door. He stopped there, his bulky frame filling the space. He staggered a moment, then caught the oak trim of the doorway, and that kept him upright. But his jaw went slack and his knees began to buckle. Her hair coming undone and slipping down her back,

Rose Newsome ran to him. Sinking with him, his wife shielded him from the awful sight, pressing his face to the black velvet of her dress. Her body shook with the force of his howls.

Mr. Benchley instructed me to close the doors.

★ ★ ★

There were detectives, Mrs. Newsome informed us, on the premises. They must be found and brought to the library. She told Mr. Benchley their names and where they were stationed. Her husband did not speak, lost in his grief.

The four of us were still in the hallway that stood between the library and the ballroom. I said tentatively, "Shall I look for Miss Charlotte?"

Mrs. Newsome stared at me. "What do you mean, look for her?"

His jaw rigid, Mr. Benchley said, "My daughter would seem to be—"

Then the far door opened and a voice called out, "I'm sorry, I'm so sorry! Is Norrie furious with me?"

My first thought was that it was not Charlotte who walked toward us, but a different woman altogether. Then I thought, no, she only *looked* different. Maybe I had dreamed the events of the last two hours, and the Benchleys and Newsomes, having just finished dinner, were now on their way upstairs to dress for the ball.

And that's when I realized: Charlotte was wearing her dress from dinner.

Tugging at her gloves, she said, "That *awful* Beatrice Tyler, I can't believe—"

She looked up. Her sharp eyes took in the faces of the Newsomes and her father. Noted the absence of Norrie.

"No," she said. "Oh, no . . ."

7

There were eleven major newspapers in New York City, and every one of them carried the story of the Newsome murder on the front page. Among the glad holiday tidings and the stores' colorful enticements to spend, the announcement of death in one of the city's most prominent families struck an ominous chord.

Some of the accounts were sober and matter-of-fact, stating only what was known. Others took a more dramatic tone. The *Herald*, for example, reported:

> Robert Norris Newsome Jr. was found murdered in his family's Fifth Avenue mansion last night. The identity of the assailant is unknown, but authorities suspect the horrific Christmas Eve slaying may be the work of ANARCHISTS.
>
> The Herald has learned that the Newsome family had received several death threats in recent weeks. The notes made reference to the Shickshinny Mine disaster, which resulted in 121 deaths, including 8 children.

While Mr. Newsome was absolved of all blame, the incident has become a rallying cry for subversive elements.

Killing and anarchists are inseparable in the minds
of most of us. Mysterious destroyers of life and of property, merciless men who have pledged their lives to some
nefarious cause or another.

Silence pervaded the Benchley household. Both mother and
younger daughter were sedated under doctor's orders. Mr. Benchley was barricaded in his study. On the street outside the house, a
ragged group of reporters waited in the cold for some vulnerable
member of the household to emerge. The cook had found herself
surrounded when she tried to attend Mass, and a delivery boy
had been pulled off his bicycle. I was glad for once that we were
short-staffed.

Louise was not sedated. Or rather, it was as if she had naturally
sedated herself when she heard the news. She had not come to
breakfast, but spent the morning in her room, taking each of her
dolls in turn on her lap. She fixed their hair, drew their sleeves
down to their wrists, straightened the fronts of their smocks. Once
as I passed, I overheard her murmur, "You've been a bad girl. It
was *wrong* what you did—"

I waited to hear more, but Louise went quiet.

As I unpacked Charlotte's case from the party, I cursed to see
that only one of the dresses had come back with us, the one she
had worn to dinner. Probably it didn't matter; Charlotte would
never want to see the dress again. But I was exhausted and irritable, and wanted to take my frustration out on someone. So I went
in search of Mary, the new maid who had been so excited to
attend the Newsome ball.

I found her in the drawing room, halfheartedly polishing a
brass lamp. As a junior member of the staff, she had not been
granted a day off, and the downstairs' Christmas festivities had

been canceled along with the upstairs'. Her dull, slack demeanor coupled with the missing dress angered me, and I snapped, "Where is Miss Charlotte's dress?"

Blinking, she said, "Miss Char—"

"She had two dresses," I reminded her. "One for dinner, one for the ball. Where is her ball gown?"

"I couldn't find it."

"That's no excuse."

"But it was ruined, miss."

"Ruined?"

"Yes, miss. That's why she had the other one on. Someone'd spilled on her. She was upset because it was midnight, and she kept shouting at me to hurry up."

So that was why Charlotte was late to the library. Unwilling to relinquish my outrage, I said, "You should have packed it. Perhaps it can be cleaned."

"I don't think so, miss. Red wine all down the front, soaked through."

Surprised, I asked, "Did Miss Charlotte say what happened?"

"No, miss. But she was in a real rage about it."

I could imagine. If someone had spilled wine on Charlotte's dress, it was a miracle there hadn't been two murders last night. But who would have done such a thing? A memory flickered of Beatrice Tyler, her hand reaching for Norrie's.

I nodded. "All right. Thank you, Mary. I'm sorry I shouted at you."

Unwilling to go back to polishing, she said, "It's awful to think, isn't it, miss? That we were in a house with a murderer."

"It is." For a moment, I thought of asking Mary if she had seen anything unusual—a wild-eyed man covered in blood shouting *Death to the bosses!* for example. But she had been upstairs, and the killer would have likely left by the kitchen or cellar. That was the Pinkertons' theory, at any rate, when last night's search for the murderer—or the weapon—had turned up empty.

I looked out the windows at the group of reporters outside. "You know not to speak to them, right? Whatever they offer, it won't be worth your job."

She shook her head. "Oh, no, miss, I wouldn't." She added regretfully, "I don't have anything to tell 'em."

"That wouldn't matter, they'd just make it up."

I wandered into the kitchen, where the cook listened as Bernadette read aloud from a newspaper.

"'The dashing young man, known as Norrie to his family and *many* intimate acquaintances, was one of the city's most eligible bachelors. While he has squired several of society's loveliest debutantes, it was recently reported in these pages that young Newsome's heart had been won by Scarsdale siren Charlotte Benchley. This dark and bloody tale is still unfolding, and *Town Topics* will be the first to get you the whole truth and nothing but!'"

Settling her chin on her hand, the cook said, "Miss Charlotte won't like them saying that about Scarsdale."

"She'll be lucky if that's all they say about her," said Bernadette.

Giving her a sharp look, I said, "Get rid of that. What if the family sees it?"

But it was not the last newspaper to make its way into the house. That night after dinner, Mr. Benchley handed me a fistful of grimy paper and said, "Dispose of these, please, Jane." He did not look at me as he said it.

"Of course, Mr. Benchley."

I turned to go upstairs, but he added, "And Jane? A detective is coming tomorrow to speak with Miss Charlotte. I would like you there."

"Will I have to answer questions, sir?"

He shook his head. "Only if asked. I would prefer to keep the members of this household out of the investigation as much as possible. But you will be more aware of Miss Charlotte's actions that night than I am. She's in a state of shock and might not be able to recall everything correctly."

"She wasn't near the library when it happened—what can she remember?"

He said, "Exactly." And that was all the explanation I got.

I meant to throw out the newspapers. Yet when the family had gone to bed, I took them to my room. I washed, got into my nightgown, and under several blankets. Then I laid the grisly sheet out on the bed.

NEWSOME DEATH THREATS MADE PUBLIC!
Dark Vows of Revenge for the Shickshinny Mine Disaster
Which Claimed 121 Lives, Including 8 Children

On January 19, 1899, 121 workers died in the Shickshinny Mine in Schuylkill Township, Pennsylvania, when an explosion caused a cave-in shortly before noon. The roof collapsed, choking the galleries, and making rescue difficult. One man who managed to escape reported hearing the voices of several boys trapped near a ventilator shaft. A cry went up to save the boys, who ranged in age from 7 to 10 years old. But the Elkins Mining Company, a subsidiary of the Newsome family holdings, said it would be unsafe to attempt rescue in that part of the mine. The boys' bodies were discovered a week later; all had suffocated. Claw marks in the tunnel wall and bloody, broken fingers gave evidence of their fight for survival. A witness reported, "They were lying together, arms around one another for comfort, as if asleep. You never saw such a pitiable sight."

COULD THE BOYS HAVE BEEN SAVED?
Many accused the Elkins Company of saving money

over lives, arguing that the boys might have been saved. An investigation was launched, and the manager of the mine, Howard Coogan, was fired for negligence.

MURDEROUS NOTES

This paper has learned that on the 10th anniversary of the disaster, a note arrived at the Newsome home in New York. It bore the date of the mine collapse and a bloody handprint, a symbol common in anarchist circles. "They began to arrive on the 19th of every month," said a source close to the family. The next one read *Blood for Blood.* Another, *Justice for the Shickshinny Eight.* The next listed the names of the boys who died. The final note, which was delivered just prior to the Newsomes' Christmas Eve Ball, read, *You murdered our children. Now we'll murder yours.*

To some, it will seem that a terrible vengeance has been taken.

There were images of the disaster. Men standing helplessly around the mine, women held back by local policemen, rows of bodies covered by tarps. At the bottom of one page, a row of bodies smaller than the rest; they were not under tarps, but their eyes were covered by cloths. The image recalled mothers putting a hand over their children's eyes to shield them from things they should not see. I folded the paper, pushed it under the bed. Then I extinguished the light and pulled up the covers.

But in the dark, there was nothing to think about but death. Nothing but Norrie's shattered face in the firelight, the fingers crooked and stiff on the rug. The boys, their eyes covered, hands crossed on their chests. My wandering thoughts caught and snagged: had Norrie's eyes been destroyed as an echo of the boys' covered eyes? That shadow I saw in the courtyard, searching for Charlotte. Josef Pawlicec asking, "You work for the Newsomes?"

> *Killing and anarchists are inseparable in the minds of most of us.*

I sat up and lit a candle. My hands were shaking with cold and nerves, and it took me several tries. When I had achieved a weak, flickering light, I opened my door. The house was dark and silent. The candle threw shadows everywhere. As I passed the floor where the family slept, the stairs creaked, and I stepped as lightly as possible.

I made my way to the first floor. Right outside the kitchen, there was a low-ceilinged passageway that served as a pantry. It was also where the servants' telephone was kept, as the cook could survey what she had while calling in orders to the butcher or the dairyman. (Mr. Benchley might have been penny-pinching in some things, but he was a firm believer in making use of the latest inventions.) This phone was to be used for household business only. But it was understood that the staff might make the occasional personal call.

I felt nervous as I reached for the telephone. I imagined tomorrow's detective standing over me, demanding, "Did you call this number the previous evening?"

"*I did, sir.*"

"*Do you know this number belongs to one Salvatore D'Amico?*"

"*I do, sir.*"

"*And that he is the uncle of Anna Ardito?*"

"*Yes, sir.*"

"*Are you aware that Anna Ardito is an anarchist?*"

To which I would have to answer yes.

"*What was your business with Anna Ardito?*"

"*I had no business. We are friends.*"

Picking up the telephone, I asked to be connected. It was late, but Anna's uncle stayed open late. It was some time before a man came on the line. It was not her uncle, who knew me. Faltering, I asked, "Is Anna there?"

There was a pause. Then, "No."

"May I leave a message for her?"

Another pause. "Okay."

Carefully, I spelled out my name and the number she could use to reach me. From the other end of the phone, I could feel the man was impatient to get back to his customers. Still, as I finished, I added, "Tell her . . ."

"Yeah?"

"Tell her I'd like to hear from her," I finished, and the man hung up.

★ ★ ★

Some might find it surprising that a full day had passed before the police interviewed one of the key people concerned in the Newsome murder. But those people will be unfamiliar with the state of the New York City Police Department at that time.

It is true that twenty years earlier, the department had undergone a reformation under Theodore Roosevelt, who insisted that police walk their beat, refuse bribes, and be in good physical condition and not mentally defective. But Mr. Roosevelt had gone on to higher office, and New York's police had once again fallen into bad habits. (Our current commissioner, James Church Cropsey, would resign the post, saying he was pressured to hire men of no competence whatsoever.)

The most visible policemen were the celebrity crusaders, those heroes of the tabloids who swore to bring the city's villains to justice. One such warrior was Inspector Thomas J. Blackburn, who had pledged to the Almighty to rid the world of anarchists, because they were "the enemy of all right-thinking, law-abiding, decent people."

For Inspector Blackburn, the murder of Robert Norris Newsome Jr. was a call to arms. It was, he informed the *Herald*, "a grievous, dastardly act, typical of the anarchist." Why, hadn't the anarchist Berkman attempted to murder Henry Clay Frick in his own office? The Newsome murder was proof that anarchists were growing stronger, bolder.

Even those who viewed Mr. Blackburn's antics with distaste may have felt that the Newsome murder had shown he was not altogether incorrect. The brutality of Norrie's death, that it had happened in his home, was shocking. Possibly Mr. Blackburn's superiors decided there could be no harm in assigning a man able to look the part of a dauntless investigator. And so he arrived at the Benchley house.

The interview was conducted in Mr. Benchley's study. The room was paneled floor to ceiling in dark wood. Heavy velvet drapes shielded us from the gaze of the outside world. Turkish carpets muffled distracting sound. Armchairs sat on either side of the fire. Charlotte was dressed in a gray day dress with a shawl around her shoulders for cold. She was pale, her eyes tired. Her face was drawn, her hands thin and fluttering. She was seated in one of the leather armchairs. I could see she was nervous.

Inspector Blackburn was on the small side, but quick and tightly knit. He was bald, with bright blue eyes and a sharp nose. Offering his handkerchief, he added his profound sympathies on her loss.

"I understand you were engaged to be married," he said.

Charlotte nodded, tears in her eyes. The handkerchief was pressed, but it had been doused with an unfortunate cologne, and she declined.

"Had Mr. Newsome told you anything about these notes, prior to the night in question?"

Charlotte shook her head. "He didn't take them seriously."

"I see. And what time were you to meet your betrothed?"

"Around eleven thirty. In the library. He was going to give me his grandmother's ring."

"But you did not meet him."

"No. I was . . ." Charlotte glanced at her father. "I was delayed."

"By who?" said Blackburn sharply. "Someone you knew?"

"Yes. Beatrice Tyler."

"*Not* an associate of anarchists," Mr. Benchley informed Mr. Blackburn.

"What did Miss Tyler want?"

"Want?" Charlotte licked her lips. "Nothing."

"But you must have told her you had to meet your fiancé."

"She didn't care," said Charlotte. "We quarreled. Beatrice, Miss Tyler, was jealous, you see, she said . . ."

Mr. Benchley interrupted. "I'm sure the detective isn't interested in personal matters not pertaining to the case."

"No, indeed," Blackburn assured Charlotte, as if she had spoken. "Can you tell me what time your conversation with Miss Tyler occurred?"

Agitated, Charlotte shook her head. "After eleven. But I can't recall exactly."

"And were you near the library before the tragedy occurred?"

"No. Miss Tyler saw fit to ruin my dress, and I had to change."

Blackburn turned toward Mr. Benchley. "Were you near the library, sir?"

"I was. I assumed my daughter would be there and wished to escort her back to the ball for the announcement of her engagement."

This, I thought, was almost true. Or not untrue. Apparently, Mr. Benchley did not wish to tell the inspector Charlotte had been thought missing.

"But you didn't see anyone leave."

"I did not. There are two entrances to the library. I assume the murderer left by the other door. It leads to the kitchen and would have provided a quicker exit point."

"And who found the body?"

If Mr. Benchley was going to mention the fact that I had discovered the body, he would do so now. I held my breath.

"Mrs. Newsome," said Mr. Benchley. "By the time I reached the library, she and her husband were already there."

Satisfied, the inspector turned his attention back to Charlotte. Did she know of anyone who had a grudge against her fiancé?

She shook her head.

Had he done anything out of the ordinary lately?

Glancing at her father, Charlotte said, "Well, he went to Philadelphia."

Mr. Benchley explained, "I'm sure you're aware that the family has mines in Pennsylvania."

Had Charlotte noticed anyone suspicious? Anyone she didn't recognize?

"There were so many people," she whispered.

It seemed Inspector Blackburn was finished. But then he turned on his heel and said to Charlotte, "Forgive me for this personal question. But are you familiar with a medication known as Pep Pills?"

I kept my face still by staring at the clock. The pills. Mrs. Benchley had brought them. What had happened to them? She'd offered them to Charlotte. Charlotte refused.

Louise reaching. *Here, Mother, give them to me.*

I heard Charlotte say, "I am not."

With that, the interview was over. Inspector Blackburn shook Mr. Benchley's hand and gave him his card. I moved toward the door, ready to show him out.

But as Blackburn passed, Charlotte caught his hands and said, "You will catch them, won't you? The people who did this to Norrie?"

Bending down, he pressed her hands in his. "Miss Benchley, I shall not rest until the foul assailants of your fiancé have been caught, tried, and executed."

I flinched at the word "executed"—it seemed brutal to mention death to a young woman so recently acquainted with it.

But Charlotte, for the first time since Norrie's murder, smiled.

★ ★ ★

When the inspector had gone, I led Charlotte back upstairs. Despite the brightness of the day, her bedroom was dark, the curtains still closed. I went to open them, but she shook her head.

"Do you need anything, Miss Charlotte?" I asked.

"Yes." Sitting down, she pulled her shawl tighter around her shoulders. "I need clothes."

I glanced at the wardrobe, which I knew to be stuffed with dresses.

"I have nothing in black, and I don't want to be seen in public until I do. And I'll need something for the funeral."

It was not for me to tell Charlotte that it would be irregular for her to wear mourning for Norrie Newsome. Not only were Charlotte and Norrie not married, their engagement had never been formally announced. It was by no means certain that the Benchleys would even be asked to attend the funeral.

I said carefully, "Perhaps we should wait until we hear what the funeral arrangements will be."

She gave me a sharp look. "Norrie was to be my husband. I want people to remember that."

Her phrasing struck me as odd, but before I could think why, we heard a cry from outside. "Newsome murder! Grisly new details! Newsome murder! Get it here first!"

Charlotte went white and gripped the shawl to her throat. I hurried down the stairs and out the servants' entrance. On the avenue, I saw a newsboy outside the Benchley house. He was maybe six years old, dressed in short pants, which showed grimy shins. His coat was out at the elbows; his lump of a hat had been gnawed at by mice. The crowd of reporters had left with Inspector Blackburn, giving the boy free rein in the street.

He shouted, "Extra, extra! Robert Norris Newsome Jr. murdered!"

Approaching, I said, "Take your wares the next block over or I'll call the police."

Holding his batch of newspapers firmly under a broken shoe, he turned his back on me. "Newsome murder! Eyewitness account! Not fit for ladies or the weak of heart!"

That got him a sale from two girls. As they hurried on down the street, one opened the paper and said, "Ooh, they bashed in his face . . ."

I was about to tell the boy he would sell more papers if he moved a few blocks to the more crowded commercial streets when a man strolled up and said, "That's fine, Joe, you head on downtown." He handed him a dollar, and the boy ran off.

I knew the voice immediately, but couldn't place the name. Then I saw the face. The happy brown eyes, the black hair coming loose from under the brim of a shabby derby. The broad, self-satisfied grin.

"It's Jane, right?" he asked. "Jane Prescott?" He gave me a slight tip of the hat. "Michael Behan."

"Why aren't you waiting tables? Because you're not a waiter. I knew you weren't."

"These big parties, you have to hire extra staff. Sadly, not all of them are well trained."

"What newspaper do you work for?"

"*Town Topics.*"

The worst of the scandal sheets. I turned to go.

"You'll want to talk to me, Miss Prescott." I kept walking. "For one thing, I can make Louie stay away. Or I can make him come back. And, boy, is he loud."

I stopped.

"Be a shame if Miss Benchley had to hear the details of her beloved's murder shouted out in the streets."

"What do you want?"

"To talk to you, Miss Prescott. After all, you found the body. Didn't you?"

It's a strange moment when you learn you are the focus of someone's interest. Strange—and oddly compelling. I had a brief memory of the day Mrs. Armslow offered me a job, that confused, exhilarated feeling that life could be entirely different.

It could also be quite dangerous, I thought, remembering the warning I gave to Mary. "You're right. I should talk to the police. And while I'm at it, I'll ask them to send someone to the house. Around the time Louie's here. Police and newsboys don't get along very well, do they?" Running off newsboys was a favorite pastime of policemen. It didn't require much effort, involved no danger, and yet they could say they were disposing of a public nuisance.

I started walking back to the house. Behan ran ahead of me. "Your little lady's in the papers, Miss Prescott. And some of the things I'm hearing . . . *well.*"

"An anarchist killed Norrie Newsome, Mr. Behan."

"There's many who say so and some that don't."

That stopped me. "What do you mean?"

"Young Mr. Newsome was a complicated fellow. There's a few people I can imagine wanting to take a swipe at him." He lowered his voice. "Talk to me, Miss Prescott. I'd like to help."

He sounded sincere, but the Irish are skilled at faking sympathy. Saying, "I'm sure," I made to go around him.

He dodged left. "Mud sticks, Miss Prescott. A lady's name

shouldn't be in the papers at all, but it's not so bad if she comes out the pure-hearted soul robbed of her happiness and innocence by the foul hand of—"

"Is that your headline?"

"It could be," he said. "Come on, Miss Prescott. Don't you think a young lady could use a friend?"

"Yes, but not you," I said and moved to turn the corner.

He pulled something from inside his coat. "Have a look at the latest edition."

The ink was still wet, and I took it gingerly. I unfolded the paper to the front page. The newsboy had promised horrible new details, and the paper delivered on that promise. The lead story was a gory reverie on the state of Norrie Newsome's body. *Savage beating! Eyes mashed to pulp! Once-smiling mouth a broken, bloody ruin!* I knew it was all true, that the eyewitness had seen what I saw. But who was the eyewitness?

Then I saw on the lower part of the left page a smaller, insinuating headline:

STRANGE NEW EVIDENCE FOUND AT THE
SCENE OF THE DREADFUL CRIME!
What do Dr. Forsythe's Pep Pills have to do with the
murder of Robert Norris Newsome Jr.? Our sources tell
us that a bottle of them was found near the unfortunate
young man's mutilated body. Popular among the fashionable set, Pep Pills are known to impart fresh energy, bright
eyes, and a singular glow to ladies in need of renewed
vim. They are not commonly used by gentlemen.
WHY WERE PEP PILLS FOUND NEAR THE BODY
OF ROBERT NORRIS NEWSOME JR.?

So this was why the inspector had inquired about Pep Pills. If *Town Topics* knew that Mrs. Benchley was a fan of Dr. Forsythe's remedy, it was keeping it quiet for now. And it was essential I do the same. Thrusting the paper back at him, I said, "Thank you, but no."

He didn't take it. "Michael Behan. *Town Topics*. Remember, Miss Prescott, if you ever have something to say, I'm your man."

★ ★ ★

Normally, someone in my position should speak to no one higher than the housekeeper, who might then convey my thoughts to the mistress of the house. But we had no housekeeper, and I did not think Mrs. Benchley would make anything useful of what I had to say. Still, the family had to be warned that a newspaper had set its sights on Charlotte. So that night, I resolved to speak with the head of the household.

As a rule, servants are supposed to simply enter a room, our presence so discreet as to be unnoticeable. To request permission to enter is an intrusion into the employer's consciousness. But I had never approached Mr. Benchley before, so I knocked. There was a long pause. Then I heard a cautious "Come in."

"I'm sorry to disturb you, sir." Approaching his desk, I laid the copy of *Town Topics* on his desk, open to the Pep Pills story. "But a reporter gave me this, and I thought you should see it."

Touching a finger to the very edge of the page, he pulled the paper toward him. He cast his eyes over the sheet for a few moments. "Yes. Thank you."

"Mrs. Benchley has used the product," I said carefully. He nodded. "I think the reporter might pursue the story further."

Mr. Benchley pushed the paper from him. "There won't be a story to pursue for much longer. Anarchists are careless. Someone will give him up."

I did not think of Anna as careless, but there was no point in saying so. Careless people returned messages. Careless people told their friends what they were doing, shared their opinions of recent

events. Reassured you that they had not been arrested for murder—or indeed committed murder.

To date, Anna had done none of those things.

* * *

A day later, the venerable Mrs. James Newsome arrived in New
York, and it was announced that the funeral would take place at
the Newsome estate in Rhinebeck. The Newsomes let it be known
that they would be staying at their estate for a time after the inter-
ment. The press attention had grown intolerable. Several of New
York's finest families would be in attendance; to our great relief,
the Benchleys were among those included. Charlotte and Louise
were even invited to stay on after the funeral.

Given Norrie Newsome's youth and celebrity, you might have
expected his funeral to be elaborate, with a service at St. Bar-
tholomew's, the cream of society acting as pallbearers, and police
holding back crowds eager for a glimpse of the eminent guests.
You might have expected the upper class to make a great show of
their power in defiance of those who wished to destroy them.

But upon her arrival, his grandmother had decided that quite
enough attention had been paid to the Newsome family, and that
Robert Norris Newsome Jr. would be remembered privately,
among his own people. How they remembered him, what they remembered, would remain . . . private.

8

The Newsome mansion and its attendant gardens had once been described as "a most idyllic spot in this our fallen world," by a particularly florid writer for *The New York Times*. Built under the auspices of the first Mrs. Newsome, the mansion had fifty-four rooms and was designed in the Beaux Arts style. I had seen this imposing limestone temple of wealth during my time with Mrs. Armslow. Set upon a seemingly endless flow of green lawn, the Hudson River flowing behind it, the house appeared to dominate the natural world, as if gods might emerge from behind the vast Roman columns to banish storm clouds or summon winds.

The gods were nowhere in evidence the day we arrived. Gray clouds hung heavy; the river ran icy and whitecapped; the grounds were patchy with mud and frost. The celebrated rose gardens were bare. The family vault where Norrie's mother was interred—and where he would lie—stood some distance from the house, a pale, solitary structure with the name Newsome carved in stone.

A Pullman train had been arranged to escort the coffin and Norrie's immediate family. Mrs. Newsome Sr. requested that close friends and members of the service travel separately; the Pullman was to be for blood relatives. There was an anxious day at the Benchleys as we waited to hear whether Charlotte would be included in the Pullman group. She was not. Norrie's grandmother was making her influence felt.

So the Benchleys traveled separately, with their staff and luggage going ahead on the train. On the omnibus from the station, I sat squeezed in between Matchless Maude and Mr. Benchley's valet, Jack. We were met at the back of the southern end of the house by a Mrs. Farrell, who was the housekeeper. She was an older woman, in her late forties, thin and sharp-eyed, her faded brown hair well threaded with gray. There was a disdain in her manner, and I felt accused, as if I were a butcher passing off poor meat for good or a scullery maid who'd been caught with her hand in the jewelry drawer. I could do my job without her help, but it's useful to have the housekeeper's goodwill when you're visiting, as she has the power to make things like laundry easy or difficult. I wondered why I hadn't seen her on the night of the ball. But as Charlotte told the inspector, there had been so many people. And my mind had been otherwise occupied.

Leaving Maude and Jack in the room given to the senior Benchleys, Mrs. Farrell took me to the rooms selected for the girls. Charlotte had been given a beautiful bedroom overlooking the river, and I said, "It's very thoughtful of the Newsomes to give Miss Charlotte such a lovely room."

Mrs. Farrell pulled the drapes open with a sharp motion. "There was a fine battle over whether to have Miss Benchley at all, I can tell you."

"Oh?"

She crossed to the second set of windows, clearly torn between the call of discretion and the desire to put me in my place. Arrogance won, and she added, "Mrs. Newsome was completely against it."

"Rose Newsome?" I said, surprised.

"Mrs. *James* Newsome," she corrected, referring to Norrie's grandmother. "Said Norrie had no business being engaged to her and she'd been here, it never would have happened."

"Well, she wasn't and it did," I said.

"And didn't that turn out well?" She opened the door to the bathroom, showing me the location of that essential room.

I asked, "So who should the Benchleys thank for the invitation?"

"*Her.*" I could see to even say the name Rose Newsome irritated the woman. "Said Norrie had chosen her to be his wife and to not have her would be to dishonor his wishes. Mrs. Newsome said that's exactly what his wishes deserved. But like calls to like, and Rose Newsome took up for your girl."

"Thank you, Mrs. Farrell," I said. "I can manage from here."

I was not a member of the household, so I did not witness the funeral, which was held the following day. Normally a funeral would be followed by a reception, but Mr. Newsome was too ill to receive a multitude of mourners, so the family and their houseguests simply returned to the estate after the service. From Louise's window, I caught a brief glimpse of Mr. Newsome as he walked up the path. He had aged a lot in the space of a week; his face and body sagged as if anticipating his final return to the earth. His young wife held him by the arm as they made sad, careful progress into the house.

Lucinda walked with her grandmother. The old woman relied on her cane but seemed vital enough. If anything, Lucinda leaned on her, her homely face heavy with grief.

The Benchleys followed at a distance.

The evening was spent in that strange limbo that follows a big event; officially, there is nothing left to be done, and yet no one feels ready to go back to their daily lives. Everyone was exhausted and miserable. It would have been much better had they all retired to their rooms for the rest of the day. But conversation must be made, dinner served and eaten, books read, puzzles worked on, sad memories shared.

I waited in Louise's room to hear the first footsteps on the stairs. At around nine o'clock, I heard the creak of floorboards. From the sound of it, a young woman was slowly making her way up the stairs. I went to the door. But as she came into view, I saw that it was not Charlotte or Louise. It was Lucinda Newsome. Curious as to what she was doing in the guest wing, I closed the door to a sliver.

She stood at the top of the stairs, gazing around the hallway as if she were in an unfamiliar house. Watching her, I wondered how I would style her to compensate for the weak chin; low, sloping bosom; and heavy buckteeth. Her eyes were large and fine, the dark hair thick, if a little coarse.

She was looking for something, gazing at each door for a moment before moving on. Then, stopping in front of Charlotte's door, she opened it. From where I was, I could just see inside, Charlotte's nightgown already laid out on the bed, her satin slippers on the floor.

Lucinda took hold of either side of the door frame, her fingers curling tensely on the oak molding. She stared hard into the room, her breath coming ragged and quick. Then she reared her head back and spit, a terse, irrevocable mark of contempt.

Then she closed the door and hurried back down the stairs.

★ ★ ★

The next day, the senior Benchleys left. Whether out of defiance or an unwillingness to let go of this last part of Norrie, Charlotte was determined to stay, seemingly content to sit by the parlor window, her hands resting on an unopened book.

Louise spent the morning similarly occupied. But after lunch, she came upstairs.

"I told them I wanted to take a nap," she said. "I've said

absolutely everything I can remember about birds—Mother told me it was the thing to talk about in the country. But no one seems interested."

"They have their minds on other things," I told her. "And I would imagine they don't know any more about birds than you do."

"And you won't believe who's coming to dinner tonight. Of all people . . ."

My mind sifted through the possible names, arriving with dread at the answer just as Louise said, "The Tylers."

She added, "William Tyler was a pallbearer. I didn't know he and Norrie were friends."

"Oh, yes," I said absently. "Mrs. Armslow's Newport house was close to the Newsomes', and the Tylers often came to stay. William, Beatrice, Lucinda, Emily . . . and Norrie spent summers together."

I remembered one summer after I began tending to Mrs. Armslow. By then, she was unable to leave her bed. The Tylers were staying with their aunt for the month, and with three young Tylers—Beatrice, Emily, and William—and the young Newsomes often visiting, the house was full of youthful energy. I saw William Tyler more than the others because he alone visited his great-aunt every day. His father had been a favorite of hers, and she took a special interest in the son. He answered her halting questions about his school. No, he had not been accepted to this club, as his father had, but he had joined a different one with some fine fellows in it. Yes, he did play on the football team, as his father had . . . well, not quite *on* the team itself. But he was the team manager, responsible for making sure they had what they needed at matches, and next year, the coach felt he might be able to play in an actual game.

Only when Mrs. Armslow asked if he saw a lot of Norrie, as he was at the same school, did William's good humor falter. But he recovered, saying, "Yes, he's tremendously popular, but I manage to see him sometimes."

He happened to catch my eye as he said it. In that moment, I knew that he had lied, and was worried about being caught in the lie—even by a servant. Out of sight of Mrs. Armslow, I smiled and he relaxed.

One morning from Mrs. Armslow's bedroom window, I caught sight of the pack racing outside. Norrie and the Tyler girls ran ahead. Lucinda lagged a little behind. Then I saw William, hands in his pockets, head down, walking down the path. Lucinda called, "Come on, William!" and Norrie shouted, "Yes, move, you slow old Willy Billy Bear," and there was a burst of laughter. At that, he took one long step forward, but then slowed again, as if he wanted to please, but the heart wasn't in it.

Another day, I heard crying near the carriage house. I looked around the corner and saw William crouched there, his face red and damp with tears and mucus.

"Mr. William?"

Panicked, he knuckled his cheeks as if that could hide the evidence of tears. I had a clean washcloth I had meant to use for Mrs. Armslow's bath. I held it out to him.

He took it gratefully, rubbing his face as he rose to his feet. He wore long shorts, a white shirt, and a light seersucker jacket. His straw hat lay on the sand.

He said, "I'm sorry."

Embarrassed, I said, "You don't have to be sorry, Mr. William."

Then, on impulse, I added, "And don't let them bully you. It's only because they're bored and can't think of anything more intelligent."

Then I froze. I had insulted one of . . . *them* was the only grouping I could think of. I would be shouted at, probably fired. I wasn't sure which was worse.

But William smiled. "He isn't very intelligent, is he?"

We didn't speak again for the rest of the visit. But at the end of the month, William sought me out and handed me five dollars. "For your kindness," he said stiffly. Then he stammered, "I'm sorry it's only money. It seems vulgar to . . . I'm not good at putting things . . ." He blew air in frustration. "I wish it was more."

Then he burst out triumphantly, "I'll see you at Christmas!"

★ ★ ★

Louise broke into my thoughts. "Do you know William Tyler, Jane?"

I saw that she had gone pink. "Somewhat. I think he's an excellent young man, Miss Louise," I said truthfully.

Charlotte was surprisingly calm at the prospect of seeing Beatrice. When I went to her room to dress her, I found her fussing at her jewelry box. "Did you pack my onyx earrings?"

"Yes, Miss Charlotte." I pointed them out.

Holding them to her ears, she said, "If that old woman asks me about Scarsdale one more time, I won't be responsible. And of course, she's invited the Tylers to dinner. Just to remind everyone who Norrie *should* have married."

Her tone was light. But her jaw was set, her eyes fixed, and in that moment, I saw a very young girl who was fighting for composure.

Looking at her jewelry box, I asked, "What color were you wearing when Mr. Newsome proposed?"

"Blue. Norrie liked me in blue."

I selected a pair of sapphire earrings, brilliant and flashing. "Then perhaps you could wear these for him."

The earrings would invite comment from the elder Mrs. Newsome. But Charlotte smiled. As I fixed them in her ears, she said softly, "Thank you, Jane."

When the ladies had gone down to dinner, I set out their slippers and nightgowns and settled into a chair in Louise's room for a nap. I woke hours later, to hear Charlotte's voice. I opened the door to see Louise pale and shaking and Charlotte bright with rage.

She hissed, "I hope the Newsomes throw him out of the house."

Louise gulped. "He only said what was true."

"How *dare* you . . ."

As she took a step toward her sister, I said, "Miss Charlotte. Miss Louise?"

"Yes, ask her," Charlotte told me. "Ask her to repeat what that criminal idiot said."

"Miss Charlotte, your voice is raised."

She wheeled on me. "I don't care. I don't care who hears me. It can't be any more obscene than . . ." Crying, she made her way to her room and slammed the door.

It all came out as I brushed Louise's hair, as she sat in her nightgown, her head swaying under the force of the brush. "It is my fault," she began. "I never know what to say, and I always end up saying the wrong thing."

"I'm not certain there are many 'right' things to say on such an occasion, Miss Louise."

"But I said the exact wrong thing." She looked up at me, a swath of light brown hair banding across the side of her face. "Because I wanted to impress him."

"Who, Miss Louise?"

"William Tyler," she said, blushing. "He was talking about workers' difficulties and strikes and how they're not really treated very well. I thought he was being sort of marvelous. So I wanted to show him, I don't know, that I understood—even though I don't. Like an idiot, I blurted out, 'Oh, like the notes.'"

I suppressed a sigh. Of all the wrong things one could say at a dinner after a funeral, Louise had indeed chosen one of the very wrongest.

"And then Mrs. Newsome—the old one, not the new one—

said she wouldn't have it talked about, that the notes were just malice and envy. People who were jealous because I don't know, they hadn't got what the Newsomes did because they were lazy . . ."

"And then?"

"Well, then it got very quiet for a while. Charlotte asked old Mrs. Newsome if she'd had a good crossing, and Mrs. Newsome didn't answer her, and new Mrs. Newsome said yes, the sea had been very calm, and then William said . . ."

She swallowed.

"What did he say, Miss Louise?"

"Then William said, 'I forget now. How many children died in that mine?'"

That stopped my breath.

"Then poor Mr. Newsome stood up and shouted that William was a guest in his home, and William said yes, and he was sorry, but it was absurd to pretend that Norrie had died because people were jealous over candlesticks. Then Charlotte said that Norrie was the finest man alive and the scum who murdered him would get the chair. And Mr. Newsome said William wasn't too old to thrash, and for a moment it looked like he was going to try, because he started struggling out of his chair . . ."

"Oh, dear."

"But then new Mrs. Newsome had the servants clear, so no one could really say anything. And William apologized. But Mr. Newsome said, 'I do not accept your apology.' So we all sat there."

I resumed brushing. "It's not your fault, Miss Louise."

"But I mentioned the notes."

"Mr. William would have found a way to make his point whether you mentioned them or not."

She nodded absently, and for a while seemed to put the evening out of her mind as I worked the tangles out of her hair.

But as Louise slid under the covers, she said, "When you see Charlotte? Will you tell her I'm sorry?"

Her tone was so serious that for a moment, I wondered what she was talking about. But clearly, Charlotte had made her feel she had committed a terrible wrong. "I will, Miss Louise. Don't worry about it any more."

Going across the hall to Charlotte's room, I found her sitting at the dressing table, already in her nightgown. The dress she had worn that evening had been left on the floor like a bad memory. I gathered it up and laid it across a low bench by the door.

"Miss Louise is very sorry, Miss Charlotte."

Charlotte sighed, her head on her hand. Under her breath, she said, "Louise." The way you might refer to a dog who has soiled the carpet. And might have to be shot because you cannot teach him otherwise.

When Charlotte was settled into bed, I turned down the lights. In the darkness, I heard, "I did love him. No matter what anyone says."

"I know you did, Miss Charlotte." I eased the door closed.

A moment later, I saw William coming up the stairs.

He smiled with relief on seeing me. "Jane." He looked toward Charlotte's room. "I wanted to apologize."

"I think you'd get something thrown at you if you tried." I lowered my voice. "What were you thinking?"

He looked guiltily at the doors of the two sisters, then said, "Care for a cigarette?"

9

It is here I must confess a great weakness, one that might have gotten me arrested in New York if I had done it in public. I—very occasionally—smoked cigarettes. In my defense, I only smoked in the company of one William Tyler. The habit started one Christmas a few years back when the family was visiting Mrs. Armslow. I had found William in the backyard, furtively inhaling. "Don't tell your aunt," I said. "No," he said. "You neither." Then he offered me a fresh cigarette from the box.

We wandered out onto the grounds of the Newsome estate, our breath turning to clouds. Catching sight of the mausoleum, starkly pale in the moonlight, we turned and took a different direction.

We soon found a private spot, a wrought-iron bench under an arc of hedge. It was cold but beautiful, with the night sky filled with stars. Hugging our coats tight, keeping one hand free, we sat like the near-children we'd been when we met.

William smoked the first cigarette in silence, then pitched the end into the darkness. Lighting the second, he said, "It was stupid, I know."

"It was stupid. And unkind."

William inhaled deeply.

"I know you didn't mean to be," I said.

"No, I did. They were all so . . . smug. As if Norrie Newsome was some saintly young hero. Do you know what I thought? When I heard he'd been killed? I thought, *Good*."

After inhaling and exhaling, I said, "He wasn't very nice to you."

William smiled bitterly. "Charlotte doesn't realize how lucky she is." He sighed. "Or Bea. Anyway, it doesn't matter, he's dead."

He took another drag, then dropped the remains onto the grass. I reminded myself to pick them up before we went inside. It wasn't like William to be thoughtless. Normally, he was at pains not to cause work for others.

Lighting another cigarette, William smiled at the slim white tube in his hands and said, "Funny—Norrie preferred cigars."

"Did he?"

"Oh, yes. Remember that summer at my aunt's? He would steal them from his father and make a big show of 'sharing' them. 'Take it, smoke it. What are you, a girl?' The whole first two weeks of that visit, he ignored me. Then one afternoon, he said, 'Let's sneak out after dark and have an adventure.'" William's mouth twisted. "I was thrilled."

"Most people would have been."

"The first time, I got sick. Threw up all over the sand after two puffs. Norrie laughed his head off. Then he offered me brandy and said, 'Have this and try again.'"

"You got sicker." I guessed.

"Eventually, I got the hang of it. I was so pleased with myself. Look at me, friends with Norrie Newsome." He stared out into the darkness.

Then, lifting his arm, he pulled back his shirtsleeve and showed me the inside of his wrist. In the dark, I could make out a small pale circle of flesh. I had a few on my arm from ironing; I recognized burn scars.

William tugged the shirtsleeve back into place. "That was the first time."

"The first."

"It was a dare. The kind of things boys do. How long can you stand it? Does it hurt if I do it on your arm? Your leg?"

He broke off. In the dark, I could see his hand was shaking.

"Every so often, he'd do it to himself, touch it to his hand, his ankle. Once he pulled down his pants and held it over . . . Well." He pitched the half-finished cigarette into the dark.

Gathering himself, he said, "So I'm damned glad he didn't marry Bea, and I'm damned glad he didn't marry Charlotte, and I'm damned glad he'll never marry anyone."

William kept his head down. But he edged closer to me on the bench; the broad stretch of his back curved near my hand. I found myself touching it in a strange impulse to see it not so abandoned.

Then just as quickly, I pulled back. I turned slightly and considered my cigarette.

"Thank you," I heard him say.

"Of course."

"Don't tell anyone."

For a blind, stupid second, I thought he meant my brief touch, then realized. "No, of course not. Never." What a story that would be for Michael Behan. THE STRANGE PRACTICES OF WEALTHY YOUNG MEN.

William stood. From the safety of height, he said, "Should I walk you back to the house?"

"I think it's best if you go on your own."

"I'll leave the kitchen door cracked for you." Giving me an extra cigarette, he turned to go.

Then he turned back. "Maybe when I'm in the city, I'll call on Louise Benchley."

"She'd like that." Louise would disintegrate with joy.

He set off toward the house, leaving me to smoke. Drawing on my cigarette, I wandered and mulled what William had told me. Tales related to tobacco and not. I shuddered at the memory of the pale patch of skin on William's wrist. What a hell Charlotte Benchley had escaped.

A question drifted into my head. Then, like the cigarette smoke wafting into the night air, it spread thin and vanished.

"Pssst." Startled, I turned, feeling I was back in the world of childhood, and saw Rose Newsome in a man's overcoat, her head wrapped in a scarf. She might have been anonymous, but the large, shining eyes, the beautiful mouth, and the lock of hair blowing free of the scarf gave her away.

The Greek myths are full of stories in which gods appear to astonished mortals. I had some sense of how those mortals felt as she approached, saying, "A fellow sinner! Thank God."

She held up a small box. "Care to try these? Gauloises. They're hideously strong. My husband objects to the smell, so I have to sneak."

I held up my own half-finished cigarette as an excuse. "No, but thank you, ma'am."

Thinking Rose Newsome would want to enjoy her gardens in peace, I nodded a deferential good night and made to step away.

"You needn't go." There was something in her voice beyond kindness, an actual need. "Stay. Please."

"Are you sure?"

"Very sure. You might be the one person who isn't furious with me this weekend."

Lighting her cigarette, she murmured, "I'm always babbling at servants. Robert tells me I must stop. But part of me keeps feeling I should be one of you. A girl from Schuylkill in a house like this? She belongs in the kitchen, doesn't she?"

I felt that those words, or words close to them, had been

spoken to her, probably by a member of her new family. "You'd be very out of place in the kitchen, ma'am."

"Tell me, how is poor Charlotte?"

I thought, then answered truthfully, "Mourning."

"I was going to her room, but I found myself waylaid by Beatrice Tyler, who was *also* in a dreadful state because I had asked Charlotte to stay. I almost told her, 'You should speak with my mother-in-law. She agrees with you entirely.' I thought the Tylers and the Benchleys were such great friends."

"They were."

"I see." She inhaled. "No one's really explained it to me, but I gather there was a romantic misunderstanding?"

She was fishing; clearly Mr. Newsome had not thought his new wife worthy of hearing the complicated histories of the Tyler and Newsome families.

I said, "The Newsomes and Tylers have been close for many years. There was an expectation that young Mr. Newsome and Miss Tyler . . ."

She nodded. "That's the difficulty with expectations, they're so seldom realized. Apparently, the young ladies had words at the ball." Taking my silence for ignorance, she added, "Things were said, dresses damaged. Hair may even have been pulled. All I know is there's a great, horrible stain on my carpet."

The wine Beatrice threw at Charlotte, I thought.

"And of course," she continued, "Lucinda's been angry with me since . . . well, *my* wedding. And Norrie just hated me from the beginning. Stupid of me to think that if I took his side over Charlotte, he might think better of me. All it did was enrage everyone else. Of course Lucinda would never have been rational about anyone he married."

Then she smiled. "Oh, dear, that wasn't very discreet of me. You're very easy to talk to, Jane. People must tell you that all the time."

I smiled. And wondered what Mrs. Newsome meant when she said Lucinda wasn't rational on the subject of her brother.

I asked, "Have the police made any progress?"

"They have the notes. A handwriting expert's looking at them. They took fingerprints. Another expert's looking at *them*. But since the man got away . . . well, it's hard to find one anarchist in an entire city. They're almost certain he had help, a network, they call it. So he could be in Chicago by now. Or Canada. Inspector Blackburn says his informants will hear if anyone boasts about it." She inhaled agitatedly. "He says there's a good chance they'll try it again."

"Have there been more notes?"

She hesitated. "Yes. One. It arrived yesterday. It said, 'Now your son is dead.' And the police aren't really sure, does that mean they won't stop there or—?" Suddenly she seemed to feel the cold and pulled her coat tight around her. "Please don't tell that to the Benchleys. I haven't even told my husband. His doctors say it's essential he be kept calm."

"How is Mr. Newsome?" I asked.

"Not well," she said. "He and Norrie had their fights, but there's no stronger bond, is there? I lost my father young. It was the end of the world."

Finishing her cigarette, she said, "I had better go back. Come—I'll open the back door for you."

As I followed her to the back of the house—what an unusual sight she made, wandering the grounds in her man's coat—she said mischievously, "I saw William Tyler coming in as I went out. Was he your smoking companion? He seems to have quite a passion for the working classes."

We reached the back door, which William had left open as promised. Rose Newsome frowned. "That's not safe."

She was right, it wasn't. Someone was threatening to kill the Newsome children—and there was still one left. Two, if you took the jokes about Rose Newsome being young enough to be Mr. Newsome's daughter seriously.

Mistaking my guilt for anxiety, Mrs. Newsome said, "We have security men watching the house. You don't have to worry. We're ridiculously protected."

It occurred to me that they had had security the night of the Newsome ball, but it had not been enough. I did notice she was careful to lock the door once we were inside.

Then, as if unable to resist a last indiscretion, she said in a low voice, "My mother-in-law seems to be coping by unleashing bile in all directions. I long to apologize to Charlotte; she's been particularly poisonous to her. After dinner, I did say to the *elder* Mrs. Newsome, 'You realize Charlotte Benchley didn't actually kill Norrie.' Do you know what she said? 'Didn't she?' You see— insane. But you can't argue with those old women."

I swallowed the sudden, hard lump in my throat. "No."

As we made our way through the cramped downstairs, I wondered if Mrs. James Newsome could be aware of *Town Topics*'s snide references to Pep Pills. It seemed insane that anyone would suspect Charlotte of murdering a young man who had offered her such a glittering future. But some people might think it insane that she would presume to marry that young man.

Passing the laundry room, I remembered that whoever murdered Norrie had likely had bloodstains on their clothes.

I said, "Mrs. Newsome?"

She turned.

"Did you ever find Miss Charlotte's dress? The one she wore to the ball? It's embarrassing, but I forgot to bring it back with us."

Rose Newsome's eyes widened. "No, I don't believe we did. You might ask Mrs. Farrell."

10

The following day was much like the one that preceded it. Gray winter skies, silent rooms, animated only by the crackling of the fireplace and the relentless tick of the clock. Louise tried to make herself pleasant, but she often "forgot" things in her room and had to retrieve them—sometimes taking quite a while. It was perhaps out of kindness that Lucinda Newsome asked her to walk. Louise hated exercise, but gratefully accepted.

Charlotte gave the elder Mrs. Newsome nothing to criticize as she read and murmured to Rose Newsome about the weather. (I had the distinct impression that lady was yearning for her Gauloises.) But I could tell the older woman's dislike was as strong as ever. Did she really believe Charlotte guilty? Or had she simply meant that by marrying beneath him, Norrie had invited some kind of cosmic destruction? I thought of Mr. Behan and the Pep Pills story. He had hinted there were other stories he could tell about Norrie; anything about his romantic entanglements would be bad for Charlotte. Between newspaper innuendo and society gossip, Charlotte might well be finished in New York. Not to mention tried for murder.

The missing dress disturbed me. A household as well run as the Newsomes' would not discard an expensive dress. So where was it now? I didn't feel I could ask the formidable Mrs. Farrell—but there was someone else. The very woman who had ruined the dress in the first place.

I took Louise's walk as my opportunity to ask Charlotte for permission, if I was not needed, to pay a visit to the Tylers. I said her mother had loaned Mrs. Tyler something and now wanted it back.

Located closer to the center of Rhinebeck, the Tyler summer house was not nearly so grand as the Newsome house. In comparison, it felt almost like a cottage. The front hallway was snug, but richly furnished. One side led to a cozy dining area and kitchen; the other took you down a hallway that branched off to Mrs. Tyler's tiny study and the parlor. I knew the upstairs bedrooms to be small, but pleasant and airy.

I was a little apprehensive of my welcome, but Mrs. Tyler greeted me with the same slightly predatory good cheer she had always shown me. "Oh, Jane, it is good to see you. But I'm afraid if you're here to ask for a job, we're in no position to offer you one."

"No, thank you. I'm very happy with the Benchleys."

"Oh," she said. "Well, that makes one of us." She let that hang in the air a moment, before saying, "I hope you're not here to bring William's head back on a platter to the Newsomes. I'd give it to you, but he left this morning."

"I'm actually here to ask a favor of Miss Beatrice."

The expression on Mrs. Tyler's face told me I would have had better luck asking for William's head. "You can try. Anything to take her mind off things." With an airy hand, she encompassed Norrie's murder and her daughter's broken heart. "She's upstairs. Third door down. Oh, and I wouldn't mention Charlotte if I were you."

The upstairs of the house was even more humble than the downstairs, with plain wood floors covered in rugs that were threadbare in patches. The roof was angled, and I had to be careful of my head. Going to the third white painted door, I knocked. Hearing, "Yes?" I called, "It's Jane, Miss Beatrice." In the pause, I prayed that Beatrice would remember I had worked for her great-aunt and not associate me entirely with the Benchleys.

From her manner when she opened the door, I saw that she did remember . . . in both cases. Once her mother had told me she found "my Bea heavy going," and I responded, "It's those dark eyes, Mrs. Tyler. They look right through you." Those eyes were looking right through me now. But she let me in and shut the door behind us. She was dressed in a drab blue day dress and looked as if she were not sleeping well. Her hair was brittle, her skin dull.

"I wanted to offer my condolences for Mr. Newsome's death, Miss Tyler."

Her eyes narrowed. "Why would you say that to me?"

"Because you were fond of him."

"I wasn't fond of him—I hate that phrase. I loved him."

Startled by her candor, it took me a moment to say, "Yes, I see that."

"Do you? Most people seem to have missed it." She got up and then sat on a wooden chair near a small desk. "I can't believe she has the gall to wear black." She glared at me. "You know better than that, Jane. You should never have let her." Then, with affected indifference, she asked, "Do they mean to go after the money? I would have thought they had enough of it already."

"I wouldn't know," I said.

She looked at me. "Really? Isn't that why she's here? Playing the part of the bereaved widow? I don't know how the Newsomes can stand it."

Taking a deep breath, I said, "I came about Miss Charlotte's gown. The one she wore to the ball. The one that was damaged."

Beatrice shrugged one shoulder. "What would I know about it?"

"Because you damaged it."

"I . . . damaged? Oh, for God's sake. It's hardly anything. I'm sure you can cope."

"I was told the dress was soaked."

"That's absurd."

"With red wine."

"With . . ." Beatrice turned in her chair to face me. "Do you imagine I would be swilling red wine at the Newsomes' ball? Which I then, what, hurled at Charlotte Benchley? Is *that* what she's saying?"

I had to think. It was not only Charlotte who said the dress was ruined. Mary had seen it as well. And Mary had no reason to lie. "One of the maids said the dress was ruined."

Beatrice turned away. "Well, I didn't ruin it."

"But you did quarrel with Miss Charlotte."

"If you mean I challenged her insane fantasy that Norrie Newsome was going to marry her, and she turned shrew, then yes, we quarreled."

I chose my words carefully. "Surely, Charlotte Benchley was not the only person with that fantasy."

"Oh, she managed to talk some people into it. So much so that Norrie was almost considering going through with it—can you imagine? It rattled people, he liked that. But I knew he would never actually do it."

"That would be a very callous way to treat a young lady who'd never done him harm."

"Never done him harm?" She took up a penknife on the desk, tapping its slender blade on the surface. "Who do you think leaked all those awful stories about them to the press? Charlotte Benchley, that's who. Who kept at him all the time? Asking when was he going to tell his father? When was he going to give her a ring?

When could she tell everyone? Honestly, how he kept from slapping her, I'll never know."

I could hear Norrie's voice in Beatrice's account. Obviously, he had soothed Beatrice's feelings with complaints about her rival.

"Are you saying he never actually proposed to her?" I asked.

The penknife stilled. "He might have. Maybe she led him into it. 'You should marry me, Norrie.'" Her imitation of the voice Charlotte used with men was cruelly accurate. "'Then you'll never have to listen to your father again.' Norrie probably liked that idea—until he realized it would mean listening to Charlotte Benchley for the rest of his life."

I had said Beatrice Tyler had eyes that looked right through a person. Apparently I didn't, because I couldn't tell: Was this the truth? What she hoped was the truth? Or a flat-out lie to conceal she herself had reasons for wanting to harm Norrie Newsome? What if, on the night of the ball, he told her that while he might not enjoy the sound of Charlotte's voice, he intended to marry her and her money anyway?

Trying to sound as simpleminded as possible, I said, "I admit, I was surprised when Miss Charlotte told me she was engaged to Mr. Newsome. Mrs. Armslow had always told me he would ask you—"

I broke off, as if shocked by my own impertinence. But it was enough to provoke Beatrice, who said, "Maybe he did. Maybe I said yes."

Curling her arms around the back of the chair, she added, "And maybe that's what he told Charlotte Benchley on Christmas Eve. And maybe that's why she killed him. Because she did, and you know it."

"I don't know that at all, Miss Beatrice."

"Don't you? Well, I know for a fact that Norrie was not going to announce his engagement to Charlotte Benchley. He told me

so himself. I know that's why he's dead. And that's why it's an obscenity the Newsomes have Charlotte Benchley under their roof."

★ ★ ★

It was a long, cold walk back to the Newsome estate. Shoulders
hunched against the biting air, chin buried in my scarf, hands
deep in my pockets, I thought about what Beatrice Tyler had said.
I wondered if she believed it. If she had told the police her suspicions. Or the tabloids. God knows the Tylers needed money.

But Beatrice was nowhere near the library when the murder
had taken place, so she couldn't have been the person who told
Behan about the Pep Pills. And why had she been so insistent that
she hadn't ruined Charlotte's dress? The answer came to me with
startling clarity: the dress was viciously expensive. If Charlotte demanded compensation for the damage, it could wipe out the Tyler girls' clothing allowance for years. Perhaps Beatrice had hidden
the dress, so there could be no proof that it was destroyed.

The servants' entrance was on the north side of the house.
As I walked the gravel path, I scanned the grounds for signs of
Louise and Lucinda out walking. Or Rose Newsome taking her
husband for a stroll in his wheelchair. But I saw no one. Until I
approached the mausoleum.

She stood alone, a black-velvet-clad Antigone before her
brother's tomb. Instinctively, I stepped from the gravel to the grass
so she would not hear me. But Lucinda's gaze was fixed on the
bronze door, its image of an impassive angel hovering over a man,
lost and despairing, his hand reaching for paradise, even as he fell.

I went on my way.

★ ★ ★

Beatrice Tyler had denounced the obscenity of Charlotte's presence under the Newsome roof. It did not continue much longer.

The next day, a newspaper clipping arrived in the mail, forwarded from the house in Manhattan. It read:

BATTLE OF THE BEAUTIES!
DID NORRIE NEWSOME'S ROVING EYE
COST HIM HIS LIFE?

This newspaper has faithfully reported the secret engagement of Robert Norris Newsome Jr. and nouveau nymphet Charlotte Benchley. But was Miss Benchley the only rose in his garden?

An eyewitness who was present at the ill-fated Christmas Eve fête tells us that a contretemps de coeur broke out the night of the murder as two delicately reared young ladies unsheathed their claws and had at it over the affections of young Mr. Newsome. The words "promise," "marriage," and "liar" could be heard quite clearly.

What did Norrie Newsome promise? And to whom? And did those promises have anything to do with the grisly discovery made later that night?

Everyone thought it best for the Benchley girls to return home that afternoon.

11

We returned to the city to find the Benchley home under siege. Reporters crowded the pavement, peering in windows, knocking on neighboring doors, and shouting questions at any individual who emerged from the house. Was it true that Miss Tyler had struck Miss Benchley? Had Miss Benchley known of Norrie's affection for Miss Tyler? The throng of newspaper people was magnified by the idly curious, craning their necks to catch a glimpse of the woman at the heart of the city's most notorious murder case.

Inside the house, it was chaos. A recently hired housekeeper had quit. A hysterical Mrs. Benchley was under the care of Matchless Maude, who seemed to be partaking of the brandy and doling it out to her mistress in equal parts. Mary dawdled by the back door, being charmed by a bucktoothed young man with a notebook. Jack, Mr. Benchley's valet, was chatting in a low voice on the downstairs phone, and Bernadette and the cook were goggle-eyed over a spread of papers in the kitchen.

I placed a finger on the phone to cut Jack's connection, pulled Mary from the door, swept up the papers, and instructed the cook to make lunch before Mrs. Benchley started singing sea chanteys. Then I went upstairs to unpack.

Charlotte was sitting on the edge of her bed as if it were the only safe spot in the house. She had been strangely calm when the elder Mrs. Newsome told her it would be wise for her to go home—and stay home—until this latest unpleasantness was over. When Louise tried to show sympathy on the ride home, Charlotte said, "I won't have it talked about. It's a lie, of course. There's no need to say another word."

Now her fists were tight, her eyes bright with anger. As I came in, she murmured, "I'll bloody her."

"Miss Charlotte?"

"Beatrice Tyler. I know she's the one who went to the newspapers. She's desperate for money, and she'll do anything to humiliate me."

I took a deep breath. "Miss Charlotte, forgive me for mentioning it, but do you remember the dress you wore Christmas Eve?" I could see she knew exactly the dress I referred to. "The one that had wine spilled upon it."

She shrugged. "I've no idea. Anyway, what does it matter now?"

"I only wondered if it could be saved."

"It was beyond saving, believe me."

"Then we should present the Tylers with a bill."

She stood and went to her bureau, an act of irritation—and avoidance. I said, "So strange. I never knew Miss Beatrice to lose her temper when I worked for Mrs. Armslow."

Charlotte turned. "Don't you take her side. You should have heard what she said to me."

"What did she say, Miss Charlotte?"

For a brief moment, she wrestled with herself. But the need to blame was too strong. "She actually grabbed my arm and said Norrie and I couldn't possibly be engaged. I said she could judge for herself whether we were engaged or not at midnight, and that she'd look pretty silly when, forced to make a choice between her and my money, Norrie chose my money."

"And that's when she threw the wine?"

Charlotte hesitated, then admitted, "No—I did that myself. She'd torn the dress when she'd taken hold of me. There was no time to fix it, and she'd made me late. I didn't want Norrie angry with me. So I thought, let her take the blame. Let him see what a harridan she is."

It was possible she was telling the truth; the fabric had been exceptionally delicate, and a rough hand could damage it. "What did you do with the dress, Miss Charlotte?"

She flushed. "I stuffed it under the bed. In a far corner so no one would find it. I could see from the dust the maids didn't clean the guest rooms."

"Do you think it's still there?"

"It might be." She looked at me. "Why on earth do you ask?"

Because some might say you spilled wine on the dress to cover up the blood.

I smiled as if it really didn't matter. "No reason."

The next day, *Town Topics* revealed that Charlotte had never received an engagement ring, hinting strongly that the ring might be on the hand of another lady, presumably Beatrice Tyler. As a result, Charlotte became more determined than ever that the world see her as Norrie's intended, and so I was sent to Macy's for more mourning attire.

Herald Square was a place I detested at the best of times, and a wet, bone-chilling afternoon hardly came close to best. An icy drizzle had started, and despite my efforts with the umbrella, rain ran off the brim of my hat and down my neck, dampened my coat, and left my feet cold and wet. The Sixth Avenue train clattered overhead, rattling my nerves. Crowds of harried shoppers shoved me this way and that. I was thankful to get under Macy's awning.

The grand windows had been made festive for Christmas. One displayed a red-cheeked Santa soaring through a painted night sky in a sleigh packed high with brightly wrapped presents. In another a model train raced up and down a dizzying array of metal track set against a daubed backdrop of Herald Square. A sign implored shoppers to GIVE THE BOY SOMETHING HE WANTS!

Another showed a beautifully decorated tree, surrounded by rows of dolls, still in their boxes. All the dolls were of the same size, dressed in the same white pinafore; only their hairstyles differed. Some were blond, some dark. Some with curls, others bangs or long straight tresses. They lay with arms at their sides, open eyes staring upward. Louise would enjoy this, I thought, but I found the little bodies in their boxes unnerving.

When I had purchased three outfits and two toques suitable for mourning, and given the Benchleys' address for delivery, I left the store. Under the awning, I wrestled with my umbrella. The rain was still coming down and the umbrella seemed to have given up the ghost. The Benchleys were less than a mile away, but it seemed like a very long journey home.

A man appeared in front of me, bearing a large umbrella, which, unlike mine, seemed to work. He smiled invitingly; I was about to look away to avoid the flirtation when I realized it was Michael Behan.

Holding up a hand, he said, "Just a cup of tea, Miss Prescott. You don't have to say anything. I'll do the talking."

I looked up and down the street; where had he come from? "Did you . . . are you following me?"

"I'm afraid so, Miss Prescott. That nice girl Mary told me where I might find you."

I was about to plunge into the bad weather—working umbrella or no—when I remembered the Pep Pill story. Mr. Behan had a point. Charlotte could use a friend in the press. Because she had enemies— at least one of whom might be feeding *Town Topics* its stories.

And it was raining very hard.

So I found myself sitting at Porter's Café. While not an actual saloon, it was a shabby place with sawdust on the floor and long tables with benches on either side. As I was the only woman present, Mr. Behan allowed me the side that let me keep my back to the wall, rather than being brushed by other patrons passing by.

Behan called to the man behind the bar, "Beer, please. And a dozen oysters." He looked to me, and I shook my head.

"I have ten minutes," I told him.

"Right." The beer arrived, and he drank. Then, setting down the glass, he said, "So. Pep Pills."

"A lot of people use Dr. Forsythe's remedy," I said.

"Not so many men, though." He still had the trace of an accent. "Though" was practically "dough."

I was about to point out that any number of women at the ball could have dropped that bottle. But I realized that would lead us to the question of which women at the party might have had Pep Pills, and that was not a question I wanted to raise. It still bothered me that I couldn't remember seeing the pills that night.

Changing the subject, I said, "Did you write that story about the engagement ring?" He grinned. "Why on earth would you say such a thing?"

I waited for him to tell me who had given him the information. But he only sipped his beer and asked, "Why, have you seen a ring on her finger?"

"Who was your 'eyewitness' for the story about Norrie's body?"

"I've got a pal at the morgue."

"A man of great sensitivity and discretion."

He raised an eyebrow. "Do you know what a man gets paid to lug a body that's spent three days in the East River, Miss Prescott? Well, it's not so much that you can't blame him for a little private entrepreneurship."

"And who told you Pep Pills were 'found' nearby?"

"Ah, there, I cannot reveal my source." Then he leaned in and whispered, "Cops figure out yet that you're the one who found the body?"

I shook my head.

"Didn't think so. The press doesn't have to be your enemy, you know."

"What does that mean?"

"Well, it could mean, why give the police the scoop for free when my associates would be happy to pay you for it?"

I made to stand up, but Behan put a hand on my wrist.

"Your uncle runs that mission on the Lower East Side, right?"

"How do you know that?"

"Because I'm a good reporter. Sit down, Miss Prescott. I can see you're a young woman of high moral principles who wouldn't take a dime for your story, and I almost admire that. But I bet your uncle could use the money for his fine work among the fallen women of this city."

"He could, but he wouldn't take it."

Beaten, he sat back and blew out his cheeks. Dropping his brash reporter's tone, he said, "I can't figure you out, Miss Prescott. You're here, so you must want something—what is it?"

"I want to know who's feeding you stories."

"I talk to a lot of people."

"The story about the fight at the party—who did you talk to for that one?"

He shook his head. "Can't tell you."

"Can't or won't?"

"Does it matter?"

I tried a different tack. "All the other papers are writing about anarchists. People who might be angry with the family over the Shickshinny Mine."

"Oh, the dark and terrible notes sent to the Newsome family? Well, those boys at the *Times* and the *Herald* have the anarchist side all sewn up. They've got the money to send people over to Pennsylvania to talk to the miners' families, and even if my paper had that money, they're not going to send me. I've got no pull with the Newsome family flunkeys on the police force. So I'm going with the women's angle. True heart scorned, that kind of thing."

"What makes you think there's a true heart scorned?"

"Well, the young ladies didn't start pulling hair over politics, did they?" He leaned in. "You have any idea how much I could have written about Norrie Newsome these past few years, only it was too hot to print? Let's put it nicely and say he had a way with women. And not all his ways were pleasant."

"So you're starting rumors about an innocent young woman simply because it makes for a good story."

"Simply nothing, Miss Prescott. It's my job. Between you, me, and the wallpaper, did those wounds look like the work of an anarchist to you?"

"How would I know?"

"Maybe I read too much of that yellow journalism, but I had the idea they went in for bombs or guns."

"Bombs and guns make noise. Maybe the killer didn't want to attract attention."

"Strange they haven't found the murder weapon yet. Think he took it with him? Dripping all that blood?"

I swallowed. "It could have been a hammer. Small, easily concealed. The sort of thing a workman would have."

"Maybe. Or maybe the killer used something in the house, something easy to hand, that could be left in the house unnoticed afterwards."

"What if they did? What difference does it make?"

"Well, surely our vengeful anarchist came prepared for the task."

I thought of Mr. Pawlicec at the door, the heavy iron tongs he used to carry the ice. "There were many people there that night. Anyone could have slipped in. You did."

"That's right, I did. But this feels like a sudden crime to me, Miss Prescott. Sudden and ugly and passionate."

In spite of myself, I felt drawn to Behan's vision. Forgetting the need for discretion, I said, "And how do you think a young woman overpowers a strong young man like Norrie Newsome?"

He held up a finger. "You make a good point, Miss Prescott. Let's think again about those Pep Pills. Maybe someone slipped Mr. Newsome a little something to make him go quiet."

And there it was, his big story: a rich, callous young man makes an unsuitable match. He jilts the unfortunate girl on the evening their engagement is to be announced. In return, she drugs him and bashes his head in.

"I can write a different story, Miss Prescott. If you tell me something you remember about that night, one little thing that proves I'm wrong—I'm not a man who slanders those who don't deserve it. It must be said, sometimes the deceased had it coming."

Remembering Norrie's ruined eyes, I said, "No one had that coming, Mr. Behan."

"What were you doing in the library, Miss Prescott?"

"I was looking for Miss Charlotte."

"You sure?" His voice was soft, his eyes concerned.

"Yes."

"There's nothing else you want to tell me?"

I hesitated, images from that night flitting through my mind, too fast and fragmented for comprehension. It was like seeing a shape in a cloud, then losing it with the slightest breath of wind. I shook my head.

Behan sighed. Then he reached into his pocket and handed me his card. "See, my theory is the people who cook the food and clean the clothes see and hear a lot more than the people they work for. And my further bet is, you see more than most. May I escort you to the trolley?"

He made good on his promise, holding his umbrella over my head all the way to the trolley stop. "What brought you out on a day like this?" he asked.

It seemed rude not to answer a man who was keeping my head dry. "Mourning wear for Miss Charlotte."

"Anxious to look the part?" She was, but I gave him a look anyway.

The trolley rolled up. Tipping his hat, Behan said, "Oh—one other thing. Did your young lady happen to take a trip to Philly shortly before her intended's demise?" He pronounced it "de-meese."

"Why?"

"Because Mr. Newsome did—and when he checked into the hotel, he brought a friend." He grinned. "A lady friend. If you remember anything about that night, give me a call, will you? My landlord will thank you."

★ ★ ★

Half an hour later, I arrived back at the Benchley house wet, cold, and dispirited. Shucking off my damp coat in the servants' cloakroom, I tried to sort through the tangle of what might be true, what people believed, and what people could be made to believe for some sense of real danger to the Benchleys. I put my mind back to that night, skirting the memory of Norrie's face. I thought of the rug, the legs of a low table, a blanket left carelessly over a chair, the leaping, irregular light of the fire. I didn't see Pep Pills, but maybe I missed them. Whenever an image or a feeling became too clear, my mind would shut down, as if slamming the door on something unpleasant.

As I trudged up the backstairs, I heard a clatter of feet overhead.

I looked up and saw Louise. Her arms were raised in happiness, her long camel face alight.

"Jane! They said you were back."

"What are you doing backstairs, Miss Louise?"

Louise held out a small package wrapped in blue paper with a silver ribbon. "I wanted to give this to you. We didn't really have Christmas, did we? So . . . Merry Christmas, Jane."

Dutifully, I opened it. It was a comb, a lovely thing and not inexpensive. It looked to be silver. A row of small dark purple jewels—I hoped they were paste—was inlaid along the edge.

"I thought the purple, with your hair and eyes. If you don't like it—"

"I own nothing in the world as nice as this," I said truthfully. "Thank you, Miss Louise."

Perhaps some small part of me should have felt insulted. Anna would have said that Louise was trying to buy my affection when diligent service was all she had a right to. But it was impossible for me not to feel moved by a girl so lonely she could be made happy by giving her maid a present. Louise wished to be generous. If I was the only person in the house capable of receiving that generosity, I couldn't feel ashamed of that position. But perhaps that position gave me the privilege to ask a question.

"Miss Louise, do you remember those pills your mother gave you the night of the party?"

"I suppose so."

"I wanted to put them back in her cabinet, but couldn't find them. Do you know where they might be?" Louise shook her head. "Perhaps you gave them to someone?"

"I can't remember. That night was so . . ." She trailed off.

It's never a pleasant thing to know you are being lied to. Still less pleasant when every possible reason for the lie is disturbing. I could not connect Louise to those reasons. And yet I knew she was lying.

And now I lied to her, saying, "Oh, well, we can order more. Thank you again for the gift, Miss Louise. I'll cherish it."

Before going upstairs, I went to the kitchen. It was nearly dinnertime, and the staff was in a flurry of chopping and stirring, poking and carving. It was not the best time to bother the ill-tempered cook with questions, but I could not help asking if I had had any calls while I was out. I held my breath, hoping Anna had finally phoned.

"No calls," she barked over her shoulder.

12

Over the next week, the newspapers avidly followed the search for Norrie Newsome's killer. Several articles educated readers about the savagery of the anarchist. Others speculated on the murder weapon itself, which had still not been found. Inspector Blackburn was daily on the front page, raiding anarchist "strongholds," hinting at secrets revealed to the department by informants, and promising a significant break in the case any day. I saw Anna's name nowhere, but that didn't stop me worrying.

The "feminine angle" was generously covered by *Town Topics.* There was speculation as to the state of relations between the intimidating grandmother of the deceased and his young stepmother, a spread on the latest in funeral fashion, and discussion of what sort of flowers had been used in the service. The paper also hinted at Norrie's past "romances." There were rumors of a grieving waitress in New Haven and an aggrieved coat check girl at the Waldorf-Astoria. So far, there was nothing more about Charlotte, but I felt it was only a matter of time.

Meanwhile, I wrestled with the possibility that either the young

woman I worked for or my oldest friend might be guilty of murder. Anna. Charlotte. Pep Pills. Once my mind had worked itself
around to reassurance on one subject, it leapt back to the other to
fret again. Lack of activity fed my anxiety; there was too much
time to worry. None of the Benchley ladies were going out, and
there were few visitors. Publicly, the Newsomes might be standing
by Charlotte, but the rest of society was not as generous.

Could Charlotte have killed Norrie? As I sewed, ironed, or
folded, I wrestled with the idea. Chief against her was the fact that
no one had seen her at the time of the murder. No—chief against
her was her fiancé's behavior. Insulting her in the weeks leading
up to the party. Flirting with Beatrice at the party.

But Charlotte had come through the door opposite the library.
She couldn't have made it through the ballroom after murdering
Norrie unnoticed; there would have been blood on her dress.
Then I remembered the library had two doors, one leading to the
kitchen and the backstairs. She might have gone that route and not
been seen; staff was accustomed to adopting an invisible posture
when the employer class was present, and that often involved
looking the other way. Upstairs she could have changed her dress . . .

No, chief against Charlotte was the fact that she changed her
dress. Why had she done that? And where was it now?

Then there were the pills. They promised energy, not lassitude,
but who knew their effect when taken with a lot of alcohol? Louise had had the bottle, but I could easily imagine her pressing
them on Charlotte at some point in the evening. With Norrie
dead, she might be hiding that detail to protect her sister.

And then there was Anna. I could think of any number of
things that argued for her guilt.

One endlessly long afternoon, I approached Mrs. Benchley
and said Louise was in need of a hair tonic; might I go out and get
some?

Then I added, as if it were a new thought, "And while I'm at the pharmacist, perhaps I could get you some more Pep Pills. Unless you have enough . . ."

She brightened. "That's an excellent idea, Jane! I've been searching everywhere for my bottle, but I suppose we left it at the Newsomes', and I certainly can't ask them now. Thank you, Jane, you think of everything."

That afternoon, I left the Benchley house and headed down to the Lower East Side. As I walked to the elevated, I passed a news-stand located by the stairs that led up to the platform. Several tables were laden with copies of the dozens of newspapers and journals sold in the city, everything from the *Herald* to the *Gaelic American* to the *Staats-Zeitung*. The Newsome murder was on the front page of many of them, but I paused to examine some ladies' magazines displayed on the rack and saw one hairstyle that might suit Louise. But as always, the "effortless" ideal involved a lot of painstaking labor.

As I started to walk up the stairs, I was confronted by an ad for Floradora Cigars featuring the lovely Floradora Girl. That put me in mind of the last time a crime had dominated the papers: the murder of Stanford White by Harry K. Thaw, who was taken by a fit of jeal-ousy over his wife, the gorgeous Evelyn Nesbit, one of "Gibson's Girls," whose face had been on the cover of *Vanity Fair, Harper's Bazaar,* and *Ladies' Home Journal.* Nesbit's testimony about her rela-tionship with White, begun when she was only fourteen, had shocked the country. As I waited for the train, I wondered what had ever happened to Evelyn Nesbit, who had once been so famous.

As always when I visited the Lower East Side, I was struck by the vast difference between this world and that of the Armslows and Benchleys. You might have been in different countries. There, the abundance of wealth stood in stark contrast with the marked absence of effort, as if the comforts of life grew organically from the earth. On those streets, quiet. A strolling ease among the people. One could hear the trees of the park, the murmured greetings of passersby. To hurry or raise one's voice would be an unseemly sign of urgency. Barter and negotiation were below-stairs matters.

Whereas here, barter was life. From storefronts and pushcarts, from windows where women called to men, from gangs of boys whose fingers fiddled at your pockets, everything was the pursuit of more—because people had so little. Everywhere you went there was assault, from shouting, elbows and shoulders, the smell. You didn't walk down these streets. You put your head down and pushed through.

The world of the Benchleys knew the city's tender care. Police patrolled to make sure no one lingered who should not be there. The streets were cleaned. The streetlamps were lit. Here, the gutters were full of sewage, rotting food, and the occasional dead horse, left splayed and stiff on the street. Not an inch of space was unused. Laundry flew overhead. Old mattresses were crammed onto fire escapes for an extra bedroom. Every stoop was crowded with neighbors. Here, street and sidewalk were the same, as carts and horses and cars and people rushed through whatever route was open, bumping, shoving, even trampling one another as they went.

I headed first toward Block's Pharmacy on Second Avenue. I had always gone there for tonics and remedies my uncle's charges needed. Aspirin and bicarbonate of soda for hangover, cocaine drops for toothache, sometimes more stringent treatments for ailments I need not discuss here. When I got there, I bought a bottle of Pep Pills and was about to ask the questions I had rehearsed on the ride down. But then I reconsidered. The pharmacists at Block's knew me. They might have heard from my uncle who I was now working for. I could not ask them my question without possibly drawing attention to the Benchleys.

Thwarted, I wandered aimlessly until I found myself on the streets where many of the store signs were in English and Hebrew. One had a sign illustrated with the age-old apothecary image of a mortar and pestle. Looking in the window, I saw that the store was empty. Which was ideal for my purposes. And no one would know me here anyway.

The store was not nearly as palatial as many pharmacies. There were only two counters lining the sides, and one in back. A few cracked and dusty stools stood empty by the counter on the left. Only one man seemed to be working, and he stood with his back to me, arranging bottles in the far cabinet.

"Excuse me," I said, hoping he spoke English.

He turned. "Yes?" He was very tall and thin, with a long face and outsized ears. His dark hair was cropped close to his head, and he wore small spectacles over large, light gray eyes. He reminded me of a ball of dough rubbed between the hands until it becomes a long wobbly strand. But if his looks were odd, his expression was intelligent. And his white coat was spotless.

I approached. "My employer has been told by her friend that she should try Dr. Forsythe's Pep Pills. But she's elderly, and I'm concerned they may not be suitable for someone in her condition. Do you know if they can cause any harm to the heart?"

"Forsythe's Pep Pills?" He had a slight accent, but I couldn't place it.

I put the bottle on the counter. He reached for them, then hesitated with his fingers above the cap. "May I?"

"Yes, please."

He unscrewed the cap and tipped one of the capsules onto a clean white slab. Taking a scalpel, he neatly sliced it in two so that the powder spilled onto the surface. Touching his pinky to his tongue, then to the powder, he tasted it.

"Gelatine," he pronounced after a moment. "Sugar. A very small trace of cocaine. But not enough to do anyone any harm." He picked up the bottle. "What does Dr. Forsythe charge for these?"

I told him the price. He raised his eyebrows in disbelief. Handing me the bottle, he said, "Well, I don't think they'll do your employer any harm, but I don't think they'll do her much good either. If you tell me a little about her, I might be able to recommend something."

"She is very set on these pills," I lied. "My concern is she may get confused and take too many. Or combine them with something she shouldn't. Would that have an ill effect?"

"Too much of anything can have an ill effect," he said. "So can a poor combination. But to be frank, the good Dr. Forsythe has put so little of anything substantial in these capsules, the worst your employer might risk is diabetes." He peered at me. "And you will make sure she does not overdose?"

"Oh, yes, of course. I was only worried because I thought maybe a mistake might be made at the factory; who knows what gets into food and medicines?"

"It is against the law," he said gravely, "to tamper with or misbrand food and drugs." Then, in a friendlier voice, he added, "But it's a recent law and honored more in the breach than the observance."

I had no way of knowing if it had been honored on the night of Norrie's murder. But it was sounding unlikely that Pep Pills were involved in his death.

Putting the bottle back in my bag, I said, "Thank you very much, Mr.—or is it Dr.?"

"Almost doctor in Lodz." He said it as Wudge, and I must have blinked. "A city in Poland. But it's Mr. here. Mr. Rosenfeld." He bowed very slightly as if we had been introduced in a parlor. "And you are?"

"Miss Jane Prescott."

"Miss Jane Prescott. Not from Lodz."

"No." I smiled. "Thank you again."

As I walked toward the door, I heard Mr. Rosenfeld call, "Perhaps you are concerned because the pills are connected to the recent Newsome murder."

I turned, surprised. "Oh—are they?" I said, then corrected myself. "They are?"

"Oh, yes. A bottle was found near the body. 'Its contents spilled upon the floor in the flickering firelight that also illuminated the dead man's face.'" He waved his fingers in comic dramatic effect.

"But"—I tried to echo his joking tone—"you don't believe the pills had anything to do with his death."

"No." Then added, "Of course, they might have been left by the murderer. I hope the police bother to look for fingerprints. But they seem settled on their anarchist story."

Fingerprints. I had not thought of fingerprints. But everyone that night had worn gloves. Except Louise, of course.

"The papers said it was a very large party," I said. "Anyone could have dropped them."

"And not picked them up? Such 'valuable' medicine?"

"Are you a follower of yellow journalism?"

"Of crime," he said. "Which is often the subject of yellow journalism, so yes, in a way, I am."

"What aspect of crime?" I asked, drawing closer to the counter.

"The science of it."

"The science?" Crime seemed a brutal, unthinking thing, far removed from the intellectual processes of science.

"Oh, yes. Don't you read Sherlock Holmes?"

"Those are just boys' detective stories."

"Not anymore. Fingerprinting, chemical tests to establish the presence of bloodstains, or certain chemicals in the bloodstream, analysis of bullets that can tell you what sort of gun they were fired from. In France, they have created the very first crime laboratory. And in England, an American doctor was just executed for the murder of his wife. He poisoned her, cut off her head, and buried her in the cellar. Do you know how they caught him?"

Caught up in his gruesome story, I shook my head slightly.

"He had covered the torso in lime, I assume to hide the smell, but the lime preserved the tissue—as well as the traces of the poison. When the police found her, they were able to take a sample from her liver and extract the alkaloid. They placed a few drops on a cat's eye, and when the eye dilated, they knew it was a certain type of alkaloid that indicated the poison hyoscine. *And"*—he finished happily—"they were able to identify the body as his wife's because of a scar on her abdomen."

"I would have thought a headless body in your basement and a missing wife was incriminating enough."

"Enough to catch, not enough to prove guilt." He smiled. "What is your interest in the Newsome case, Miss Prescott?"

"Oh, idle gossip, I suppose."

He nodded. But I knew I hadn't been entirely convincing.

Then he stuck out his hand like a twelve-year-old boy who's been told it's the proper thing to do. "Well. It is unlikely, but I hope we meet again."

"Yes," I said. "Good day, Mr. Rosenfeld. Thank you."

★ ★ ★

So Pep Pills had played no role in Norrie's death. That eased my mind on the subject of Charlotte's guilt. But there was still Anna to worry about.

As I walked to her uncle's restaurant, I told myself I was wasting my time. Anna wouldn't be there. She would be busy with work. But I wanted to hear from her uncle that was all she was busy with. That she was not failing to return my calls because Inspector Blackburn had taken her in for questioning.

I was so convinced she would not be there that it was a shock to walk through the door of Morelli's and see Anna sitting at a table with a group of two other women and three men. One of them I recognized as Mr. Pawlicec. Her uncle stood at the back of the room. Seeing me, he looked away, and I knew he had given my messages to Anna.

Mr. Pawlicec rose to his feet with a smile and extended hand. "Miss Prescott, good to see." But Anna stayed seated, said nothing.

Blundering into her silence, I said, "I'm sorry. I didn't mean to interrupt. I only wanted to see that you were . . ."

Safe. Not in jail. Or in danger. Or dangerous.

"Clearly you are," I said. I turned and left.

I was halfway down the block before I heard, "Jane Prescott!"

I stopped.

Catching up to me, Anna said, "I'm sorry I did not answer your calls." Her voice was mechanical, not in the least sorry.

"I was worried," I told her.

"I know."

"Have the police talked to you?"

"About?"

I looked at her.

"Oh, that," she said tiredly. "The Newsome murder. So funny that they call it that. One hundred and twenty-nine people die at Shickshinny, it's a mine disaster. One rich man dies—*now* it's a murder."

"I saw the body," I said. "It was murder."

"You saw the body?" I nodded. "I'm sorry. I'm sure it was terrible."

"It was."

She hesitated. "You want to tell me about it?"

"Do you want to hear?"

"No," she said. "If you ask me to be honest, I don't. That's why I didn't answer your calls. Because I knew you would want to talk about it—as if it matters. And it doesn't." Then, as if to be kind, she added, "Not to me."

Thinking of the daily headlines about anarchists, I said, "I don't see how you can say that."

She misunderstood my meaning. Throwing up her hands, she said, "One. Boy. One stupid, worthless, rich boy. One boy like this dies and oh, the screaming, the crying, the why, God, why? I don't have to ask why. I don't care."

I wanted to ask, *You don't care or you know why?*

"The family did get death threats . . ."

"Did they?" she said sarcastically. "Have you seen these threats?"

"Of course not."

"But you're certain they exist."

"They were in the newspapers," I said and felt foolish.

"Enough. I am sure this death matters very much to your Benchleys. And so of course, it matters to you. It's what you want to talk about. Or if we don't talk about it, it's what you'll be thinking about, even as you smile and ask pleasant questions. I won't be talking to Jane, I'll be talking to . . ."

She drew her hand in front of her face.

Then she put that hand on my arm and said, "Look, when this is over, and you don't worry about it, and your Benchleys are back to . . . whatever it is they do with their days, then we have dinner. And we really talk. I don't want you to pretend. And I don't want to pretend either. Okay?"

She kept her eyes on mine as she said it, and I felt there was nothing . . . untrue in what she said. But words were missing, things unsaid.

I asked, "Did I interrupt some kind of meeting?"

"Yes."

"What was it about?"

"Do you want me to tell you?"

I must not have, because I didn't answer. Anna nodded and turned back to the restaurant. When she was almost at the door, she turned and said, "I am sorry you saw the body. I would not have wanted that. But—believe me. You should be happy he's dead."

Then she went her way and I went mine.

* * *

When I got back to the house, Bernadette said, "You had a phone call while you were gone. A man." She raised an eyebrow. "Didn't sound like a relative."

She handed me a piece of paper with a number written on it. I didn't recognize the number. When I was connected, I heard, "Michael Behan."

I exhaled angrily.

"Jane Prescott?" he guessed. "Don't hang up."

My hand stopped above the phone.

"You remember anything yet?"

"Yes. I remembered I like having a job. Good-bye, Mr. Behan." This time, I nearly managed it. But just before I cut the connection, I heard "There's more." I put the phone back to my ear. "I've got more."

"What?" I knew it had been too long since Charlotte's name was in the papers.

"You can either talk to me or read about it on the front page."

Blackmailed, I thought. I was actually being blackmailed.

Behan said, "I can tell you've got doubts about the anarchist story."

Remembering Anna's words—*You should be happy he's dead*—I thought, *Fewer than I had before*.

"It's not a 'story.' The notes made it very clear—"

"The notes made it very clear that someone hates Robert Newsome's guts and that he's a lousy boss. But Robert Newsome wasn't the one who got killed."

"They said they'd go after his children."

"Okay, sure. That's one story. Then there's my story. Which one makes more sense to you?"

"Neither. She didn't do it." As I said it, I realized I wasn't sure which she I was referring to.

"Then help me prove it. Tell me what you remember."

I tried to reassemble the image in my head, but all that came back was a feeling, a throb of *not right* that was oddly disconnected from the death.

Frustrated, I said, "I don't remember what I remember."

There was silence on the other end. Having got myself in this far, I said, "There was something . . . strange. About the scene."

"Aside from the dead Newsome on the floor."

"I remember thinking, *How did that happen?* But I don't remember what I was looking at."

"If you saw it again, do you think you'd remember?"

"What, the room?"

"I can do better than that, Miss Prescott. You remember my pal at the morgue?"

"Yes."

"If he shows you something and it helps you remember, will you tell me?"

"What on earth would he show me?"

"Will you? In return, I tell you the other thing I've got on your girl."

I considered. "And you tell me who your source is."

"No. Not worth it."

I very much wanted to clear the Tylers of complicity in the story. "If I give you a name, can you tell me if it's *not* them?"

"One name," he said. "We have a deal?"

I wasn't sure. Behan had said he would show me something to make me remember. The other night, I had dreamed of Norrie Newsome walking toward me, that stiff hand outstretched, his face a mass of broken flesh and feeding maggots. The eyes, red sightless wells . . .

I swallowed. "We have a deal."

13

And so it was that I met with Michael Behan a second time—
this time, at night. Our destination was Chrystie Street and Rivington. It was an area I knew and avoided. Some of the women
at the refuge had walked these streets, and they had told me if
you wanted someone's neck broken or their ear chewed off, you
could find someone here to do it for you, provided you had the
money. There had been sporadic gun battles between rival gangs
such as the Eastmans, Five Pointers, and Yakey Yakes. At one point,
as many as a hundred gangsters had gathered to shoot at one another, sending any policeman who attempted to stop them running. And we were not far from where the murder of Bow Kum, a
young woman once owned by the Hip Sing Tong, had reignited
the bloody war between rival gangs in Chinatown.

As we walked down the block, I asked Behan, "Couldn't we
have done this during the day?"

"My friend has the night off. And you work during the day."

The streets were mostly quiet, but I felt increasingly anxious as
Behan stopped in front of one tenement building and rang. As we

waited in the close vestibule, I tried an old game from childhood, easing nerves by touching first the white floor tile, then the black. From behind the door, I could hear a baby crying, someone shouting, then the heavy tread of footsteps on the stairs. I looked up and saw an enormous man—it seemed as if his stomach were a separate person, moving slowly and deliberately before him— coming down the stairs. He looked about forty, with a graying fringe around his red, sweating face. His swollen hand gripped the rickety banister tight. His shoelaces were untied, and his shirt unbuttoned to reveal a grimy undershirt. When he opened the door, I caught the combined smell of stewed cabbage and under- arm.

Mr. Behan held one hand toward me, the other toward the gentleman. "Mr. Clops Connolly, this is Miss Jane Prescott."

I tried to smile. "Mr. Connolly." I got a sour smile and a nod in return.

He led us up two flights. The stairway was dimly lit; one floor was in total darkness. As I stepped, I could feel there was refuse on the floor and tried to put down as little of my shoe as possible. At one point, my foot settled on something soft and movable; I heard a cry. Looking hard in the gloom, I saw I had stepped on a child's bare foot. It—he?—she? The hair was long, and I decided she. She stood in a stained dress, eyes bright in a dirty little face, sucking on the sleeve of her gown. I looked, but saw no parents. The child seemed completely alone.

Behan pulled on my arm, and I resisted, saying, "We should . . ."

Then I realized I had no idea how to finish that sentence and let myself be led upstairs. I glanced back as I went up the stairs, saw the child was following me with her eyes. She didn't seem surprised to be left.

On the next floor, most of the doors were open to extend the apartments into the hall, and several people stopped their conver- sations to take our measure. I nodded politely. Behan touched his hat. Mr. Connolly said nothing. Finally we reached his door, which he opened with a meaty twist of the doorknob.

There were only two small rooms, a kitchen and another room off to the side that seemed to serve as a bedroom. The kitchen was crowded with a scarred wooden table and two chairs. But we did not move from it.

Connolly said to Behan, "It's the suit you're wanting."

"That's right," said Behan. "The one we talked about."

As Connolly lumbered into the other room, I glanced at Behan. But he was watching Connolly as he opened a trunk.

"How do I know it's the real thing?" Behan called.

"Oh, it's real." Connolly returned to the kitchen, a pile of dark cloth in his hands. Right away I could see it was excellent fabric, and I winced at the thought of it bundled against that soiled undershirt.

But it wasn't until he laid it out on the table that I understood what I was looking at: the clothes Norrie had been wearing the night he was killed.

"The shoes took a walk," Mr. Connolly said, "but the rest is here."

"Why weren't his clothes given to the police?" I asked.

Mr. Connolly shrugged. "They never asked. I guess it was obvious it was the skull-cracking what killed him. They didn't look further."

Behan arranged the items so that the shirt was under the jacket, waistcoat over the shirt, evening pants below—all neat and tidy. Except for the wrinkles. And the blood, which had dried brown and rust on the collar and bib of his white shirt.

Stepping back, he said, "Take your time. Take a good look."

I tried to connect what was before my eyes right now to that flash of comprehension I had when I first saw the body. But nothing in what I saw took me back to that moment of *doesn't fit*. And yet the moment had happened.

What had I seen? I pressed myself. What had been so out of place? I struggled, sifting through images in my mind, one more useless than the other.

Then all of a sudden, one picture came—still indistinguishable, but brighter, more insistent, and I cried, "There. On the lapel."

Behan looked. "What?"

Surprised he couldn't see it, I pointed. "The stain, right there."

He leaned in, squinting in the poor light. I put my hand over the spot without touching it. Perhaps it was difficult to notice if you weren't used to cleaning clothes. But I could see clearly the pale brittle film of a spilled drink, now dried, in the dark cloth.

It had been damp, I realized, on the night of the murder, and hard to distinguish from blood against the black jacket. But the spread of the stain had been different, broader, looser. Not a spatter, but a spill. Now that the liquid had dried, it was clearly not blood.

"It's not blood," I explained.

Behan frowned. "Man was soused. I've been known to spill a drink or two when I'm soused."

"Not that soused. I saw him only half an hour before. He was speaking clearly." And cruelly, I thought, remembering his remarks to Rose Newsome. "People don't generally spill drinks on their front unless their arm is jogged." I knew this well, having had to repair Louise once after a devastating encounter with Freddie Holbrooke's elbow that left punch all over her décolletage. I demonstrated, hoisting my elbow with one hand and flinging my arm back.

Behan nodded. "All right. So someone bumped into him. Or he bumped into them."

"Or he passed out." This was not helpful to Charlotte—but in my excitement at having found the thing that bothered me, I couldn't resist saying, "Didn't you say one way for a weak person to overpower a strong young man would have been to slip him something?"

I pointed to the clothes again. "Norrie's drinking. Holding his glass like so." I lifted my hand to my waist. "Suddenly, he feels strange. Dizzy. He sways—I bet if they had examined that rug, they would have found spills to match this one. He falls back, the drink falls with him. And you have—"

I gestured to the stain.

"Maybe it spilled when he took the first hit," Behan said.

I remembered the time Emily Tyler slapped Henry Pargeter for pinching her, how his head lurched back and the glass of champagne erupted all over Mrs. Pargeter's rug.

"It would have fallen on the floor and his pants. I don't see anything on the pants. A shame you don't have the shoes."

I could tell Behan was excited, but he said, "Still—we don't know anything was in the drink."

Mr. Rosenfeld's words came back to me. *Fingerprinting, chemical tests to establish the presence of bloodstains, or certain chemicals in the bloodstream . . .*

Mr. Connolly was right: the coroner had seen the blows to Norrie's head and looked no further for the cause of death. I couldn't think of anything I could say that would prove otherwise. I stared around the room. Noticing an empty jar on the counter, I said, "I need something to cut with."

Connolly instantly gathered up the clothes, saying, "No, you don't."

He raised his eyebrows at Behan, who sighed. "What's the price?"

"I told you before."

Behan pulled an envelope out of his inside coat pocket and handed it to Connolly, who promptly put it in a drawer. As he did, I mouthed to Behan, "Where did you get that?"

He mouthed back, "Newspaper."

Connolly found me a knife. At first I thought of trying to scrape the film off, but then decided I would need to give Mr. Rosenfeld more to work with. As I picked up the jacket, Behan asked, "What do you mean to do?"

"I have a friend who studies this kind of thing. I'm going to give it to him and see what he finds."

"Careful when you cut," he said. "That jacket's going on our front page."

As carefully as I could, I sliced a three-inch scrap of cloth from the lapel. Then I put it into the jar and screwed the lid tight for safekeeping.

Taking my arm, Behan thanked Mr. Connolly, who sarcastically thanked him back. Then he said, "Miss Prescott—how about I buy you dinner?"

When we went back down the stairs, I looked for the child. But she was gone.

★ ★ ★

A little while later, I found myself in a modest but comfortable restaurant that clearly catered to an Irish clientele. Seeing Norrie's clothes had left me feeling unsettled, and when Mr. Behan told the waiter to bring me a whiskey, I drank it. Slowly, disliking the taste. But I drank it.

When the whiskey had done its work, I said, "All right. I did what you asked. Tell me what you know about Miss Charlotte."

Behan tapped his finger on the edge of the table. Finally he said, "Let me ask you something. You think Newsome really meant to marry your girl?"

"Why?"

"Because a friend of mine puts him in a Philadelphia hotel with a young woman not long before he got his head bashed in."

"So?"

"Well, since Charlotte Benchley was in New York, we know she wasn't the girl in Philly."

I shrugged. "If there was another girl, I'm sure Charlotte knew nothing about it. Even if she did, I'm not sure she would have cared. She once told me she was going to marry Norrie Newsome and nothing would stop her."

"Here's the thing, though. He signed them in as Mr. and Mrs. Robert Newsome Jr."

"Well—isn't that what young men do?"

"Is it? What if it happened to be the truth? What if he was *already* married? And he broke the news to Charlotte Christmas Eve? What if that's why he went to Philadelphia, to get married in secret?"

"I congratulate you on your imagination, Mr. Behan. Really, you ought to write novels."

"Any guesses on who the real Mrs. Newsome Jr. might be?"

"There is no Mrs. Newsome Jr.," I said, keeping memories of Beatrice's accusations at bay. "It's probably some girl he met in the city. I doubt he remembered her name the next morning."

"Well, it'll be awkward if she turns out to be the heir to the Newsome fortune."

"Stop it. You're not actually going to write this, are you?"

"It's a good story."

"But people will think . . ."

"What will they think, Miss Prescott?"

I lowered my voice. "You're giving Charlotte Benchley a motive."

Behan whispered back, "Maybe I didn't give it to her. Maybe her intended did." He sat back. "Anything good from the funeral?"

I thought. William's confession, Lucinda's vengeful spit, Beatrice's malice. The new note Rose Newsome had told me about. What had it said? *Now your son is dead.* So clear in its meaning, but vague in its intent. Now *your* son is dead? Now your *son* is dead? Meaning the killer might move on to the next family member?

I asked, "Has your paper heard about any more threats to the family?"

"No. Why?"

I looked at him, unsure of how much to tell.

"You think they're going after the daughter?"

I thought of Lucinda standing in front of the mausoleum as if waiting for permission to enter. "Eight children died at Shickshinny. Is one Newsome death enough?"

"Well, but it depends on what the murder was meant to avenge. Eight kids or one girl in a hotel room?"

"The Newsomes were very kind to Charlotte," I argued. "They don't seem to share your suspicions."

He grinned, tipped his glass toward me. "Bet you the old lady does."

Trying to make a joke of it, I said, "She'd probably rather Charlotte murder Norrie than marry him."

Behan pretended shock. "Miss Prescott!" He moved my long-empty whiskey glass out of reach. "No more of that for you."

As he paid the bill, I looked at the wrapped bundle under the table. "Is that really going on your front page?"

"Certainly is, after what my boss paid for it."

"And in the meantime?"

"How do you mean?"

"You're not going to write some story about infamous infants and mysterious marriages, are you? What proof do you have? One hotel clerk's word?"

He stood. "I'm afraid I've got better than that. My friend kept the sheet from the registry. Either I take it or he sells it to someone else. I told you, young ladies caught up in murder need a friend."

"If you take it, what will you do with it?"

He shrugged, making no promises. Then he said, "Come on, I'll take you home."

"You don't need to do that."

"Miss Prescott, I'm not letting a young woman wander through the city at night on her own. I may be a newspaperman, but give me credit for some morals."

As we walked to the el, I said, "You said you would tell me the name of your source."

"I said I'd tell you one name that was not my source." He wasn't stupid, I gave him that.

I gave him Beatrice Tyler's name. He immediately shook his head.

"You're sure?" I pressed. "Maybe someone connected to her . . . ?"

"I am sure it is not Beatrice Tyler," he said precisely.

I made him leave me on the platform of the train station closest to the Benchleys', partly so I wouldn't be seen with him near the house and partly so he didn't have to pay a second fare.

Putting his hands in his pockets, the bundle of Norrie's clothes under his arm, he said, "This friend with the hobby—you'll tell me what he says about the stain?"

"Don't be too hopeful. Norrie probably just wiped his hand on his jacket."

"But you'll call me, no matter what?" He widened his eyes in a poor imitation of a pleading suitor.

"I'll call."

"Because I'd be brokenhearted not to see you again, Miss Prescott. Really I would."

★ ★ ★

It did occur to me not to tell the Benchleys that there was a document that could incriminate Charlotte in Norrie's murder.

They could, I reasoned, read about it when Mr. Behan published his story. But loyalty is a peculiar thing. It hurt my heart to think of Mrs. Benchley and Louise exposed to damaging scandal. Even Charlotte, if I was honest. So much of people's bad opinion of her grew from the fact that she was "a la Scarsdale," as *Town Topics* might put it. Also—it was my job to make these ladies look attractive. It would be a failure of duty to let them be pelted with mud. Any proof of marriage would be damaging to Charlotte. A girlfriend could be overlooked, but a wife was a killing offense. Even if she were never charged, the suspicion would stay with her.

And there was something more complicated than loyalty. A feeling that had started when Mr. Benchley gave me the newspapers to destroy and asked me to be present during Charlotte's questioning. He had dismissed my concerns about the Pep Pills story, but he hadn't rebuked me for telling him. *Show them* about summed it up. I wanted to show them—and myself—that I was capable of more than tending clothes and dressing hair. I knew things, could find out things I didn't know. Anna and my uncle had always said I should think of myself as more than a servant. Perhaps it was true. At any rate, you'd never catch Bernadette on Chrystie and Rivington at night. Or bargaining with a reporter for information.

So the following evening, I knocked again at Mr. Benchley's door. He listened to my story without comment. If he was angry with me for meeting with Mr. Behan, it didn't show on his face. When I was finished, he picked up a pen and scratched idly on a piece of paper. "And this registry sheet, does the reporter have it?"

"Not yet. But his newspaper seems willing to buy things they feel will be of interest to their readership."

"I see. And this reporter means to write about it."

"Yes." I hesitated. "I know it seems ridiculous, Mr. Benchley. But the police haven't found the anarchist yet, and the newspapers are simply making up their own stories to fill their pages. I'm afraid they've decided Miss Charlotte is a good story."

I was afraid I'd gone too far. But Mr. Benchley nodded in agreement.

"I did warn the reporter you might sue."

Mr. Benchley surprised me by shaking his head. "Then the lawsuit becomes the story. 'Outraged father defends slandered daughter.' No, thank you."

Sitting back, he said, "However, if young Mr. Newsome did enter into a 'secret marriage,' in Philadelphia, I want to know about it. And I certainly want that registry sheet before the newspaper gets it."

"Will you hire your own investigator?"

He sat up, hands on the edge of his desk. "No, Jane. I'm going to hire your reporter friend. Find out what he makes at the newspaper, and I'll decide his price."

Behan would welcome the chance to follow Norrie's trail. Still, I said, "Wouldn't a private investigator be more discreet?"

"An investigator will find what the highest bidder wants him to find," he said cryptically. "I want my own people."

"But how can you trust the reporter?"

"I won't. I'll be trusting you." He looked up. "That's not a mistake, is it?"

"No, sir."

"Good, I didn't think so. Mrs. Benchley's widowed sister lives in Philadelphia. She'd welcome a visit from her niece. Obviously, Charlotte is not yet ready for travel, but it would do Louise good to get away. You will travel with Miss Louise, meet this reporter in Philadelphia, and get the registry sheet."

"He may want money for it."

"Of course he will. Also, I want you to find out what Norrie Newsome was doing in Philadelphia and if there's any other proof of . . . adventuring."

I was both excited and puzzled. Why didn't Mr. Benchley just hire a private detective agency, such as the Pinkertons? Perhaps he didn't trust them not to answer to a higher bidder. Whereas Michael Behan was a nobody. I was a nobody. If we proved untrustworthy, we could be destroyed without comment. Still—it wasn't ironing.

"Do you have this fellow's telephone number?"

"Yes, sir."

"Please give it to me."

"Yes, sir."

★ ★ ★

A few days later, I had another telephone call. When I answered, Behan said, "Sounds like your boss is a little nervous."

"If you knew him, you wouldn't say that." The cook was lingering in the hallway, suspicious of my frequent phone conversations. I frowned at her, and she moved on.

"So, we're going to Philadelphia, Miss Prescott. What do you think we'll find?"

Images flashed through my head. Charlotte toying with the onyx earring. William as he flicked cigarette ends onto the grass. Rose Newsome smiling through smoke. Beatrice, her dark, uncompromising eyes. Louise going pink when she asked about William.

And Mr. Pawlicec. *Miss Prescott, so good to see.*

And Anna, who hid so much, and yet made so much clear. Horrifyingly clear.

"I don't know, Mr. Behan."

★ ★ ★

The day before we left for Philadelphia, I returned to the Lower East Side and Mr. Rosenfeld's pharmacy. When he saw me, his face brightened and he said, "Miss Jane Prescott not from Lodz."

"Yes." I approached the counter, the glass jar in my bag. "Do you . . . is there a place we might talk in private?"

"Certainly," he said, as if it were no surprise to be asked. He took me through a door, which led to a small office with a desk and two chairs. Gesturing to one of the chairs, he sat in the other. "Now, what is this condition that requires privacy?"

I had a sudden flash of other women who had sat in this chair discussing "private" ailments. Shifting uncomfortably, I said, "It's not a condition, but it does require privacy. Even secrecy."

He nodded, understanding.

I set the jar on the desk. "You said you liked mysteries."

"I do."

"You also said there were ways . . . tests to find out if certain chemicals were . . ."

He supplied the words. "Present in the blood."

"Or clothes?"

His eyes on the jar, he echoed, "Or clothes."

I pushed the jar in his direction. "Do you think you could find out what chemicals, if any, were on this piece of cloth?"

He picked it up and examined the cloth through the glass. "Do I know what I'm looking for?"

"A sedative of some kind." I decided to risk it. "Strong enough to render a young man unconscious."

Mr. Rosenfeld looked at me.

I assured him, "Whatever you tell me, if it's important, I'll go to the police."

"But you don't want to go to the police now. They have tests, too."

"No." Should Mr. Rosenfeld discover the worst, the Benchleys would need time. "But I will. No one is harmed by my not going now, I promise you."

He nodded. "I will cut the cloth in two and run my tests on one piece. If I find something . . . interesting, the police will have enough left to test themselves."

"Thank you. How long will it take?"

"If a sedative was used, it will depend on what kind. It may be weeks, it may be tomorrow." He handed me a card. "Call me in a week. I may know something then."

14

Mrs. Amelia Ramsay, formerly Shaw, was, in appearance, a near copy of her sister: not tall, with a plump, rounded figure, and shining hazel eyes. But where Mrs. Benchley's eyes were kind and eager, Mrs. Ramsay's eyes were sharp and critical. Where Mrs. Benchley had the habit of fretting the air with her hands when she was anxious, Mrs. Ramsay used her hands to emphasize and correct. Mrs. Benchley's mouth, when it was not speaking a mile a minute, was either smiling or half open in confusion. Her sister's was set in a thin, disapproving line. I did not envy Louise having to keep her company for the week.

Amelia Shaw had not married half so well as her sister. She lived in a rather modest town house in a quiet street in a lovely residential area. Philadelphia itself was altogether a more conservative city than New York. Here, there was no glamorous impropriety, no titillation. The realms of proper and improper were strictly defined, and woe betide those who crossed the line. Louise crossed it the moment she entered her aunt's house. Mrs. Ramsay took one look at her trunk and narrowed her eyes at its size.

"Whatever do you need so many clothes for?" she demanded.

"Oh . . ." Louise looked doubtfully at her trunk, which she had had no hand in packing.

"We were worried about the weather," I said. "Miss Louise has a weak chest."

"Perhaps if she stood up straight, her lungs would have room to expand," said her aunt.

"That's what Jane says," said Louise weakly. "Although not the part about the lungs."

Louise's main activity was to be reading to her aunt. Not that the week was to be entirely free of festivity. The two ladies would attend a string quartet concert, hear a lecture on the social ills of intemperance, and pay calls on Mrs. Ramsay's eminent acquaintances. If Louise's behavior was exemplary, she might be allowed to indulge in some needlepoint.

That evening, as she watched me unpack her things in a small upstairs bedroom, Louise said, "I wish you didn't have to visit your relatives. I didn't know you had family in Philadelphia."

I felt bad lying to Louise. She believed anything, which made it even more despicable to deceive her. But Mr. Benchley had been firm on this point, and he was paying for the trip. "I didn't either," I said. "They just contacted my uncle recently. It's very kind of Mr. Benchley to allow it."

"I bet they're more fun than Aunt Amelia," said Louise, glumly examining a copy of *Pilgrim's Progress*.

Mr. Behan had traveled to the city separately and was staying in a hotel. The next morning, he presented himself at Mrs. Ramsay's door as my cousin Henry. Mrs. Ramsay looked disbelieving, but she had been instructed by Mr. Benchley to let me go, and so she did.

When we were safely away from the house, Behan asked, "How's life with Auntie?" He was bright and cheerful, like a dog on the scent.

"Poor Louise. She's certainly suffering to clear her sister's rep-utation."

"Philadelphia matrons can be real gorgons. Especially the Main Line ladies."

"She's hardly Main Line."

"Aren't you the snob?"

Anna had once accused me of the same thing. I changed the subject. "You didn't tell me where we were going."

"To Norrie's hotel, of course."

The driver drove us into the center of town and dropped us off on the Avenue of the Arts, in front of the Ritz-Carlton. It was Phil-adelphia's newest and most fashionable hotel, situated in the for-mer Girard Trust Company. The building had been inspired by the Pantheon in Rome; looking up at the massive Roman columns that lined the front of the building, I felt very much like a Christian about to encounter lions. I was not dressed for such surroundings. Yet Michael Behan in his shabby hat was making his way up the marble steps, ignoring the appalled looks of the hotel patrons.

I followed, whispering frantically, "I'm not dressed, I don't have the right hat."

"Just stay close," he said, as we passed two very intimidating doormen in black Ritz-Carlton livery. He strode through the lobby, right up to the front desk, where he addressed the clerk with a sharp clearing of the throat and a "See here, my good man!"

I expected the clerk to instruct one of the hotel detectives to have us thrown out. But when he looked up, he smiled and offered his hand for an exuberant shake.

Behan asked, "Time for a drink?"

"Give me ten minutes and I'll meet you outside." Noticing me, he raised an eyebrow, and Mr. Behan raised a hand, apparently assuring him I was strictly business.

Ten minutes later, we were in a noisy restaurant, and the clerk was introduced to me as Mr. Behan's cousin, a Eugene O'Reilly.

He had a round, pink face, a pudgy nose that put me in mind of a piglet, and thinning dark hair, slicked straight back. Upon making my acquaintance, he shook my hand with a "Meetcha."

"So," said Behan, "about this boy." He slid a copy of *Town Topics* with Norrie's photo on the front page onto the table, and I understood that Mr. O'Reilly had been the one to tell him about Norrie's visit to the hotel with the mystery lady.

Mr. O'Reilly ran a finger around his collar, as if his throat were being squeezed. "Now, none of me in the papers, Michael, I could lose my job."

"No, no. This isn't for the paper anymore. My employer is someone whose name I cannot . . ." He thought for a moment, then finished with "reveal."

"You and he require anonymity," I said, wanting the poor man to breathe easier. He smiled thanks, but didn't look any happier. I nudged Behan to put the paper away, and he did, sliding it back into his coat.

"Well," said Mr. O'Reilly, "he was there. On the day I told you . . ." He looked at Behan, who whispered the date to me. It fit the time Norrie had told Charlotte he would be in Philadelphia, and I nodded.

"And the woman?" Behan said.

"There was a woman, yes."

"Can you describe her at all?" I asked.

"She was dark."

Beatrice Tyler, I thought. But then an ugly thought came to me: Rose Newsome was also dark.

To be certain, I asked, "Tall or short?"

"Tall," he said promptly. "I noticed it right away."

Rose Newsome was not short, but she was not noticeably tall. Whereas Beatrice's height was often lamented by her mother, who worried it made her appear unfeminine. My stomach turned. Until that moment, I hadn't realized how much I had been

counting on Beatrice's claim to Norrie's affections being merit-
less. Of course, Lucinda's beige coloring might pass for dark. And
it was possible that Mr. O'Reilly had written Mr. and Mrs. rather
than Mr. and Miss by accident.

I was about to ask if the lady had been attractive when
Mr. O'Reilly said, "She'd had a few, pardon me saying so."

Almost certainly not Lucinda, I decided. But still shocking to
think it might be Beatrice. A woman of the Tyler/Armslow family
tipsy and being signed into a hotel with a man for the night. Beatrice's general contempt for the human race had sometimes shown
itself as defiance of its customs, but never to this degree.

Unless Behan was right and she and Norrie had gotten married that day. Which was a shock of a different caliber.

"And the young man in the paper, you're sure it was the young
man you signed in?"

"He did the signing."

Even if he'd been inebriated, I thought, the handwriting would
probably be close enough to match.

"You have the sheet, right?" asked Behan. O'Reilly nodded.
"On you?" He nodded again.

At that point, two envelopes were placed on the table. Behan
slid his toward O'Reilly; O'Reilly slid his toward Behan. Each man
tucked an envelope into his inside coat pocket.

"And this is the only copy?" Behan asked.

"'Course. If you'll excuse me . . ."

As Mr. O'Reilly went to relieve himself, I nodded to the table
where the envelopes had crossed and said, "What happens to
that?"

"Your boss paid for it, so it's now his property. Better to have
any 'relevant documents' where they can't do any harm, seems to
be his logic. I can see his point."

So any hard evidence that Norrie had enjoyed another woman's
company was shortly to be in Mr. Benchley's keeping. But that

didn't prove no marriage had taken place. I thought back to my talk with Beatrice, her hands in her lap, on the top of the chair. I hadn't seen a ring.

When he came back, I asked, "Mr. O'Reilly. Since the lady was . . . the worse for wear, did you think to ask for proof that they were married?"

O'Reilly swallowed. "No. No, I didn't."

Behan half smiled. "Did the gentleman indicate it'd be worth your while not to?" O'Reilly didn't answer directly, but from the look he gave Behan, I felt pretty sure money had changed hands. That was promising; Norrie would hardly have had to bribe a hotel to admit his wife.

O'Reilly said, "I did notice, she kept her gloves on."

"Did she say anything?"

He thought. "Yes. She laughed a bit and said, 'What would Mother say?'"

Not "What will Mother say?" Which is what Beatrice would have said if she were speaking of a marriage. "Would" indicated news Mrs. Tyler was never to hear. We would have to go to city hall and check the public records for a license. But I began to relax, feeling there was now little to prove that Charlotte had a powerful motive for murdering Norrie Newsome.

At the same time, I felt a pang for Beatrice, a young woman whose pride was so important to her. Yet, out of love, she'd allowed herself to be used by a young man who took pleasure in causing embarrassment and misery to others. Love—and perhaps desperation to hold on to the young man who was so central to her family's hopes.

Then I had another thought. If Norrie had promised her he would drop Charlotte, and then gone back on his promise the night of the ball, Beatrice would be enraged—and frightened. To know that such a secret was in the hands of someone with no scruples whatsoever would be an intolerable level of helplessness. One that I couldn't see Beatrice accepting.

I heard Behan ask, "What'd they do the next morning?"

"The lady left. She didn't stay."

"And the gentleman? Any idea where he went or how he spent his time?"

"Mostly calling room service and having a grand old party," said Mr. O'Reilly. "Ah, now wait. I called him a car once. I remember because it was a strange, out-of-the-way place he was going. Couldn't think what was there to interest him. Long drive, too. I told him so, but he said he'd got the cash."

"Where did he go exactly?" Behan asked.

"I don't remember." He raised a finger. "But I know a man who will."

As we walked back to the Ritz, I tried to catch Behan's eye. Our next stop should be city hall; where Norrie went on his sordid adventures shouldn't concern us. But he kept his gaze straight ahead.

O'Reilly led us to a row of Elmore cabs lined up to take the hotel's guests wherever they wanted to go. Mr. O'Reilly walked down the line, stopping at the fifth car, and called, "Burt."

The driver looked hopefully at me and Mr. Behan.

Behan said, "We're trying to track down a gentleman. Swell young fellow, handsome, brown hair." Burt looked uncertain. "You took him quite a distance about a month ago."

Burt nodded. "I remember."

"Think you could take us where you took him? We'll pay you for your time, of course."

"Yes, I take you."

I said, "Excuse us a moment," and pulled Mr. Behan to one side. "What are you doing?"

"Your boss told me to find out what Norrie Newsome was doing in Philadelphia. That's what I'm doing."

"He meant anything that might be connected to Charlotte." I poked his coat, heard the rustle of paper. "We have what we came for. We should go to city hall and see if there's a license on file."

"And we will. But we're also going to find out where Norrie went after his romantic evening."

"That's in *your* interests, not Mr. Benchley's."

"The two are the same, until proven otherwise. I gave up a good story with that registry sheet, Miss Prescott. But something tells me I might find another if I look in the right places. You don't have to come with me if you don't want to."

He started walking back to the row of cabs. In a moment, he would be in one of them, going off God knows where with Mr. Benchley's money and learning God knows what about his potential son-in-law. I had been told to keep an eye on him; now I knew why Mr. Benchley had sent me along on this journey.

I ran and pushed into the backseat beside Mr. Behan. Then I asked Burt, "Will it take very long? I have to be back before dark."

"Ja, we make it back. Hour there, hour back." He held the door open for me.

As we rumbled out of the city, I felt distinctly uneasy. For one thing, I was in the company of two strange men, headed who knows where. Also, I was not comfortable in cars. They went too fast, as much as a mile a minute, and they felt perilously flimsy. People were using them for everyday trips more and more, but I still thought of them as big toys for wealthy young men to speed around in and, as often as not, crash.

Keeping my grip tight on the edge of the door, I leaned toward the driver's seat. "Was the young man traveling alone?"

"Alone," Burt confirmed, then turned his eyes back to the road.

I sat back. Where could we be going? What would Norrie want to see in Pennsylvania that was not a fancy hotel—or a club of some kind? If a stately home, why had he not taken a train and been picked up at the station by his hosts?

The car jumped as it hit a bump in the road. I seized the seat edge, and Behan wondered aloud, "What was Newsome doing taking a cab? I thought he had his own fleet. Not to mention Papa's car and driver."

"He may not have wanted 'Papa' to know what he was up to," I said. Then, remembering his response to Charlotte's request for a drive, I added, "And he had a habit of breaking his toys, so Papa was keeping him on a short leash with money."

As we drove past a field, I saw a horse-drawn wagon coming toward us on the road. As they passed, I saw the wagon had sacks of grain and other farming supplies, a shovel, rope, a pickax. And then I remembered the business Norrie had supposedly come to examine: the Newsome mines. At the time, I had dismissed the idea that Norrie could be at all interested in anything work related. But perhaps he really had visited the site of the disaster that likely cost him his own life.

We drove a long while. I shivered in the cold, wrapped my arms tight around myself. The surrounding countryside did not look like a mining town. Our road was taking us through a lovely village, well kept, with substantial homes dotting the landscape. No sign of poverty anywhere.

As we rolled down the main street, I asked, "What's the name of this town?"

"It's called Haddonfield," said Burt.

Haddonfield. The name was familiar to me, a tickle in my brain, but I couldn't make the connection.

Finally I heard Burt say, "There."

I looked up. Before us was a handsome white building that resembled a small hotel. Dark green shutters braced the windows. A dark green door led the way in. A few girls dressed in matching skirts and hats hurried indoors from the cold.

This was not a mine haunted by the ghosts of trapped and dying children. Or a church for a clandestine wedding.

It was Phipps Academy for Girls. Attended for over a century by the daughters of wealthy men, such as Lucinda Newsome.

And, very rarely but every so often, the daughters of less fortunate men.

Such as Rose Newsome. Née Briggs.

15

"A *girls' school?*" *said* Behan. "What the hell was he doing at a girls' school?"

We were in the dining room of the village inn. Burt had been paid to wait in the tavern across the road. I suspected Behan would have preferred to be with him. But it had been a long morning, and I wanted a real lunch.

Now he asked me, "Another girlfriend, you think?"

Norrie Newsome had never expended that much effort to see any girl. "His sister went there. But she left the school last year."

"He doesn't strike me as the devoted sibling."

"No." I remembered the lonely figure in front of the mausoleum. "She is. Still, he didn't come out here to see her."

"Who else would he know here?"

I hesitated. "His stepmother went to the school as well."

"Ah, right." He chuckled. "I forgot the girlies were classmates."

The door of the restaurant opened. There was a gust of frigid wind and a burst of happy chatter and giggling. I looked over and saw that a group of girls had arrived. They rubbed their arms and stamped their feet against the cold. They also wore Phipps Academy uniforms.

Neither Behan nor I said anything as they took a table in the back. From the excited whispers and glances around the room, I guessed these girls were supposed to be in school but had escaped for an unsanctioned lunch out. They looked perhaps seventeen, old enough to dare such a thing. Also old enough that they might remember Lucinda Newsome.

But they were young enough that they went to the ladies' room in pairs. And when they went, I followed, waiting by the sinks for the girls to emerge. They took no notice of me as they tumbled out of the stalls, fingers flying to their masses of sleek hair.

Trying to keep my voice steady, I said, "Do you attend Phipps Academy?"

In the mirror, the girls glanced at each other to see if they should answer—and how. One was long limbed with clear skin and large eyes, the other short through the waist and neck. It was clear which was leader and which follower.

Sliding her eyes toward me, the taller one said, "That's right."

Her voice was defiant, but nervous; I realized they thought I was going to report them to some adult authority.

"I wonder if you could help me."

Appealed to, they were calmer, but haughtier. There was an almost imperceptible lifting of the nose, a delicate rearing of the shoulders. *They always want something, these people.*

"My employer is seeking information about a former student at Phipps." There was a spark of interest, although they tried to hide it. "He's considering a marriage. Of course, he wants to make sure the young lady has nothing . . . disreputable . . . that might be connected to her. He's willing to compensate anyone who can be of assistance." I dangled the last piece of bait. "Her name was Lucinda . . . ?"

From the way the girls looked at each other, I knew they knew her. They hesitated only for a few seconds; then the taller one blurted out, "Oh, God, there's nothing scandalous about that old stick—except how boring she is."

The other one let her jaw go slack and heavy, her eyes half-lidded in imitation, then giggled. "You can't *ever* imagine her with a boy."

"Except her brother," said the first girl, and they burst out laughing.

I pretended ignorance. "Her brother?"

"She has an older brother. She's very fond of him," explained the tall girl.

"Had," corrected the mimic.

"Oh, that's *right*." She looked at her with grudging respect for recalling this fact. "That's right, he was murdered. Something political."

"It'd be funny if *she* did it."

The other girl's mouth quirked. "It's those twisted spinsters-in-training you've got to look out for."

"It's all bottled up."

Having shocked themselves, they shrieked with laughter. I was practically forgotten, but I smiled along. "Did her brother visit her often?"

"He had better things to do, I'm sure."

"Oh, but don't you remember?" said the small girl excitedly. "He was here this winter. Betsy Cameron-Dodge had to stay in for the holidays—"

"She says her family's abroad, but you know they're just too poor to afford the train."

"And she saw him. Talking to Mr. Mayles, the music teacher—"

"*That* disgusting creature. I hate how he looks at me."

"I know. But Betsy saw them, and she told everyone how she'd seen Norrie Newsome right before he died. It was all she talked about."

The tall girl rolled her eyes. "Well, there you see. When did her beloved brother come to the school? *Not* when Lucinda was here. And it'd be the same for any man. So as long as your employer or whoever doesn't mind being bored to death, I'd think he can go right ahead with the match."

When the girls had gotten their money and left the restaurant, Behan said, "So?"

"Norrie talked to a man named Mayles. He teaches music at Phipps."

Behan raised his eyebrows in admiration. "So how do we get in touch with Mr. Mayles?"

"I don't know. A school like that won't let us through the door."

Behan's mouth bunched in agreement. Then he raised his eyes as our waitress passed. "Excuse me, ma'am."

The woman was old enough to merit the ma'am and to suspect the tone of the man who offered it. She stopped but did not smile.

"You know the school nearby?"

She nodded.

"Where might we find a person who works at that school? My sister"—I was indicated—"is anxious to be employed by that establishment. I thought perhaps if she could introduce herself to a member of the faculty, they'd see what an excellent candidate she would be."

The waitress glanced at me. I tried to look excellent.

"You're looking for one of the teachers?" she said finally.

Behan nodded.

"You want a teacher, there's only one place to find 'em." She nodded across the way. "And that's the bar."

★ ★ ★

I couldn't go into the saloon, so Behan went while I drank more tea and grew increasingly jittery. Why would Norrie come all the way out here to ask a music teacher questions? He had never seemed interested in his sister. Of course, Lucinda was not the only member of the family to attend Phipps Academy.

Just then I heard Behan cry, "Here she is!"

He came to the table with a thin, balding man. "This is Mr. Mayles. Mr. Mayles teaches music at Phipps Academy."

As Mr. Mayles extended his hand, I saw that it was pale and long fingered; the nails were well cared for, the skin smooth. But he did not so much shake my hand as feel it. His gaze made me feel inspected rather than greeted.

"Mr. Mayles here is a friend of our friend," said Behan. "The one who visited about a month ago."

"Very nice to meet you, Mr. Mayles. Would you like some tea or coffee?"

"Coffee, please." He gave me a brief smile. His eyes did not move.

Coffee was brought. I pushed a tea cake toward Mr. Mayles, careful to withdraw my hand before he touched the plate.

"Now, Mr. Mayles, why don't you tell the young lady what you told me?"

Mayles looked reluctant, as if he felt himself too good for the bargain he had clearly made. Finally he said, "He wanted to know about a certain student at the school."

He took a sip of his coffee. I glanced at Behan, who said, "Don't make us guess which one."

Another sip. "A very *beautiful* student."

That could not be Lucinda. "Who later married quite well?" I guessed.

Mr. Mayles pointed to me as if I were a bright pupil who'd got the right answer. "The young man was curious to know how she came to be at the school. As we serve only the finest families, our education is out of reach for all but the most blessed in our society." He gave the words a mocking twist.

"Were you able to tell him?" I asked.

"I was. The gentleman who handles the school's finances is a particular friend of mine. We belong to a string quartet." He emphasized the *T*'s in the last two words; I had the impression it was code for something less musical. "It seems the young lady had a benefactor. My friend was able to tell the young man the mailing address used by the Samaritan."

"And the Samaritan's name?" asked Behan.

"There was never a name," said Mayles. "Make of that what you will. The checks were signed by an attorney."

"And you gave this address to the young man?"

Mayles nodded.

I knew I shouldn't be antagonistic, but I couldn't resist asking, "And you had no qualms about giving out this young woman's private information?"

"No," said Mayles. "Not when I gave it to the young man a month ago, and not when I gave it to him"—he nodded at Behan—"half an hour ago. Proper young ladies have no need for privacy, do they? If they're . . . proper?"

"This young lady seems to have made quite an impression on you."

"Oh, yes." He sat back. "She was very memorable."

I had the distinct sense he would have chosen another adjective had I not been present. I wanted very much to tell him that after we left, I would be contacting the school and telling them that a member of their staff was selling secrets about their students—in particular, one who was now a member of a very powerful family and in a position to do the school great good or harm, should the mood take her. I disliked his casual selling of Rose Newsome. I disliked how his tongue moved about his mouth when he spoke of her. I disliked that I could not pour scalding tea into his lap.

"Oh," he said. "One other thing, and I'll give it to you for nothing. My friend also noted that the memo line of the checks specified that they were for the care and education of Rose Briggs. Except that one time, the lawyer made a mistake and wrote for the care and education of Rose Coogan. I've always wondered about that."

★ ★ ★

On the drive back, Behan said, "So. This stepmother."

I pretended not to hear. The conversation with Mayles had turned my stomach, and I wasn't in a mood to talk.

But Behan kept his eye on me, waiting. In a low voice, I said, "Her name is Rose Newsome. Or Rose Briggs, if you prefer."

"Or Rose Coogan."

The name pricked something in my memory. But when I tried to attach a face or event to it, I couldn't. Maybe one of the many girls who came and went at the Benchley house had been a Coogan.

I said, "Why would a girl change her name from Coogan to Briggs? It's hardly an improvement."

"It's not the choice of name, it's the fact that she changed it."

I knew he was right, but I felt stubborn about admitting it. "What does it matter? We know Norrie probably didn't marry Beatrice Tyler in secret. So we know there was nothing to prevent Charlotte marrying him—except good sense, which she doesn't possess. Our job is done."

"Was that a shot at the Benchleys?" Behan sounded amused.

"No. Yes, I guess it was. I'm tired."

I was more than tired. I was upset. The way Mayles talked about sixteen-year-old Rose Briggs—or Coogan—implying that no virtuous woman should need privacy while he himself was drunk, leering, and indiscreet, made me angry. The way he disposed of her dignity as if it were trash was insulting. If he could do that to her, what would he do to me? That stupid, malicious, meaningless . . . music teacher.

And Behan—he would never dare go after Mr. Newsome or even Lucinda Newsome in this way. But Rose Briggs, a poor girl who had the nerve to marry well, she was fair game. No doubt the Coogans were embarrassing hicks with wonderfully awful stories to tell, but there was no great clue to the murder here. Norrie wanted to make mischief by tracking down the people who knew Rose . . . Briggs? Coogan? . . . before she became Rose Newsome. Tomorrow, Behan would find those people and do what Norrie never got to: show everyone what a tacky little fraud she was.

I thought of the women at my uncle's refuge. Many of them went on to have jobs. Marry. Have children. What if one day some reporter decided one of the women's pasts would make a wonderfully seamy story? What would the likes of Behan and Mayles have made of her life—of *her*—then?

"I know when a woman's cussing me out in her head, Miss Prescott. You might as well say it."

I faced him. "You're very casual about a woman's reputation, Mr. Behan. You can say a lot about a girl and stop well short of accusing her of murder. But you'll have ruined her life just the same, simply because she's got a selfish streak, or loves her brother more than she should, or had a sad, degraded childhood."

I expected Behan to come back with a joke, a bold statement that he could do what he wanted, write what he wanted. But he didn't. For many miles, we rode in silence.

Finally, as we drew close to the city, he said, "I'm sorry."

"For what?"

"I don't know."

"Oh. Well, then." I turned back to the view.

Shifting in his seat, he said in a rush, "I'm sorry Mayles was dirty. He didn't . . . he didn't insult you, but he didn't treat you with a whole lot of respect. And I didn't tell him to, because I wanted him to keep talking."

I took that in. "Well, we didn't drive all the way out there so we could listen to him play piano."

"No."

We had reached Mrs. Ramsay's house. Getting out of the car, Behan signaled to Burt that he would be a moment. Then he stood in front of me with his hands in his pockets, head down.

"Here's another thing I'm sorry about. I'm going to that address, and whatever Newsome found out, I'm going to find out. Because I can't not. The story leads there. I can't start and not finish."

I was about to say he could very easily do that when he added, "Look, if you saw a . . . a crease on Louise Benchley's dress, you'd go after her and fix it, right? Even if maybe you were the only one who'd notice?"

"It's my job."

"Right. And you don't leave your job half done. Norrie Newsome came here to find out something about his stepmother. I want to know what he found out. And I want to know if it got him killed."

"It didn't."

"Then she's got nothing to worry about. It won't matter if I go to that address tomorrow. Or if I go digging in whatever mud hole she comes from—"

"Schuylkill," I said, remembering her embarrassed admission. "She comes from Schuylkill. Her name is Rose Coogan, and she comes from Schuylkill. She's a *person*, Mr. Behan."

"Fine. Then come with me and let's find out who that person really is."

"Where?"

"The address Mayles gave us. Or to Schuylkill, whichever. Both."

I hesitated. As little as I wanted to concede the point, Mayles had left me with questions. Perhaps there was no ugliness in Rose's background; Norrie had just assumed there must be because she didn't come from one of the four hundred acceptable families. But I realized that I did want to know if the change in her name had been on purpose or a careless error by a bank clerk.

And ultimately, Mr. Behan was right. I didn't like to leave a job half done.

"Schuylkill first." I didn't want to begin where Norrie had begun. It made me feel we were following a path he had laid for us.

I turned to the Ramsay house. "I should go in. I don't want Mr. Benchley having to answer Mrs. Ramsay's questions as to why he lets a loose woman tend to his daughters."

16

The next day, at my insistence, Mr. Behan and I went first to the Philadelphia City Hall and confirmed there was no marriage license issued to Robert Norris Newsome Jr.

Then we began our journey to Schuylkill.

We went by train. I would have preferred to sit by myself, but Behan took the seat next to me without asking. However, he was preoccupied with his notes and was, for once, not in the mood to talk.

In less than half an hour, we were well into the countryside, far beyond the genteel neighborhoods that surrounded the city. We rode for miles and saw nothing but potato fields and endless pale sky. At other times, we were swallowed up in the silence of trees surrounding us on either side. I suddenly had the realization that I was, for all intents and purposes, alone. I felt the breath leave my body in a single exhalation of freedom. I tilted my head to see the sky, aware that I had two hours with absolutely nothing to do.

"They're only trees," I heard Behan say.

"Maybe to you," I answered, not taking my eyes off the view.

The view changed as we got close to Schuylkill—and not for the better. As we stepped off the train, I was tempted to ask if we had actually arrived at the station, as the only indication was a platform of broken, warped boards and a small ticket shack that stood empty. But then the stationmaster returned from the outhouse.

The man found us a horse and buggy that would take us into town. The roads were bumpy, and Behan cursed as we bounced over rocks and deep puddles. The trees thinned out. The land was scraggly, mud and brush and tree stumps. Our driver matched the landscape, so thin he appeared all gristle; his patchy beard was graying; his eyes had deep lines. He could have been anywhere from thirty to ninety.

At one point, Behan called up, "You don't know the Briggs family, do you?"

The driver didn't turn around, but gave a sharp shake of the head.

"Or the Coogans?" I asked.

That didn't even get a shake of the head.

The main street had brick buildings and wooden pathways along the storefronts. There were some signs of modernity. Electric poles leaned this way and that. But many of the houses were rough, hastily built from raw wood planks, with gaps that must have let the wind whip right through the house. Poorly dressed women and children stared as we passed. A store owner came out to inspect us. An elderly man removed his pipe from his mouth to get a better look. I wondered where the other men were.

We stopped the car outside a largish store. Behan paid the buggy driver extra and asked him to wait. Then he turned to me and said, "Well, Rose Briggs certainly came up in the world, didn't she? Anyone with any brains up and left this place a while ago. All you got here is bullheads and suckers."

Darting my eyes to indicate the bullheads and suckers might

be listening, I said, "Let's ask the store owner if he knows how to find the house."

It was a general store, offering everything from canned food and flour to hammers and oilcloth. Behan approached the owner, who was a thin, sandy-haired man in his forties, although the hair had retreated to the sides of his head. Behan bought a small bag of hard candy and said, "We're looking for the Briggs house."

The store owner shook his head. "Don't know it."

Behan and I looked at each other. I tried, "The Coogan house?"

The man gave me a hard stare. Disconcerted, I said, "The family did live here, didn't they?"

"Oh, they lived here," he said. Pointing, he told us, "You take a left at the end of the road, keep going up the hill. After maybe a mile, you'll see a white house with a weather vane shaped like a rooster. Turn right there and go another quarter mile. It'll be there, third house on the right. Can I ask your interest in the Coogans?"

Behan shrugged as if to say it was our business.

Outside, Behan dispensed the candy to children who had surrounded the car. He was casual about it, teasing them in a way that made me think he must have had younger brothers and sisters. As I looked around, I thought there was something disquieting about the town. It wasn't only the poverty; I had seen that in New York. This place was silent, as if condemned. Maybe Behan was right. Maybe anyone of any spirit had abandoned the place and all that was left were the . . . survivors—the word popped oddly into my head.

At one point, Behan gave me the bag of candy so he could go in search of the buggy driver. Handing a piece to one little girl, I asked, "Is your mother at home?"

She nodded.

"And your father, he's at work?"

She nodded again.

"What does he do?"

Speaking around the hard lump of sugar, she said, "He works in the Shick—"

But she couldn't quite get the word out. Shifting the candy to the other side of her mouth, she finished, "Shinny mine."

And that was when I remembered where I had heard the name Coogan.

★ ★ ★

"Her father was the manager of the mine," I told Behan as we waited for the buggy. "The company blamed him for the cave-in."

"Where is he now?"

I shook my head. "The store owner said they lived here, not live. But we might find a neighbor who knows where the family went."

"You think the father's still alive?"

"Her parents are supposed to be dead. She told me she'd lost her father young. Although I see now why she might say that—and why she changed her name."

Had Norrie gotten this far? I wondered. Or even farther? Had he found Mr. Coogan? Tried to blackmail Rose Newsome with that discovery?

Behan was clearly thinking along the same lines. "You think Norrie came through here?"

"I don't know. He may not know where she comes from."

"Think the husband knows?"

I shook my head. "It was a very sudden match. At the time, people were horrified that he knew nothing about her except that she went to Phipps." I remembered the red-faced bully I'd seen at the party. Not a man to tolerate complexities. "I can't believe she's told him the truth. Really, why should she?" For a second, I thought of my father, the sensation of rough wool pulled from my hand as he vanished. "People get lost easily in this country."

A tired horse clopped into view, and we climbed back into the buggy. Perhaps I imagined it, but our driver's neck looked even stiffer with disapproval than before. The houses, I saw with some relief, were more refined the farther we got from the center of town. Most of them were freshly painted blue or white. There were curtains on the windows, fences in good condition, the winter remnants of front gardens. I saw one woman vigorously beating a rug of some quality in the backyard.

The former Coogan home was a fine little two-story home. The windows were clean, the porch swept; it was a cared-for house. Behan rang the bell. From inside, I heard a woman's voice say, "Yes?"

She came to the door, and Behan took off his hat. "Excuse me, ma'am, for disturbing you, but we're trying to locate a family that used to live here."

She looked suspicious—and I could hardly blame her. "What's the name?"

"Coogan?"

Suspicion hardened into distaste. "I never knew the Coogans, and I don't know where they are now. Good day."

She shut the door before I had a chance to ask if Norrie had been here before us.

Defeated, Behan walked down the steps. "Now what?"

I began looking up and down the street. "Someone must have known them."

"It's a mining town. People don't necessarily stay."

"In these houses they do. These are comfortable, settled people. Who looks like they've lived here a long time?"

Turning, I searched the outside of the houses. Everyone, it seemed, shopped at the general store or ordered from the same catalog; there was little to distinguish one house from another. Until I caught sight of a pretty little house with lace curtains. The curtains were clean and well ironed—but they were not new. The front door had fine brass fixtures, but they needed a polish. The paintwork on the fence was peeling; the roof was worse. Whoever lived there had refined tastes but lacked the resources to properly maintain the house. Those resources were either financial—or physical. A glance through the curtains showed me a dining room with a good-sized table lovingly polished and an arrangement of dried flowers. An elderly person lived there, I was sure of it.

"That one," I said. Behan went through the gate, trotted up the steps, and rang the bell. Moments passed.

"No one home," he said.

"Wait," I whispered. "It may take a while."

Sure enough, we heard the thump of a cane on wood floors and a thin voice call, "One moment."

Then the door opened to reveal a small, white-haired woman. She wore both a sweater and a shawl over a heavy woolen skirt. Her eyes were large and blue, although one of them was filmed over.

"I'm very sorry to disturb you, ma'am," said Behan. "We're looking for a family, and we wonder if you know them."

Her good eye brightened. "Which family? I've lived here thirty years."

"Coogan."

She leaned on the cane and sighed.

"Did you know them?" I asked.

"Oh, I knew them." She swung the cane toward the parlor. "Why don't you come in?"

When we were all seated in the snug parlor, the elderly woman, who had introduced herself as Mrs. Thorskill, said, "Funny, we haven't had your sort around here for a while."

She was looking at Behan, who had inched himself as close to the fire as he could. "My sort?"

"Reporters. Not since the cave-in." She pointed to the upper floor. "I made a nice bit of money renting a room to newspapermen at the time. My Isaac was one of the few men in town who didn't work the mines, and we didn't have children, so it wasn't as bad for us."

"He is a reporter," I said. "But we're not here for a story. We need to get in touch with the Coogan family."

"Well, if you're a reporter, you must know what happened," said Mrs. Thorskill. Behan shook his head. "They blamed the whole mess on Mr. Coogan. Fired him for drunkenness and neg-ligence. The story went that he'd skimped on reinforcing the mine shaft—pocketed the money for himself. There was talk of putting him in jail, but I guess the powers that be figured once he lost his job, that was the end of it."

"Did you know him to drink before the cave-in?" I asked.

The old lady considered. "No, now that you mention it. But people can keep that sort of thing secret a long time—and Lord knows he drank after. People around here gave them a hard time. Rocks through their windows, spitting at them in the street."

"Why didn't they move?" asked Behan. He had his notebook out, I noticed.

"No one else'd hire him. When he died, that's when they got out of town."

As Behan wrote this down, I asked, "Did you know Rose Coogan?"

"The daughter?" I nodded. "She was a pretty little thing. I re-member her holding her daddy's hand to keep him steady as he weaved down the street."

I lost my father young. It was the end of the world.

"How did he die?"

"Worthless," said the old woman. "The man died drunk and broke and a burden. When he'd taken every dime and spent it, taken every nice thing his wife had and pawned it, taken every bit of dignity she had and soaked it in misery and gin, he put a gun to his head and blew his brains out. Left the wife shattered with a daughter to raise. She took off to the city, got a job working at some department store."

"Is the mother still alive?" Behan asked.

"I don't know. I heard she came into some money after they moved."

Behan and I glanced at each other. "And the daughter?" I asked.

Mrs. Thorskill shook her head. "Never heard."

Having come to that dead end, we made our way to the door. Shrugging his coat on, Behan asked, "You don't recall the name of that department store, do you?"

"I do," said the lady, proud of her memory. "It was Wanamaker's."

★ ★ ★

"Still think she's innocent?"

The train had lurched away from the rotted platform of Schuylkill and was gathering speed. I watched as the town fell away from view. It was not yet late afternoon, but the shadows were already growing. It would be well after dark when we got back. Without the midday sun, it was even more bleak. And the train's heating stove was apathetic in its efforts to keep us warm.

Finally I answered, "You think she plotted to marry Robert Newsome so she could murder his son to avenge her father? And waited ten years to do it?"

"She didn't have the opportunity to do it before. The notes gave her the perfect cover. Or maybe she wrote the notes herself, you ever think of that?"

"Why didn't she simply brain her husband on the wedding night?"

"Presumably because she'd like to get away with it and inherit the cash."

"There's still Lucinda Newsome."

"For now. How's her health?"

"Fine," I said absently, suddenly taken with the memory of Lucinda's spiteful classmates. *It's those twisted spinsters-in-training you've got to look out for.* What a hell school must have been for that plain, earnest young woman. Had it been any better for the lovely, lively Rose Coogan? They had been friends. Now Lucinda detested her.

I thought of how this journey might have felt to Rose when she left. Had she been happy? Relieved? Or was Schuylkill just one more thing she had lost? Did she have any idea that within ten years, she would be smoking French cigarettes in a sumptuous garden as she confessed she was most comfortable talking to servants?

We drew into a station, and the doors were opened. Bitter wind blew through the car. I hunched against the cold.

"Here." Behan shrugged off his coat. Offering it to me, he said, "Put this over you."

"Then you'll be cold."

"We'll swap every half hour." Depositing it on my lap, he said, "Take it."

Realizing I was holding my jaw tight to keep my teeth from chattering, I laid the coat over me. It was heavy wool, pleasantly bulky, and smelled of tobacco and something that put me in mind of cutting a man's hair: soap and the scent of warm skin laid bare when you lifted the hair off the nape of the neck.

My muscles eased as my body stopped bracing itself. I murmured, "Thank you."

And immediately fell asleep.

When I woke up, night had fallen. We were going through a small town; I could see lights in distant houses, but the view was dominated by shadowy fields and a vast dark sky. I felt lost in the middle of nowhere.

Momentarily panicked, I said, "Where are we?"

"About an hour out."

"An hour—what time is it?"

"About seven." Behan glanced at me. "What are you worried about? Mrs. Ramsay thinks you're with your benighted relatives, doesn't she?"

"What if she says something to the Benchleys?"

"Miss Prescott, the Benchleys aren't going to fire you. After ten minutes of talking with Mr. Benchley, I can assure you he respects you far more than his battle-ax sister-in-law." He frowned at something he'd written and closed his notebook. "Besides, who'd get 'em out of bed and wipe their backsides?"

Reassured, I settled back in my seat. "It's your turn for the coat."

"I'm all right, you keep it." Turning toward me, he said, "Tell me something, Miss Prescott—or can I call you Jane?"

I was wearing the gentleman's coat; it seemed only fair. "All right."

"Jane. Why don't you want to believe Rose Newsome might be guilty?"

Part of me keeps feeling I should be one of you. And so she was, I thought. A poor girl, after all.

To Behan, I said, "I'm not sure you believe she's guilty of murder so much as she's guilty of being poor and marrying well."

"What happened to her father, it's a pretty good motive."

"So good she waited more than a year. And why kill Norrie? It would make much more sense for her to kill Mr. Newsome. He was the one responsible for ruining her father's life, and, as you say, there's the money."

"It's not outside the realm of possibility that Norrie figured out who she was and tried to blackmail her, is it?"

"I thought of that. But who really stands to lose if her identity is revealed? So he tells his father. What can Mr. Newsome do? Divorce her? That would bring up the mining disaster again, and I have a feeling Mr. Newsome wouldn't welcome that. And if

Norrie tells anyone else, his father would cut him off for good. No, I can't see her killing Norrie because he threatened to tell people her father was Howard Coogan."

"So he found out something else."

"Like what?"

"I don't know. But I'm curious how a lady who worked at Wanamaker's Department Store managed to send her daughter to such a fancy school."

"You're going to track down that benefactor."

"Yes, I am."

I toyed with a button on Behan's coat. It was tightly sewed on and neatly finished. "Mr. Behan, in your quest for dirty secrets, you're forgetting one simple thing. Anarchists threatened violence against the family—and now Norrie is dead. It's less exciting, but more than likely the truth."

I took no pleasure in saying this. An image of Mr. Pawlicec rising clumsily to greet me came to mind. Anna's blank look when she saw me at the door of her uncle's restaurant, her coldness as she told me she would rather not see me until the Newsome murder was solved—it did all point one way.

"You don't sound so happy about that."

Caught, I said, "What do you mean?"

"Just now. You didn't have the ring of righteous condemnation most people do when they say 'anarchist.' Are you an anarchist, Miss Prescott? Jane? *Know* any anarchists?"

"Is it only women you think have no right to privacy? Or doesn't your newspaper pay you enough to intrude in men's lives this way?"

"I'm trying to figure you out. I guess an anarchist wouldn't be out here in God-knows-where Pennsylvania trying to help a family like the Benchleys. Most girls in your position would have sold their story and quit the next day. If Charlotte Benchley is suspected of killing the Newsome swine, what's it to you?"

"Because people don't really think she's guilty, they just don't like her. That's not justice, it's hate. Besides, I'm fond of Louise Benchley, and she's having enough trouble finding a husband. She doesn't need a sister suspected of murder as well."

"And how come you're so worried about Louise Benchley catching a husband? Don't you want a husband of your own?"

A memory came to me: feet swinging in emptiness. For an instant, the stomach-dropping sensation of being utterly alone.

"Not especially."

"Story you'd care to share?"

"No."

"Oh, now you must have some fellow. A milkman who leaves the extra bottle of cream. Or a policeman—that's it. A fine young man who walks the Benchley beat. Rosy of cheek, firm of purpose, bright of eye . . ."

"We don't see much of our local policeman. And when we do, he's drunk."

"Chauffeur?"

"O'Hara?" I laughed.

"Why do you say it like that?"

"Say what?"

"'O'Hara.' With a sneer. Like you wouldn't wipe your shoes on him." The train swerved, and he rocked a little on the seat. "You don't like the Irish, do you?"

Annoyed to be accused of prejudice, I said, "I can hardly know all of them."

"And you wouldn't want to either, I can tell. What superior swamp do you come from?"

". . . Scotland."

"That explains it. More snobbish than the English and cheap besides."

Ignoring the insults, I said, "It's not the Irish people, but the Roman Catholic Church—"

"Careful, I'm Roman Catholic."

"Oh." We sat in silence. "I suppose you want your coat back."

"No." He smiled a little. "I'll sit here in the moral rectitude and self-sacrifice which are the hallmarks of my faith. Now a Protestant—*he'd* ask for the coat back."

Just before we reached the city, the train made a prolonged stop, and Behan got out to, as he put it, "fill the stomach and empty the extremities." The station wasn't much more than a shed, and I stayed on the train. It seemed to me Mr. Behan was taking a long time. Nervous, I went into the station and found him on the phone. From the disgruntled look on the clerk's face, I guessed he had been talking for some time.

When Behan saw me, he said, "Train's leaving. Yes. Soon."

As we got back on the train, I asked, "Was that Mr. Benchley?"

"It was not." And he said nothing more on the subject.

★ ★ ★

It was late and I was exhausted by the time I reached the Ramsay home, so I was amazed and slightly frustrated to see Louise waiting up for me. No doubt it had been a long and torturous evening of *Pilgrim's Progress*, but I didn't have the strength to hear it all in detail. I braced myself, only to hear Louise say, "You won't believe what's happened!"

"What?"

"It's Mr. Newsome. Mother called to tell me after you left."

"And?"

"You know how he's been since Norrie's death—ill, agitated?" I nodded. "Well, the doctors were giving him a sedative to keep him calm. Only someone mixed up the medicines and he got too much and almost died. His valet found him just in time. Isn't it awful?"

"Awful," I echoed, realizing that, as tired as I was, I would not be able to sleep that night.

17

The following afternoon, we went in search of the benefactor—or at least the benefactor's lawyer. The address that Mr. Mayles had provided took us to the law offices of Stadtler and Carr, located on Chestnut Street in the city's financial district. The law firm kept their offices on the seventh floor of one of the more modern office buildings, which towered over the older, more sedate redbrick buildings. As we rode up in the elevator, I asked Michael Behan, "Why should the lawyer speak with us? We don't even know the name of his client. All we have is the name of a girl he once wrote checks for. He may not even remember her; she might be one of several children helped by this . . . benefactor."

"I have a feeling Norrie Newsome might have jogged his memory," said Behan.

It was true no law firm would turn down a meeting with a member of such a wealthy family. We might learn what the lawyer had told Norrie Newsome—or that he had refused to tell him anything. I admit that was what I hoped. I had decided not to tell Michael Behan about Mr. Newsome's medicinal mishap. In the

light of day, I felt there was every chance it had been an accident;
sedatives were tricky to manage. Surely, a hired nurse was responsible. Although I did not remember seeing any such nurse at the
Newsome house . . .

The firm's offices were handsome and respectable, but not of
the first class, and I didn't feel shy approaching the front desk. Still,
an officious clerk demanded to know our business.

I said, "One of your attorneys was recommended to us. We
hoped to speak with him."

He peered at us through his glasses in a way that indicated
doubt as to whether we could pay the firm's fees. "Which one,
please?"

"Mr. George Gilfoyle."

The clerk frowned, looked from me to Mr. Behan and back
again. Either I had named a senior member of the staff—or the
janitor.

"A client *recommended* him, you say?"

"Yes," said Behan firmly. "He was recommended by Robert
Norris Newsome Jr."

I could not tell whether it was that young man's wealth or death
that spurred the clerk to action. But he told us to wait a moment
and went through the dark oak door.

"He seems less than impressed by Mr. Gilfoyle's abilities,"
I said.

"Newsome's name got a reaction, though."

A few minutes later, he was back. "I'm sorry, Mr. Gilfoyle isn't
in at the moment."

This was an obvious lie. There was only one entrance, and the
sharp-eyed clerk would be able to see everyone who came and
went.

"Can we make an appointment to see him?" I asked.

"He isn't taking clients at this time." The clerk began shuffling papers around the desk with no particular purpose other than avoiding our eyes.

"Did he just tell you that?" Behan asked. The clerk glared at him. "Oh, that's right, I forgot, he's not in. Tell me, was he in when Mr. Newsome called?"

"I can't divulge—"

"Did he meet with him sometime in December?" I asked. I knew the clerk wouldn't give me a verbal answer, but from his startled look, I knew for certain that Gilfoyle and Norrie had met.

"I'd like you to leave now," he said.

★ ★ ★

"We should have told him we were a charity," I said when we were out on the street. "Hoping to approach the benefactor for a needy case. That might have been less threatening than tossing Norrie's name around."

"They would have thrown us straight out if we were a charity," said Behan, gazing down the street. "Now what?"

We walked for several blocks, thinking as we went. If we could not meet with the lawyer, we couldn't find out the name of the benefactor or what he might have told Norrie about Rose Briggs/ Coogan. I was wondering if perhaps we could ask Mrs. Ramsay if she knew the local great and good, when Behan stopped dead in the street.

"What was the name of that store? The old lady said the mother worked there?"

"Wanamaker's."

He pointed. And there it was, across the street.

★ ★ ★

It was not a shop for men. If we were going to learn anything about the Coogan family after they left Schuylkill, it would be up to me to find it out. I wandered the aisles, looking for the sort of woman Behan and I had agreed would be most likely to know anything. I found her straightening shirtwaists on a table. A saleslady, perhaps in her early forties, plump and rather genteel looking. Approaching her, I said, "Excuse me."

She turned with a "Yes, may I help you?"

"I'm looking for a woman who might work here. Or did in the past."

The smile dimmed but did not disappear. "Who might that be?"

"A Mrs. Coogan," I guessed. "Or she may have gone by her maiden name of Briggs; she was widowed."

The reaction was instant: the woman raised her eyebrows in sharp surprise and said, "I'm afraid that woman went on to her reward several years ago."

"You knew her?"

"Yes, I knew her." She picked up a swathe of brocade that had been left in disarray by a customer.

"You didn't like her?"

"It's not for me to like or dislike, I'm sure."

I launched into my prepared story. "My mother and she were friends as girls. She said if I was ever in Philadelphia, I must get in touch. My mother will be so sad to hear of her passing. The last we heard she had come into some money."

The saleswoman smiled sadly. "She didn't come into any money, dear. She came into a man."

"She married again?"

"I don't believe I mentioned marriage." The lady began folding, taking her discomfort out on the brocade. "That gentleman wasn't the marrying kind."

Up to this moment, I had had a clear picture of Rose Coogan's savior. He would be an older man, not unlike my uncle in appearance, but obviously wealthier and better groomed. He would have that rather vague benevolence, a dotty otherworldliness, that was common among the rich who chose to do good by sharing God's blessings among the less fortunate. Now I saw how wrong I had been.

Shaking her head, the saleslady said, "I shouldn't be telling you this. It's just that Mrs. Briggs shared with me her terrible story, how her husband fell to drink and met his end. We had things in common, let me say that. Although my trials continue."

So that was why a woman like her was working behind the counter; her husband was a drunkard.

"And your hope," I said.

She tried to smile. "The poor woman did have a child. But she was also the kind of woman who's known comfort and can't give it up, no matter what the cost."

"Perhaps the gentleman was kind . . ."

"He was neither kind nor a gentleman. Does a gentleman send his carriage and driver to a store after-hours? As if she were a . . . well, I suppose she was. Two nights out of every week, she went to his house. And she took that poor child with her. Said she'd no one to leave her with. Well, if you've no one to leave your child with, you stay home if you're any kind of mother."

"Maybe the child liked going," I tried.

That made her angry. Setting her fists on her hips, she said, "I remember one day the little girl told her mother she didn't want to go. Started crying. Do you know—that woman *shouted* at her. 'What do you not want? Do you not want to eat? Have a roof over your head? What is it you don't want?' Then she took that little girl by the arm and pulled her out to the carriage."

Her mouth twisted. "Once I got up the nerve to tell her she should be ashamed of herself. She got sick and quit a few months later. I don't know what happened to them after that."

"And the gentleman? Do you remember his name?"

"She never said. But I once overheard the driver telling her that

Mr. Farragut wouldn't like to be kept waiting." Her hands hovered over the cloth, even though it was now folded and there was nothing left to do. "I still think about that little girl sometimes."

I was about to say she shouldn't worry, the little girl had landed just fine. But then I wondered, had she?

Before leaving, I said, "May I ask one more question?" The woman didn't say no. "Was a young man here about a month ago, also asking about that lady?"

Surprised by the question, she said, "We don't get young men in here, dear. Although I do remember one older man. Said he was from Cincinnati. Bought a lovely beige peignoir for his wife." She smiled. "Size 40."

★ ★ ★

Behan had told me to meet him at a restaurant a block down from Wanamaker's. As I walked, I assembled the pieces of what I had learned: that Rose Coogan's mother had been . . . several words presented themselves, and I rejected all of them . . . the friend of a wealthy man who paid her bills. Which meant she might have, if she were so inclined, taken a room at my uncle's refuge.

But Norrie had not gone to Wanamaker's, so he would have been unaware of Mrs. Coogan's financial arrangements. Unless Gilfoyle had told him. I could see it, the two men, smirks barely suppressed. *So, the widow Briggs charmed Mr. Farragut out of his cash. Wonder what she offered as collateral . . .*

Behan was not sitting at a table when I entered the restaurant. Puzzled, I asked the waitress if she had seen a tall, dark-haired man. I almost said, "Good-looking," but from the way she said, "Oh, yes, he's here," I could see I didn't have to.

"He's on the phone," she said and pointed.

At the back of the restaurant, Behan leaned against the wall, the receiver to his ear. I raised a hand, wanting to let him know I was here. And as I did so, I heard him say, "No, darling, I'll be home soon. Nope, promise. Tomorrow or day after. I know you have. Me, too."

Then he looked up and saw me. Adding a last "Good-bye," he hung up the phone and looked at me. He seemed embarrassed, as if he had been caught out. But really, what did it matter? Michael Behan was married. Most men were married. I should have expected as much. No wonder that button had been so well sewn.

For a moment we stood there, awkward with each other. I was about to ask his wife's name when he said, "Hungry?" and I said, "Yes," and the time for talking about it was over.

★ ★ ★

"So, Ma was a kept woman," said Behan when I told him.

"I'm not sure she merited that status," I said. "She had a job. She only seems to have asked for help for her daughter."

"The school."

I nodded. "Maybe when she died, she made the man promise to look after Rose."

I expected brutal sarcasm, but he considered it. "Sort of pathetic, when you think about it. 'A Mother's Sacrifice.' Would that be enough of a scandal to make Rose Newsome bash Norrie's brains out? I mean, it's not the pedigree you'd ask for, but public sympathy might be in her favor."

"I'm not sure Mr. Newsome would want to be married to the daughter of a loose woman." Hence his recent accidental overdose— the thought came before I could stop it. "But he may not have known. The saleslady said the man's name was Farragut. We could find out where he lives, see if Norrie found him. Although he might be married, for all we know. It could be awkward . . ." I felt self-conscious and trailed off.

If he noticed, Mr. Behan didn't show it. "I've got a better idea. While you were shopping, I was talking to the doorman who works in that building. He said our Mr. Gilfoyle leaves every night at five on the dot. He notices it because most of the lawyers stay late sometimes. Not Mr. Gilfoyle. So I figure, we wait in the lobby and we get him on the way home."

"I suppose." Maybe it was tiredness from yesterday, but I was sick of Norrie Newsome. Of sad, desperate women and the men who let them down. And Philadelphia, I was sick of that, too. I wanted to go home.

And still, I followed Mr. Behan back to the law offices and waited with him on the street. The streetlights had just come on when the first men started leaving the building. I said, "How will we know him?"

"The doorman described him—there he is." Behan started walking purposefully toward a tall, thin man with stooped shoulders. "Mr. Gilfoyle?"

I could tell from the fearful way the man turned that he knew we were the same people who had asked for him earlier. His appearance was unhealthy, his face drawn, with bruised pouches under his eyes. His hand shook as he lifted it to his hat. "What do you want with me?"

"To talk to you, Mr. Gilfoyle."

"No." Energized by fear, he started walking again. Moving quickly, I put myself in front of him.

"We know you talked with Norrie Newsome."

"Please get out of my way, miss."

"If you could tell us what you told him—"

"You must understand that I can't."

"And you must know why we're asking," I said.

Behan said, "We know you signed the checks for Rose Coogan." Mr. Gilfoyle now looked more panicked than ever. "And we have a pretty good idea why. We want to know what you told Mr. Newsome about it."

"I can't. Please. I don't want to be rude—"

"Well, perhaps we could talk to your client, Mr. Farragut," I said.

At that, Gilfoyle froze. "No, I don't think you can."

"Why's that?" asked Behan.

"Because he's dead," said Gilfoyle. "Just as Mr. Newsome is dead. Now please—leave me alone."

I don't know how long it was after the terrified Mr. Gilfoyle had disappeared that we first heard it, the shrill, urgent cry of a boy. Perhaps it was because we were stunned, or perhaps because it was such a common sound, blending in with the other sounds of a city—horse hooves, horns honking, men and women grumbling as they made their way home in the chilly dark. Who pays attention to one newsboy trying to sell the evening paper?

But eventually, the words, repeated over and over, became clear. "Extra! Extra! Arrest in Newsome murder! Anarchist arrested in the killing of Newsome heir!"

Oh, God, I thought. *Anna . . .*

18

Mary had quit.

With both her regular maid and her sister/whipping boy out of the house, Charlotte's irritation had only one target besides her mother. After the third day of faultfinding, pointless errands, and correction, Mary walked out.

I heard all about it from Bernadette over breakfast the morning after we got back. "They expected *me* to do their hair, wash their clothes, and make a fuss. After ten minutes, I wanted to slap her with the back of the brush."

"Maybe Miss Charlotte's mood will improve now that there's been an arrest."

"That Inspector Blackburn stopped by personally to give her the news. Miss Nose in the Air was in high spirits when he left."

As casually as possible, I said, "He didn't mention the name of the person they've arrested, did he? The papers didn't say." I had searched every newspaper I could find in Philadelphia for mention of Anna. They had referred to the anarchist as "he," but with no other evidence, they would assume the killer was a man.

She shook her head. "Might have. Something foreign, I'm sure." Putting her dishes in the sink, she added, "By the way, Mister wants to see you. In his office."

"Now?"

"Now is usually when they want it."

When Louise and I had arrived last night, it had been too late for me to speak with Mr. Benchley. Now it seemed it was time to make my report. As I walked downstairs, I tried to assemble a suitable narrative of everything Michael Behan and I had learned. Then wondered: did it matter? The anarchist had been caught. Whatever happened in Rose Newsome's past—who her father was, what her mother did to get her an education—was no longer important. Norrie might never have learned his stepmother's full history; he might have only found out that her great benefactor was dead. Which wasn't shocking. Benefactors died all the time—it was one of the most beneficent things they did; look at Mrs. Armslow.

Only they didn't usually leave their lawyers in a blind panic when they did so. Michael Behan had made that very point to me on the day he told me he would stay in Philadelphia until he could find out what had happened to Mr. Farragut.

I reminded him he had told his wife he would be home tomorrow. He went quiet, then said, "She's used to it."

Then he either said my name or was about to say it, and I knew something would follow that shouldn't be spoken.

So I said, "Please give me the registry sheet for Mr. Benchley."

The door to Mr. Benchley's study was closed, as it always was. When I knocked, I heard, "Yes?" and said, "It's Jane, sir."

There was a pause. Then, "Yes, come in."

When I entered, Mr. Benchley was writing something. Without looking up, he said, "How was your trip?"

I stepped forward and placed the envelope with the registry sheet on the desk. A hint of a smile crossed Mr. Benchley's face, and I wondered if it gave him pleasure to think of the Tylers' embarrassment.

"We found nothing that would reflect poorly on Miss Charlotte," I said. "But we did learn . . ."

He waved a hand as if everything else was irrelevant. "Now that the murder has been solved, I trust that Charlotte's name will no longer be appearing in *Town Topics*. Astonishingly, Inspector Blackburn was right. The man is an anarchist. They found pamphlets in his room."

"It is a man, then?" I said, then corrected myself. "*One* man?"

"Oh, yes. Witnesses place him at the house the night of the murder. Apparently he gained access by delivering ice."

My heart felt as if it had stopped beating. Working my mouth so that my speech would sound normal, I said, "Did he send the notes?"

"It would seem. He had a nephew who died in that mining accident."

Accident, I thought, remembering Anna's words. *When poor people die, it's an accident. When rich people die, then it's murder.*

I said, "Still, they don't know for sure. Simply because he was there . . ."

"They do know. The man's confessed."

I took this in. "And they think he acted alone?"

"The man says he did, but of course they'll look at his associates."

He took up the pen again. Able servants know when they are dismissed without words. It's vulgar to continue to be present after the point of dismissal; it breaks the contract of invisibility.

Mrs. Armslow had once said of me, "I never know she is there until I need her." Her friend agreed. "That's as it should be. The best staff should be like the plumbing. You couldn't do without, but you certainly don't want to see it."

And yet I had a question. Moving my foot slightly on the rug made a gentle brushing sound. Mr. Benchley looked up.

"Do you think it was a genuine confession?" I asked.

"Genuine?"

Frustrated that he was pretending not to know what I meant, I said, "Coerced."

"I didn't inquire."

I gave him a slight smile as if to say, *Of course not, it would be beneath you to do so.*

The arrest of Josef Pawlicec had put the Newsome murder back on the front pages. BLACKBURN GETS HIS MAN! ANARCHIST CONFESSES! The break in the case had come when Mr. Pawlicec's employer contacted the police; he had become suspicious when the deliveryman asked for a change of route the night of the murder. A handwriting expert had been called in to ascertain if Mr. Pawlicec was the author of what were now being called the Shickshinny notes. With the great plot revealed, the city was even more on alert. There was a flurry of excitement when Michael Ashbury, a hotel owner, announced that he had also received threatening notes—but this turned out to be a hoax.

I couldn't deny there was a very good case against Mr. Pawlicec. And yet I felt a nagging sense that justice, whatever that was, was not being served. Every time I thought about that peculiar man with his soft, ugly face and halting English, I saw a victim rather than a killer. I could not call Anna, for fear of drawing attention to her, and I had nowhere else to go with my thoughts. In the evenings, as I turned the pages of the day's discarded newspapers for mention of "associates," I wondered what Michael Behan would make of it all. I imagined him scoffing at rival reporters' efforts or making jokes at Blackburn's expense. I was vaguely aware that this meant I was missing him. And aware of the stupidity of missing him.

The mood in the Benchley house was lighter. Mrs. Benchley could be heard asking the cook if she was familiar with the practice of placing the fish sauce in the shell of a hard-boiled egg—a trick she had seen at a luncheon of Mrs. Cadwallader's and was anxious to try. Louise came downstairs to practice her piano and, for the first time in weeks, was not shouted at by her sister. There was talk of trips in the spring, of opening the summer home.

Charlotte in particular seemed intent on having new things— new hairbrush, new nail file, new ribbons—as if throwing away last year's accessories would erase the events as well. In the days that followed, I seemed to spend all my time rushing out of the house only to return a few hours later to dump my packages and go straight out again.

One afternoon, as I was walking down the avenue for the third time that day, I heard, "Jane!"

Looking up, I saw William Tyler. His cheeks were pink from the cold air; his breath came in gusts.

I said, "Aren't you supposed to be at school?"

"I went back," he said.

"And?"

"And then I came home again." He grinned. "Are you on Benchley business?"

"I am."

"Can I walk with you? Ma's furious with me for coming home, and it's better if I'm out of the house."

"Be my guest. If you find hair ribbons fascinating."

"Oh, I do. Without question. You should hear what Nietzsche has to say on the subject."

William suggested we go through the park. Occasionally, he loped ahead and walked backward, his hair falling into his eyes. As we walked by the zoo, I said, "And why, exactly, did you leave school?"

"I uh, couldn't seem to settle." He glanced at me. "What happened on Christmas Eve . . . it was hard to think about anything else."

I nodded. I hadn't thought about much besides Christmas Eve either.

"Ma thinks I'm acting like a child. 'Look at Bea,' she says. 'She's all right, and she was supposed to marry the boy.' I see they've arrested someone and he's confessed."

"Well, they say he has."

William looked at me. "What do you mean?"

I hadn't really meant to say it. But having said it, I decided to be honest. "Just—they've been so determined to arrest someone, it's difficult not to think they might charge anyone, even if they aren't guilty."

"That's what I've been thinking!" William swung around, began to walk sideways. "Because, Jane, the Newsomes will have blood. Not Lucinda, of course, but the old man and the grandmother? You have to believe they've been talking to the governor, the mayor, screaming for results. Then the governor and the mayor scream at the police. So the police have to arrest someone."

Thrown by his vehemence, I stammered, "There were notes . . ."

"Has anyone actually seen those blasted notes? I wouldn't be surprised if they made this poor fellow write out the words—'Oh, we want to see what your handwriting looks like.' Then they'll hold them up and say, 'He wrote the notes, all right!'"

"What if he *did* write them?" I asked.

William went quiet. "Well, so what if he did? Shouldn't someone be punished for what happened at Shickshinny? Yes, they fired some lowly foreman, but the people who were really responsible got off scot-free."

As lightly as possible, I said, "William, have you been attending political meetings?"

"You don't have to go to meetings to know when something's wrong." He looked at his feet dragging through the winter slush.

"I was thinking, I might give something to this man's defense. Maybe even pay for the lawyer myself."

"That could be very expensive."

"I know. And Ma has made it pretty clear that now that Bea's prospects aren't what they used to be, I have to think a bit more seriously about my career." He stood up straight. "What do you think about me as a merchant seaman?"

"I'm not sure you can support your mother and two sisters on that pay. Much less pay for Mr. Pawlicec's defense." Then, thinking of Louise, I said, "But if you're staying in the city, you should call on Louise Benchley. I feel certain she'd be happy to see you."

William said, "Yes, I should stop by," in an absent sort of way.

As we walked, I thought how strange it was that someone like William Tyler should be the one to say what I had been thinking since I got back from Philadelphia. And that he should be so ready to *do* something. That awful quote of my uncle's, the one that had made me squirm, came to mind: *Even a child is known by his doings, whether his work be pure, and whether it be right.* So what was I prepared to do?

When we reached the store, William seemed reluctant to go. Hands in his pockets, he ducked his head and said, "I guess I can't pretend my interest in hair ribbons is all that strong."

"That's all right. I've enjoyed the company."

"I like talking to you, Jane. If I told anyone else I thought Mr. Pawlicec deserved sympathy, they'd put me in an institution."

"I think it does you credit. And if you do decide to give him money, I might know of a way to get it to him." William looked surprised, but I didn't want to explain.

Then he said, "I suppose I do feel a little badly for the Newsomes. Poor Mr. Newsome having that overdose scare . . ."

"That was shocking, wasn't it?" As lightly as possible, I added, "I thought Rose Newsome took such good care of him."

"Oh, but that's just it. Rose Newsome wasn't there the day it happened."

"She wasn't?" The picture that had been so clear in my mind began to blur.

"No, she'd gone to visit friends in Long Island and left him with the nurse. Oh, and Lucinda. She was home. She liked working with the nurses, so I guess everyone thought it would be all right."

★ ★ ★

When I returned to the Benchleys', the ladies were in the drawing room. I could hear the uncertain *plink plink* of Louise's piano practice, and Mrs. Benchley exclaiming to Charlotte about the latest glories of transatlantic travel. I went upstairs and arranged the new items on Charlotte's bureau as she liked them. Then, before anyone could call for me, I went up to my room to fetch the slip of paper on which I had written Mr. Rosenfeld's telephone number and hurried to the downstairs telephone.

When I heard Mr. Rosenfeld say, "Yes?" I answered, "Mr. Rosenfeld? It's Jane Prescott."

"Miss Prescott, yes! I called a week ago, but they said you were away."

"Does that mean you've finished the tests?"

"I have. They were very surprising. I would not like to talk about it over the phone. Do you think you could come to the pharmacy?"

It was a few days before I could make a visit to the Lower East Side. Mr. Rosenfeld was busy helping another customer when I came into his shop. For ten minutes, I examined the bottles and boxes on the shelves, declining help from another assistant. Finally the lady's problem was solved, and Mr. Rosenfeld came around the counter to greet me.

Once again, he led me to the comfortable chair in his office and sat behind the battered desk. Reaching down, he opened a drawer and took out the jar I had used to carry the scrap of Norrie's jacket. I could see part of the stain was faded now, as if it had been scraped at.

Turning the jar, Mr. Rosenfeld said, "You said you would go to the police. If I found anything."

"Did you find something?"

"I did. And now I am not sure which of us should tell their story first. Is it for you to tell me where this little scrap came from? Or for me to tell you what I found?"

In the end, I went first. Then Mr. Rosenfeld told me his story, recounting each of the elements he had found on the cloth. He used several scientific terms that I did not understand.

But even I knew what the word "opiate" meant.

19

The next day, I made another detour in my shopping and visited the offices of the ILGWU. As I waited for Anna on a wooden bench in the lobby, I reflected how much of my life I spent with women. The women of the refuge, Bernadette, Mrs. Armslow, the Benchley ladies. Beyond the wooden fence that served as a partition between the office and the waiting area was a different kind of women: women typing, arguing, talking into phones, reading papers. It was a busy, noisy world; I felt drawn to it, but could not see my place.

I got up and walked to a wall that served as an informal history of the union. There were placards from the Uprising of the Twenty Thousand—ABOLISH SLAVERY! WORKHOUSE PRISONER!— and press clippings covering the event—GIRL STRIKERS FORM BAND TO FIGHT THUGS. One sign read: "Our enemies have wealth. We have the power of reproduction." There were banners from various locals, surprisingly intricate and well made. But then, I thought, these were seamstresses and craftswomen; I shouldn't be surprised.

One banner in particular caught my eye. It was a long piece of red cloth, edged with gold trim. At the top in gold thread, it read: JUSTICE FOR THE SHICKSHINNY EIGHT. My uncle would have called it Romish, but perhaps not if he had seen the eight names embroidered into the fabric. Eight boys' names. I stared at the banner, trying to commit them to memory. *Liam Brody, 11. Erich Kessel, 11. Will Dempsey, 10. Adam Janyk, 11, Karl Peterhof, 10, Jan Pawlicec* . . .

Jan Pawlicec had been eight years old.

Was there a moment when they realized no one was coming? That they had been left? Forgotten? Did they understand that they were going to die? Or had death come on them suddenly, without warning? Left, they had just been . . . left. As children should never be left. I had a memory: rough wooden plank under my fingers, a sensation of weightlessness, swinging feet . . .

A hand on my arm. I jumped.

"It's only me," said Anna.

I looked at the banner. "I thought you had to be ten."

It was a stupid thing to say. And I knew it. But some part of my brain insisted that it was all a terrible mistake. An eight-year-old child had not died in a mine. No one had left a boy that small to die.

"Legally, you have to be ten," said Anna. "If a boy looks the right age, no one asks questions."

I let her lead me a little way toward the doors. "I've seen that banner before . . ."

"And never looked at the names. I know. Come, let's talk."

★ ★ ★

We ate in one of the German cafés. It had probably once been one of the hundreds of saloons in the area, but as the Germans moved uptown to make way for Jews who were not as enamored of lager, it had begun to balance its offerings of food and drink. I sat at a rough wooden table, making my way through a bowl of heavily spiced goulash. There was a lively, raucous crowd; I didn't have to worry we would be overheard. At first we talked of nothing, as if we had met for dinner as we used to. But small talk eventually fell to silence.

Finally I said, "Josef Pawlicec was there that night. I saw him."

"I know. He told me."

"I didn't tell the police that. Even if they'd asked, I wouldn't have—"

"I know."

Did she? I still wasn't sure if Anna trusted me.

"*Did* he write the notes?"

"You've heard him speak English. Do you think he wrote those notes?"

Someone could have written them for him, I thought.

But I said, "I think he's innocent of murder. And we might be able to prove it."

I told her about my talk with Mr. Rosenfeld. "If we told the police Norrie was drugged before he was killed, that would cause doubt about Mr. Pawlicec, wouldn't it?"

She picked at her food, unconvinced. "Because of this piece of cloth."

"Yes."

"With this drug."

"Yes, the pharmacist explained—"

"And this pharmacist will testify." She looked at me. "This nobody from the Lower East Side will get up and say these things in a court of law. He will tell one of the most powerful families in the nation, 'I'm sorry, you are wrong. Let the anarchist go free.'"

"If he has to, yes."

Anna shook her head.

"If Mr. Pawlicec can be saved, isn't our duty to try?"

"How do you know he wants to be saved?"

"Of course he does. No man could want to go to the electric chair."

"He may not want to, but he may see the necessity."

"But I'm telling you it's *not* necessary. It's letting the very people you're fighting get away with a crime they say you committed."

"And if you fight them in the courts, then they won't get away with it," she said, mocking me as gently as she could.

"At least tell him he should retract his confession."

"You want him to say he didn't murder Norrie Newsome? That he lied or was beaten until he confessed?"

"Yes."

"Then I'm sorry, I can't help you."

It took me a moment to speak. "You want him to die."

"No, not at all. It will be hard to think of him suffering. But it will be better than to think of him suffering for nothing."

"He needn't suffer at all!"

For a brief moment, Anna's face mirrored my anger. Then, taking a deep breath, she said, "You don't understand."

"No, I don't understand. I don't understand how some idea is more important to you than a man's life."

Anna was quiet for a long time. I had the sense she was struggling to control herself. Finally she said, "It's not only an idea. It's one man's life for many men's lives. Ask your uncle about this idea. He's a believer in the myth of Jesus Christ, isn't he?"

Having delivered that jab, she went back to eating. I knew she expected me to stop now. That was how our arguments generally went. One of us made a statement, the other disagreed. We went back and forth until she won—not, I couldn't help feeling, because she was right, but by saying something I couldn't challenge because I didn't know enough.

Maybe I didn't know enough. But I didn't want to stop this

time. I signaled as much by slapping my cutlery down on the table. Anna looked up.

"You always say I care about the wrong things and the wrong people—"

"I have never said this."

"You think it." That she didn't deny. "You think I spend my life worrying about rich people, the ones who need help least of all. Well, now I want to help someone with no money, no power, and all you have to say is . . . don't. Give up. There's nothing you can do."

"There—"

But then she saw my face and changed her tone. "What is it you want me to do?"

"Help me see Josef Pawlicec. He should at least know there's a chance."

Anna was quiet a long moment. "There is no chance. But I will help you see him."

★ ★ ★

Josef Pawlicec was being held at the city prison known as the Tombs. They were located on Centre Street, the prison so called because the original jail had been modeled on an Egyptian tomb. Built on swampland and poor landfill, it gave off a foul smell, nearly sank at one point, and almost burned down at another. Less than a decade ago, the building Charles Dickens had reviled as a "dismal-fronted pile of bastard Egyptian" was torn down and replaced with a gray stone building that strove to imitate a French château with dark slate turrets. The style might be more elegant, but I couldn't imagine that gave any solace to the men and women imprisoned there. The jail was connected to the courthouse by a covered throughway four stories above street level known as the Bridge of Sighs.

I was searched on arrival to make sure I had nothing I could pass to the prisoner. A matron was brought in to pat me down. Then a red-faced policeman said to me, "Follow me, miss."

As I rode the elevator down with Officer Shenck, I felt a tightness in my chest and took a deep breath. We moved out of the elevator and down a long, low-ceilinged corridor, then passed through two doors, made up of iron bars; these doors had to be locked and unlocked, then locked again once we had passed through. Hearing the rattle of keys and the heavy knock of the bolt sliding into place, it was difficult not to be aware that I was trapped.

The officer took me to a large room, which had the feeling of an animal pen. It was maybe two stories high, with a catwalk that circled it at the first story. There were long rows of narrow tables, with chairs on either side. The room was filled with men in prison garb; they were chained to the tables, which I'm ashamed to say I found reassuring. Policemen stood along the walls at four-foot intervals. They carried guns. It was difficult not to note that there were maybe twenty policemen and as many as fifty prisoners.

"We put him over here," said Officer Shenck, leading me to a remote corner. "We don't get so many young women in here. We thought it'd be safer for you."

I looked to the spot the officer indicated. There were two empty seats. I looked questioningly at him, and he said, "He'll be along shortly." Then, scratching his ear, he said, "Mind if I ask your interest in the case?"

"He delivered ice to the house where I work," I said vaguely. I had caught sight of Mr. Pawlicec. He was brought in through a side door, looking broken and shambling. Seeing me, he smiled broadly in surprise, showing the loss of not a few teeth.

When he had been seated, the guard began to chain him to the table. I said, "Do you have to? I'm not afraid."

The guard continued his business. I smiled apologetically at Mr. Pawlicec, who shrugged inside his overlarge prison uniform. It seemed to me his shaving-brush hair was patchier than it had been, his face thin and gray. Except for a large purple bruise under his eye. Still, he smiled at me as if we had simply run into each other on the street and sat down for a chat.

The guard finished and stepped back to stand against the wall; he still felt too close for privacy, but I knew he would not budge. It was hard in the din of so many people to keep my voice down and be heard, but I tried.

"I'm sorry," I began.

Mr. Pawlicec leaned in to hear better. The guard brought his baton down on the edge of the table, and he sat back.

"I'm sorry," I said more loudly. "About your nephew. I didn't know."

At the mention of his nephew, the wide, crooked smile vanished, and Mr. Pawlicec seemed to lose all liveliness. Finally he said, "I had a picture. I would show you, but they took it away."

"I'll try to get it back for you."

"Thank you. I would like it when"—he tried to smile—"at the end."

The resigned way he spoke of his own execution spurred me to ask, "Why did you confess?"

Surprised to be asked, he said, "I am guilty."

"But you're not. I know you're not."

He shook his head. "You think you know this."

"No, I do. And even if I'm wrong, and the person I suspect is not guilty, I know that you are not guilty. For one thing, Norrie Newsome was drugged. I have proof."

"The rich, they take all kinds of things. Maybe to ease their conscience."

"Norrie had no conscience. Someone gave him something to make it easier to kill him. You carry ice for a living, Mr. Pawlicec. You're very strong. You would have had no need to drug Norrie Newsome to kill him. And no opportunity."

"I had tongs. They did the work for me."

"And what did you do with those tongs? They must have been dripping with blood. How did you get them out of the house?"

"I wrap them in my coat."

"Where is that coat now?"

"I throw it away."

"I saw you at Anna's uncle's restaurant after the murder, Mr. Pawlicec. You had it then. I noticed it hanging over the back of your chair."

"After," he stammered. "I throw it away after that."

"Are you so rich that you can afford to throw away an unstained coat?"

"There were stains," he said.

"No, there weren't," I said. "Because you never killed Norrie Newsome."

He was quiet a long time. I barely heard him as he murmured, "I wanted to."

"Wanting and doing are not the same. Why did you lie to the police? Did they threaten you?"

"No, not at all."

"Then why?"

"Because they believed I had done it." He met my eye. "And that was a great gift to me."

I sat back, stunned. "How could that be a gift?"

He frowned, and I had the feeling he was struggling to work his thoughts through the words of English he knew. Finally he said, "Do you have a brother or sister?"

"No."

". . . Family?"

"An uncle."

He nodded. "My brother Leon was the oldest. He came here first. After him, me and my sister. He found us a place to live, he found us jobs. He took care of us. Like a father. You understand?"

"Yes, I do."

"He worked hard. Too hard. He got the—" He pointed his chest to indicate his lungs. "But when he dies, he doesn't have anything. So his wife, she says to Janusz, my nephew, now you have to go to work. I am in New York, I am working, I don't think about it. But after Janusz dies, I think, how did I let that happen? Leon took care of me. But I don't take care of his son. For years, I think about that.

"You can say I didn't do it. But I should have. Not the son, I would not have killed the son. But the father—I should have killed him. I switched routes so that I would be able to get into the house." He looked down at his chained hands. "But I didn't have the courage. I went into that house and I left it with that man still alive. I let Janusz's murderer live. If there were a God, I would thank him for my boss calling the police. I would thank that God for having me arrested. Because now, they will understand that we can kill also. Now they know what it is when someone destroys your children and does not see anything wrong with that. And now—they are afraid."

"Frightened people do terrible things, Mr. Pawlicec. Fear doesn't make them kinder."

"But maybe it makes them change—in order to survive. And if not, well, in the end, there are more of us."

He glanced at the guard, who had long ago turned his attention elsewhere. "Please, Miss Prescott. You would not have come here if you did not . . ."

He struggled with the words, and I said, "I want to help you, Mr. Pawlicec."

He nodded eagerly. "Yes, and you can help me. By saying nothing. Whatever it is you think, whatever proof you have, stay silent. Let me be tried, let me be guilty."

"They will execute you." He did not react. "Do you know that word?"

Swallowing, he nodded.

"It will not be quick," I said.

"I know." He nodded to himself as if to clear his head of the images that had come into his mind. "And that is why, if you could, I would like very much to have Janusz's picture. When that time comes, I will be afraid, and I might think, no, tell them the truth. Tell them you are a coward. Tell them to go to Miss Prescott. But if I can look at Janusz, and remember, I will be strong."

"You are asking me to help you die."

He dropped his head. "Yes. I am sorry."

I tried another argument. "The person who did this is probably very wealthy. Wouldn't it make more sense to show the world that the rich can be cruel?"

"The world knows. It just doesn't believe it's possible to do anything. This will show them that it is possible."

"Your sister—does she believe in what you are doing?"

His smile was sad. "She does not believe I did it either. She says she will tell everyone I am innocent. But no one will believe her."

"Do you think it's fair to her, to lose both her brothers?"

"No, it is not fair. But it wasn't my choice. I didn't surrender to the police. It was only when they arrested me and I saw there was no chance of convincing them that I was innocent that I decided not to try. For once, injustice will work in our favor." He patted my hand. "Anna can explain it better."

I knew that to keep talking was pointless. Mr. Pawlicec was convinced of the rightness of what he was doing—and even if he wavered, Inspector Blackburn was also convinced. The world had the story it wanted, and the person who had the most to lose did not care to tell them otherwise.

And yet I stayed on the hard bench, because I knew when I walked away, it would be the last time I ever saw Josef Pawlicec alive.

"Time, miss." The guard was back at the table. Hoisting Mr. Pawlicec to his feet, he added, "Say your good-byes."

There was nothing more to say, and yet when told I had to leave, I felt panicked. My hands and Mr. Pawlicec's were raised with the unconscious intention of shaking hands good-bye. But he was pulled back before our hands met, leaving the space empty between us.

I shouted, "I will get your nephew's picture back."

He nodded as he was turned around, called, "Thank you," over his shoulder. Then they led him through a metal door and he was gone.

★ ★ ★

I don't remember much after that, except the sound of the doors as they slammed behind me one after the other on the walk back. As I found myself back on the street, I was startled by the noise of the traffic, the brightness of the winter sun, the chill air on my face. Disoriented, I walked for some time, trying to shake the feeling that I had just woken up with no knowledge of what had happened as I slept.

"It's Jane, isn't it?"

A woman's voice, cultured and concerned. I looked in its direction. And saw Lucinda Newsome, bent slightly, a gloved hand raised as if to steady me.

I must have nodded, because she asked, "Are you all right?"

"I . . . yes." Dazed by the sudden appearance of a young woman I had recently envisioned spooning her father to his death, I looked up at the street signs. I had wandered to Eldridge Street, not too far from my uncle's refuge.

"You're surprised to see me here," she said, placing her hand back inside her muff.

Her frankness made it difficult not to respond in kind. "Yes."

"I volunteer at the Rivington Street Settlement House. I teach immigrant children."

"That's . . . very admirable."

"No, it's not. I teach singing, which is absurd, but it's all they'll let me do. I take a great interest in the immigrant community—working women, especially."

She made this declaration with some defiance, as if she expected ridicule. When I didn't answer, she looked down at her hidden hands and added, "Given what my family's done, it is literally the very least I can do. Coming down here is the only time I don't feel ashamed."

A reassuring pleasantry came to mind, but I resisted. The young woman wanted to be truthful—and I wanted to hear what she had to say.

She took a step toward me. "You might not believe this, but I didn't know anything about the Shickshinny Mine until the notes came. I didn't even know we owned mines. What my father did, where our money came from, it was all sort of . . . business to me. When Norrie told me about the death threats, I actually said, 'Why would anyone want to hurt us? What have we done?' He said, 'Well, the slobs of Shickshinny feel differently.' I had no idea what he meant. He wouldn't tell me either. I had to go to a library and look it up in old newspapers. Can you imagine? Such criminal ignorance?"

I was about to say I hadn't heard about Shickshinny at Mrs. Armslow's when she burst out, "We *never* spoke of it! Eight children, a hundred men dead . . ."

Emotion choked her words, and she stared at the pavement to compose herself. Finally she managed, "It eats away at you, knowing everything you have, everything you see around you, the beautiful dresses, the endless food, the warmth, is because you've used up a life and tossed it away. Our family talks endlessly about all the good we've done this country. The fact is, the world would be far better off without us."

"Did your brother feel as you do?"

"No. He didn't. When I told him I knew the truth about

Shickshinny, he just shrugged as if it had nothing to do with us. I was astonished. No, appalled. You probably think I've been unkind to Charlotte Benchley, but she brought out the worst in my brother. If they had married, I feel certain his life would have been wasted in luxury and excess."

"You tried to talk to him the night he died." Lucinda pressed her lips together and looked intently at a spot in the distance. It was no use; the tears fell anyway. "What did you want to talk to him about?"

Embarrassed by her tears, she tried to smile. ". . . Atonement?"

"You needn't feel responsible for what your family has done."

"Oh, I have blood on my hands," she said, gazing down at her muff, which, now that I looked, was indeed very beautiful and no doubt cost the earth.

20

That evening when I returned to the Benchley house, I went straight to my room, pulled off my shoes, and lay down on my bed. For a long, long time, I took in the cracked plaster of the ceiling, the brown patch of damp in the corner, the rattle of the windowpane. I thought about guilt. I thought about justice. And Norrie's ruined face, the broken, bloody teeth, the gouged holes where eyes had been.

A knock on the door brought me back. "Yes?"

The door creaked open and Louise appeared. Sitting up, I stammered, "Did you ring? I'm sorry, I didn't hear—"

"No, I didn't ring." She gestured to the desk chair. "Is it all right if I . . . ?"

Moving it closer to her, I said, "Of course, please." No family member had ever visited my room before. I wasn't certain as to the protocol.

She sat. Then said, "I'm not disturbing you? I know it's your day off."

"No, no. I . . . company is very welcome."

"Just you've been out so much since we got back from Philadelphia, I hardly ever see you."

"Miss Charlotte has kept me busy," I acknowledged.

"Yes. She got another invitation just this morning. Well, this one was for all of us. Lucinda's birthday party."

"Birthday party?"

"I know, it's very strange, but her stepmother wanted it. And her grandmother. Norrie's death has been so hard on her, maybe they think it will cheer her up."

Hard on her, yes, I thought. But perhaps not for the reasons her family imagined. Had that overwrought, guilty young woman lashed out at her brother once she realized the extent of his callousness? Was her father's overdose an accident or part of her "atonement"? If the latter, just how far would she take her crusade?

Louise broke into my thoughts, saying, "Charlotte says Lucinda's never liked her, she doesn't see why she should celebrate her being born. But Mother says we can't give offense when the whole city feels so badly for them."

The whole family would be gathered, I thought, with Lucinda the center of attention. "Miss Louise, will you tell me something?"

"Yes?"

"Do you remember your mother's Pep Pills? The ones that went missing? You told me you didn't remember what happened to them."

Louise looked away. "Is it important?"

"If it matters enough to lie about, I think it could be important. Don't you?"

"The reason I lied has nothing to do with the murder. But I promised . . ."

"Who did you promise, Miss Louise?" She looked unhappy. "It was Lucinda Newsome, wasn't it? You gave her the pills?"

"No," she said surprised. "It was Rose Newsome."

"Rose." Stupidly, I echoed the name, hoping against hope Louise would correct herself.

But she nodded. "The new Mrs. Newsome. I'd just realized I'd come down without my gloves, and I was feeling so terribly self-conscious about my hands, trying to find a way to get rid of the bottle, and she saw me holding it behind my back. She said, 'What's that? Something secret?' I never expected her to be so nice. As if we'd been friends forever."

I nodded, knowing just that tone of voice.

"And when I showed her how I'd forgotten my gloves, she laughed and told me a story about how she'd stepped out of her shoe at some important dinner she attended with Mr. Newsome. She said, 'To be honest, that's why we ran off to Europe. Like Cinderella, I'd lost my slipper! Only no fairy godmother for me to make it right.'"

"Then she said, 'But tonight I will be your fairy godmother.' And she sent one of the servants off to get me a pair of gloves."

"That was very kind of her."

"I know. So when she asked, 'And what's that little bottle there?' I told her it was Pep Pills and how I was to give them to Charlotte, only I couldn't find Charlotte . . ."

"And then?"

"She said she'd just seen Charlotte and she would give them to her. But I should stay where I was, hiding, until the maid brought me the gloves. Then she got this worried look on her face, and I said, 'What?' She said, 'Will you do me a great favor?' I said of course, because she'd been so kind to me. She said, 'Please don't tell anyone I have these.' She said there were people at the party who thought badly of her, and if I told anyone I'd given them to her, they'd be straight off to tell her mother-in-law she was taking pills."

"And you promised," I said.

"I did. But I feel badly that I lied to you about it. Was it important?"

"Yes, Miss Louise. I think it was."

There was another knock at the door. I was apparently very popular this evening. Opening it, I saw Bernadette, who said, "Man at the door for you."

I thought of my uncle. "Old?"

"Oh, not old." She smiled ever so slightly. Michael Behan was Irish, after all.

I tried not to hurry. But when I went out and saw him standing on the street, I felt the exhilaration of finding something you thought was lost, the deep relief of knowing you will not have to live without it after all.

"When did you get back?" I asked.

"A few days ago. I thought of calling, but I wasn't sure you'd want to hear from me."

"Why did you come, then?"

"Thought I might as well make sure." He smiled. I smiled back.

Glancing toward the kitchen, I closed the door and stepped outside. "Did you find out anything more about Mr. Farragut?"

"I did, as a matter of fact. Have you found out anything more?"

"I have."

"You go first."

I told him—all of it. Every memory of the Newsome murder, from the discovery of Norrie's body to my conversation with Lucinda that afternoon and Louise's recent revelation.

Leaning against the house, I said, "So, there it is, the mystery of the Pep Pills solved. I knew I hadn't seen them when I was in the room. Did you learn anything more in Philadelphia?"

Uncrossing his arms, Behan reached into his coat pocket and pulled out two sheets of paper. "Story rejected for lack of timeliness and public interest."

I unfolded the paper, read the headline: UNSOLVED MURDER IN PHILADELPHIA: THE STRANGE DEATH OF CHARLES FARRAGUT.

When I got to the part about the eyes, I swallowed bile.

"Funny, isn't it?" said Behan. "New York society run by a woman who could do that."

"We should show this to the police."

"Why? The poor slob's confessed. Although—'Humble Worker Framed for Society Murder!'"

"Would your editor be interested in that story?"

Behan shrugged to indicate it was unlikely. "I suppose the real murderer could always have a change of heart and confess."

He was joking, but I had been thinking the same thing. I wanted to believe that a small sliver of human feeling remained in that tormented individual. I just didn't know how to reach it.

Then I thought of something. "Who was your inside source, Mr. Behan?"

"What does it matter now?"

"Think about it."

He did. And told me. "You're not going to tell her what we know, are you?"

The bells at a nearby church began to sound. It was late. "I should go back."

Scrambling to his feet, he said, "What are you going to do, Miss Prescott?"

I climbed the stairs to the servants' entrance. "Lucinda Newsome is giving a little party next week. I think Louise and Charlotte will need assistance."

"Those little parties can be tricky," he said, looking up at me. "Maybe they need extra staff."

"Not for this gathering. But thank you. One thing you could do?"

He nodded.

"Mr. Pawlicec wants his nephew's picture back. The little boy who died. Someone at the prison took it. If you have a 'friend' there, maybe you could get it returned to him."

★ ★ ★

The next day, I called Mr. Rosenfeld to thank him again for his help. There were, I said, one or two terms I had not understood; could he explain them to me? He could and he did. And when he was done, I not only knew who murdered Norrie Newsome, I had some idea of how we might prove it.

21

The evening before Lucinda Newsome's birthday party, I paid a visit to my uncle. The Gorman Refuge for Lost Women was on East Third Street, close to the Bowery. It was a modest four-story town house that had once been a highly successful brothel. The madam, Mrs. Edith Gorman, had left it to my uncle on the grounds that the "game" had gotten rough with the arrival of syndicates and pimps, and most of her girls wouldn't last without her guidance and protection. She had seen my uncle wander the streets at night, inviting her employees to services at St. Mark's Church and secretarial classes at a nearby settlement house. This habit had caused a great deal of whispering among his parishioners, and so when he was offered the house, my uncle took his own chance at a new life.

The refuge could house as many as twenty women at a time, more if they did not bring children. Two of the floors were dormitories; the basement served as a nursery and laundry. The first floor was a classroom, with a dining room off the kitchen. When I lived here, my uncle and I had most of the top floor, a room for each with a parlor between us.

That evening, the refuge was full, and as I entered, I could hear the women talking in the dining hall. The talk was lively, but not too loud, which meant my uncle, or one or two of the long-term residents, were present to maintain order. These were women used to fighting for their place in the world, and that made communal living a challenge.

Stepping inside, I wondered what the murderer would have thought of these women. Of fourteen-year-old Annie, who had worked the coal boats with her friend Sarah since she was twelve, only giving up the life when her friend had her neck broken by a customer. She woke up most nights crying for her.

Or eighteen-year-old Ruth, whose parents had sold her to Mrs. Gorman because their poor English led them to believe their daughter would be trained as a seamstress. Or forty-year-old Liz, whose husband had left her for the midwife who helped her deliver a stillborn child. She didn't mind the loss of the husband, but the loss of his income had ruined her. Or nineteen-year-old Maddie, who drank terribly, but my uncle could not ask her to leave because she was seven months pregnant. Some of these women had worked in Frenchtown, as the French brothels near the university were known. They had roamed the park, doing business there, day or night. In the Italian brothels of Greene and Wooster, they had solicited customers by performing, singly, in pairs, or in groups, in front of windows. (All were adamant: they would have nothing to do with the women who worked below Bleecker in what was called Coon Town.)

Ruth was working at the front desk as I came in. She came around the desk, her arms open. Ruth was very small and very round. She had been eleven when her parents sold her, but she never had any bitterness over their dreadful mistake.

When she had hugged me, she set her fists on her hips and said, "Guess what? I got a job."

Congratulating her, I asked, "Where?"

"A factory." She nodded uptown. "Can you believe it? I'm going to be a seamstress after all. You here to see your uncle?" I nodded. "He's upstairs."

As I climbed the stairs to the top floor, I passed a framed piece of embroidery. One of the women had made it for my uncle a long time ago. It read

FOR ALL HAVE SINNED,
AND COME SHORT OF THE GLORY OF GOD.
ROMANS 3:23

When I reached the door of my uncle's room, I knocked and said, "It's me, Uncle."

He opened the door. "Jane. Is something wrong?"

I was about to say no out of habit, but hesitated. "May I come in?"

My uncle was at his desk in the parlor room. As always, he put me in mind of a terrier, one of those dogs employed to catch rats. Like them, he was small, compact, and relentless. Now he put his work aside, pushed a chair toward me, and waited for me to speak.

I had felt so desperate to talk to him, and now I didn't know how to begin. I found myself staring above his head at the wall where there were several watercolor prints depicting scenes from the Bible. One of them showed Cain and Abel side by side. Abel, blond and smiling, held a lamb. Cain, dark, stood with his vegetables pulled from the earth, the offering God had found less worthy than Abel's.

"I hate that story," I said.

My uncle turned to look at the picture. "Why is that?"

"It's unfair. They never say why God loves one more than the other. How is a lamb better than vegetables? I'd say the ewe worked harder than Abel did."

"A flawed offering wasn't Cain's sin. It was his anger."

"Why shouldn't he be angry? If Man ignores God for two seconds, He's enraged."

"And what Cain did with his anger? It wasn't Abel's fault God loved him better."

"God created that situation by pointlessly favoring one over the other, then He punishes the man He destined to fail—as if He had nothing to do with it."

"'If thou doest well, shalt thou not be accepted?'" quoted my uncle. "Cain had choices."

"Easier to be good when you're the favored son." I looked away from the picture. "Do you remember that woman who killed a man? She came to the refuge?"

I had worried my uncle would not remember. But he said, "Yes."

"You took her in." He nodded. "Because you thought she deserved protection?"

"Because she asked for it."

I felt my uncle was deliberately avoiding the point. "But she killed someone."

"And if I were a policeman, I would have arrested her. But I am not a policeman."

"But when the police came, you didn't hide her."

"Because I am also not a judge."

"And if you were?" Challenging my uncle for the first time, I felt a strange flex in my nature, a weak muscle that was now being tested. "Would you have found her guilty?"

My uncle sighed. "Those are very simple words."

"Yes, but they're the ones we use. That man had threatened her, abused her, might have killed her."

"She did not kill him because she was afraid," said my uncle. "She was very clear about that. She hated him and felt her life would be better if he lost his."

"He gave her good reason to feel that way."

My uncle said nothing.

"Doesn't that matter?" I asked.

"I don't know. Does it matter to you?" He looked at me and I felt the question: *why* does it matter to you?

I struggled. "If someone kills someone who threatens them, who is stronger than they are, don't we call that self-defense?"

"You'd have to ask that man's children. He had three."

I was about to say that clearly they were better off without him, but my uncle placed his fingers on the desk as if preparing to stand. I felt the stupidity of dismissing that loss.

Instead I asked, "Did you like her?" My uncle smiled, puzzled. "Did you feel she had any kindness? If her life had not been hard, if she had felt safe . . ."

"No," he said abruptly. "I didn't like her. She was shortsighted, filled with rage, and unaware of anyone else's pain. But that's not why I gave her to the police. I gave her to the police because she had taken a life, and I lack the arrogance to stand against man's law and God's and say 'I know better.' Murder is a final act. Something stolen can be returned. A life of sin can be redeemed. But a life taken is a life gone. Something must answer it. Someone must speak for the dead."

★ ★ ★

The next evening, we drove to the Newsome house. It was customary for a ladies' maid to accompany her employers to any affair of a certain size and level of prestige. But as I told Mr. Behan, this was to be a smaller gathering. In order to go, I had to impress upon Mrs. Benchley the necessity of my presence to provide that extra support for Charlotte and Louise on what was sure to be a very difficult occasion.

On the drive over, I could see that Mrs. Benchley was anxious. In her hands was a small lace handkerchief; she tugged on it with such concentration, I did not think it would last the evening. Charlotte's jaw was set, her gaze stark and unreadable. Louise glanced from her mother to her sister to me for reassurance, but found little. I was too preoccupied by thoughts of how this evening might end.

Going around to the back, I was greeted by the surly Mrs. Farrell—who, as it happened, was the very person I needed. As she led me up the stairs to the guest rooms, I caught a brief glimpse of Lucinda. Now in half-mourning, she wore a blouse of black and white paisley print with a black velvet collar and a slender necklace of jet beads. The shoes underneath the long skirt were high-laced boots. Though not festive, the outfit suited her far better than that awful meringue she wore Christmas Eve; she looked quite handsome as she shook hands and touched cheeks with her guests.

"Miss Lucinda looks happy," I observed as we passed by.

"The Newsomes don't inflict their private pain on others," said Mrs. Farrell.

No, I thought. *But that doesn't stop you from making a pretty penny on it.*

My second piece of luck came when she took me to the same guest room the Benchley ladies had shared the night of the party. As she was about to leave, I said, "Mrs. Farrell, I wonder if I might ask you a question."

She hesitated. "About?"

"Do you recall our talk at the Rhinebeck house?"

"I'm not sure," she said carefully.

"We talked about salaries, the rising cost of things, elderly relatives . . . ?"

We had had no such conversation, but she understood, giving the briefest nod.

"I'm so impressed by the way you've managed. Thirty years with one family—that's an achievement. I've only been working for seven years, and already I've been with two families. I hate to say it, but the second one isn't what I was used to with Mrs. Armslow."

"Of course it's not," she said. "Now you work for trash."

"I know," I lamented. "They're always getting themselves in the scandal sheets." I paused. "Which makes me wonder how loyal do we have to be?"

"You're thinking you'd like to make some extra money," she said bluntly.

"It did occur to me."

"And where do I fit in?" The woman's business sense was incredible, I thought. She would profit off any opportunity that came her way. And like a crocodile, she had teeth enough to make sure they came her way.

"If you were to steer me in the right direction, it would be wrong not to acknowledge your assistance."

"What do you need to know?"

I asked her things I knew already or did not care about. Who did she speak to at *Town Topics*? How much did they pay? What sort of stories were they interested in? Mrs. Farrell supplied all this information in a brisk, no-nonsense tone as if she were instructing me on the correct way to fold stockings.

Then, as if I had just thought of it, I said, "But Mrs. Farrell, what if I don't have the stories they want?"

"Then you don't get paid."

"But how did you find out what you know? Did you just . . . notice things, listen when you weren't supposed to?"

Now that we were to be business partners, she relaxed, sitting down on a nearby chair. "You have to gain their trust. Go for the young ones—you look after the daughters, don't you? When they pour their hearts out to you, give them the sympathy they're looking for. Ask questions. Then you've got your story."

"So you got your information from Miss Lucinda?"

"Of course not. That young woman would never discuss family matters with the staff. It was the other one, the new wife. She doesn't have the first idea how to run a house like this, and she relies on me completely. Burbles all kinds of things. When Mr. Newsome Jr. died, she couldn't keep her mouth shut, she was so frightened."

"She told you about the Pep Pills, didn't she?"

"That's right. And the fight between Miss Beatrice and your girl. She was worried young Mr. Newsome'd gotten himself tangled in something he shouldn't have and he'd bring shame on the family."

"And when the stories began appearing in the newspaper— Mrs. Newsome didn't suspect you?"

"She thought it must have been a policeman. I told you, she trusts me. And she can't afford to pick a fight with me."

Rose Newsome certainly did need Mrs. Farrell, I thought, but not in the way the housekeeper thought.

"But the fight over Mr. Newsome, the two young ladies—a policeman couldn't have known that story."

"Couldn't they? Didn't Charlotte Benchley spill the whole tawdry mess to that detective? That's why the Newsomes invited the Benchleys to the Rhinebeck house, to get her away from the detectives and the press before she opened her mouth again."

As lightly as possible, I said, "Very fortunate to have the lady of the house so talkative. People do speak of her lovely ease of manner."

"Oh, she likes to make friends, that one. Thinks she can fool anyone the way she fooled Mr. Newsome. Miss Charlotte seems very free with herself," she said, rising from the chair. "I'd start there. The other one doesn't look as if she knows what goes on two feet in front of her. You hear something worth sharing, I'll see it gets into the right hands."

"I'd be very grateful."

That I would show such gratitude in a monetary fashion was expressed in a brief smile between us. Then she left, closing the door behind her.

I took a deep breath. It helped to have a full picture of how the events after Norrie's death had been managed. So expertly that I felt sure the next step in my plan should be to remove any evidence that might point to Charlotte Benchley. The person who had gone to such lengths to implicate her wouldn't hesitate to use the dress as evidence if she felt cornered. What else she might do if she felt cornered was not something I could think about right now.

Charlotte had said she stuffed the dress under the bed. From the looks of it, this guest room was not the finest the house had to offer; it would be used largely as a changing room for parties—as it had been that night. With the Newsomes in Rhinebeck and the house in general disorder, there was every chance it hadn't been thoroughly cleaned in the weeks that followed. Dusting and mopping, yes. But only those surfaces that were visible . . .

I got on my knees and looked underneath the bed.

It wasn't there. Someone had already found it. And taken it for safekeeping.

I considered the second thing I needed to find: the murder weapon.

There was no fireplace here; the room was too insignificant for that. There had been nothing else under the bed, I was sure. Quickly, I felt with my feet along the rug. I looked behind chairs, pulled open the drawers of the heavy oak bureau. But I found nothing.

Could it have been returned to its original place? Sitting there in plain sight, the weapon the entire police force of New York City had been looking for all these weeks?

Leaving the guest room, I made my way down the backstairs to the kitchen. It was strange to see it for the first time since the night of the murder. The room was far less crowded and chaotic; a cook and two kitchen maids worked the stove and sinks as butlers came and went, bringing in fresh glassware and dainties for the party. A large cake, frosted white and piped in pink, waited to be taken out at the end of the evening.

Taking a cloth from a table, I ran it quickly under the tap. Muttering something about a spill to the most junior kitchen maid, I hurried out the door—fingers crossed that no one noticed I was not headed back upstairs. Walking with speed and purpose I hoped would discourage questions, I approached the back door to the library.

Leaning in, I listened for voices beyond the door, although I knew that was unlikely. Then I took a deep breath, held the cloth tight to keep my hands from shaking, and went inside.

The moment I entered, I could tell I was probably the first person to do so since the police completed their investigations—or perhaps the second. The air was still and heavy with dust. The drapes were closed; unlike that evening, there was no fire to give light. Reaching along the wall, I found a lamp fixture. As it glowed into weak life, I saw that I was standing right by the fireplace.

Where I saw the fire iron, exactly where it should be. But had not been the night of the murder. The poker was a blunt, ugly rod of iron with a cruel hook at one point. Remembering what Mr. Rosenfeld had said about fingerprints, I was careful not to touch it. But looking closely, I saw that it had been wiped clean.

What would you use to wipe such a thing clean? And how would you dispose of a blood-soaked rag on the night a murder was committed? Anything bloodstained would be extremely incriminating . . .

I turned out the light and hurried back upstairs. Using my memory of Mrs. Armslow's Newport house as a map, I wandered until I found a remote part of the house; the opulent silence declared it the family's living quarters. A long, richly carpeted corridor led to three doors. As I passed one room I caught a whiff of lime and cloves; masculine scents. This was not the room I was looking for.

No, the room I was looking for was at the end of the hall. There was a double door, white and gilded with gold. As I put my hand on the handle, I listened for people inside. I didn't hear anything. The maids must all be downstairs. But I rehearsed, "Oh, I'm so sorry! I must have the wrong room!" nonetheless.

It was entirely possible someone would think I was a thief. I supposed in a way, I was. I swallowed that thought, turned the handle, and stepped inside Rose Newsome's bedroom.

Marie Antoinette would have found the room suitable to her needs. Most of the gleaming floor was softened by a large carpet, covered in a riot of roses. The walls were covered in pink silk, embroidered with gold garlands. The twenty-foot-high windows were obscured by heavy damask drapes and topped with stern figures of the virtues, accompanied by the odd cherub. There was a delicate writing desk in the center of the room, and a pretty white bureau with a porcelain bathing bowl. A portrait of someone's ancestor, demure and bewigged, hung on the wall. At various points about the room, there were small paintings of charming English country scenes.

But the centerpiece of the room was the bed itself. Large enough to sleep four, it boasted a canopy and coverlet draped in the same gold-garlanded pink silk. It stood on a platform of rose velvet. Not surprisingly, there were no personal mementoes on display. Only a photograph of Rose Newsome and her husband on their wedding day.

I felt certain this had not been the first Mrs. Newsome's taste. But the room as a vision of the second Mrs. Newsome's taste puzzled me. Her dress style was modern, daring without being vulgar. Intelligent, aware of the impression it made. Mature. This room was a princess's dream—or a six-year-old child's dream of a princess.

But I was not here to criticize the lady's taste. Crossing to the bureau, I saw that the drawers were long enough to hide what I was looking for. I pulled one open and felt at the front and back. But my hand came across nothing except silk and satin. Some of the items were of an intimate nature, and I pulled my hand out of the drawer.

There was a smaller door that led off the main room. Opening it, I saw that it was a sort of closet or storage space. It was packed tight with dresses and coats. On the floor, on racks, the lady's shoes for the season—or month. At the far back, shelves with boxes put up high and away. The kind of spaces even the most devoted lady's maid does not disturb more than a few times a year.

And yet when I stood on a small stool to look more closely, I could see the faintest trace of fingerprints in the dust that had gathered on the lids. These boxes had been recently moved.

I took one box down, carefully lifting the lid with one finger. Here were items even more intimate than what was kept in the bureau outside. Also, a skirt and sweater that looked strangely pedestrian—until I noticed the emblem of the Phipps Academy. I closed the box and put it back. As I did, I pushed it close to the wall—and heard the sound of crinkling cloth. Moving some of the boxes, I found Charlotte's dress, hidden behind them.

With delicacy, I reached out and tugged at the very edge of the garment. It was fragile, and I did not want to tear it, in case it became evidence. I could see it was badly stained; the red wine had turned purplish in the weeks that had passed. The stain was heaviest on the bodice; the skirt was spattered as well.

But when I held it up, I saw a different stain. A darker, heavier patch. I reached out to touch it with the tips of my fingers, felt the stiffness of dried blood.

My heart felt as if it had turned to lead. I had to remind myself to inhale, then exhale. I looked more closely at the dress.

And all of a sudden, I was calm. My heart eased; breathing came more naturally.

The stain was wrong.

Had Charlotte been the one to batter Norrie's head in, the blood would have flown, landing randomly in drops or spatters. As it had on Norrie's shirt. And yet the darker stain was a solid smear, with a few lighter ones surrounding it, almost the way a child draws the sun and its rays. It did not have the appearance of chaos. More of . . . cleaning.

Wiping.

Wiping off something covered in blood.

Stepping down, I took the dress with me.

Then I heard, "Jane—what on earth are you doing?"

I turned. And saw Rose Coogan Briggs Newsome. A Rose Blush in her hand.

22

In such circumstances, it can be difficult to know who has committed the greater crime: the servant who has entered the sanctum of the bedroom without permission or the woman who has taken a life. Those who dictate social mores *might* find me guilty of the lesser offense. But that didn't stop me from feeling like a criminal caught in the act.

Like her stepdaughter, Rose Newsome wore black—on top at any rate. The tunic and the fall of the skirt were a black silk, embroidered with pale cream roses. But the skirt was open at the front, and the tunic was stopped short at the waist to show a glorious fall of sunrise gold taffeta. Small gold coins dangled provocatively from the hem.

For a moment, she stood there, assessing the situation. Her gaze traveled the room, noted the open drawers, then the soiled dress on the floor. She seemed determined not to meet my eye, and I had the sudden impression of a child who thinks if she does not see you, she will be invisible.

As gently as possible, I said, "Rose."

"I'll say I caught you stealing."

"And the bloodstained dress?"

"That's what you were stealing. The Benchleys sent you to get it because they knew it would prove Charlotte killed Norrie."

"And that's why you kept it. If Blackburn had ever suspected you, you meant to 'find' this dress, didn't you?"

She turned away from me and began to walk along the edge of the rose-patterned rug, delicately placing one foot in front of the other.

"Also why you kept bringing Charlotte and Beatrice together. You pretended not to understand their history, but of course, you understood very well. Another blow-up between them would strengthen your story that Charlotte murdered Norrie out of jealousy. 'Several witnesses reported bad feelings existed between the two young ladies.'"

She continued on her odd journey, and I wondered if she would speak to me at all.

"You once said I was easy to talk to. Will you talk to me now? I want to understand."

She had run out of rug and now stood blocked by the massive bed. Sitting on the edge of a chaise lounge, she brought her hands together like a nervous but attentive student. "Mrs. Benchley told me you went to Philadelphia."

"Yes. I was sorry to hear about your father."

"Oh, then you went to Schuylkill."

"Yes."

"Not much of a place, is it?"

I hesitated. "The people are poor."

"The *people*. The people are animals." The hands in her lap began to twist. "Did you see any children?"

"Some," I said, remembering the little girl, her cheek bulging with candy.

"They threw rocks at me, you know."

"Who?"

"The children. After it happened. They'd wait for me after school—and throw rocks. At my head." She tried to smile as if she had made a joke. "They screamed, called my father a murderer. And the adults could hear them. They'd cross the street, pretend not to see. Or watch from their houses, peeking from behind the curtains. Did any of them come out of their ugly little hovels to say no, don't do that? Of course not. I don't think those children had lost anyone. They just liked throwing rocks."

"I'm sure you're right."

"Once? They hit me in the mouth. I had blood all down my front. They broke my tooth." She touched her cheek. "I got dizzy and fell down. When I was lying on the ground, I thought, *They'll stop now. They'll see I'm really hurt and stop.* But they just started crowding around, shoving to be next. I can remember scrabbling in the dirt with my fingers, desperate for something to throw back. Something heavy and hard. But all I found was dust, and dust blows away into nothing when you throw it."

"How did you get away?"

"I kicked at them so they had to step back. Then I ran. When I got home, my mother said, 'Your face!' And my father just stared at me. The next day, they found him by the river."

"Then you went to Philadelphia."

"That's right. My mother got a job at Wanamaker's. We got a discount on the clothes. Nice clothes were important to her. I went to the store after school. One day, I couldn't be quiet and sit like she wanted me to, so she sent me outside to play. I was pretending to be on a tightrope, walking along a crack in the sidewalk, when a man came up to me and said, 'Careful, you don't want to fall. It's a long way down.' I thought that was very funny." She pulled at the fingertips of her glove; it was odd to see she had the same bad habit I did.

"He asked why I was alone. I said, 'I'm not alone. My mother works in the store.' 'Does she? Is she as pretty as you?' 'Oh, prettier,' I said. 'Well, this I have to see. I'll go in and say hello.'" She looked up at me. "I don't think my mother ever realized that he had met me first. Seen me first."

She continued to stare at me, and I felt uncomfortably scrutinized. Then I understood that she wanted me to look away. She didn't want me looking at her when I realized what I had known on some level all along.

"It wasn't your mother," I said. "With Charles Farragut."

"He told me to call him Mr. Charley, so that's what I called him." She pulled her glove straight. "He started calling on her, taking her to nice places. She didn't have the right clothes; he bought them for her. And for me. One day, he invited us to a party at his home. When we got there, he told my mother I would be happier upstairs; he had a surprise, something that would keep me occupied and out of the way. She needn't come up. She should stay downstairs, talk to the other guests."

"Were you frightened to be alone with him?"

"A little at first. But Mr. Charley told me it was a game. He said, 'You know, I have some friends over to dinner. Well, my most important friends are upstairs. And I want your help playing a little trick on them.' I liked that, the idea of playing a trick on someone. It felt so much better than being the fool who didn't know what was coming. So he said, 'When we get into the room, I want you to march straight over to the dining room table and stand on it!'" She smiled. "Well, that seemed very daring and naughty. My mother would have fainted if I scuffed her furniture."

"And then?"

"Just before we got into the room, Mr. Charley got very excited, as if he'd had the most brilliant idea. Bending down, he whispered, 'And when you're standing there, on the table, with all these stupid men staring at you, I want you to pull down your bloomers. And leave them there, on the table. They'll feel so silly, won't they?'

Well, obviously, that was a little more daring. But he told me I didn't have to do anything else. Just get up on the table and drop my drawers. And make those men feel silly."

Setting her arms straight, she trapped her hands between her knees. "I do remember—all of them staring. Breathing. I looked at their eyes and thought, *They know what's happening here. They wanted it to happen. If they felt silly, they'd look away. I'm . . . I'm the one who's silly.*"

"Did he let you leave after that?" I asked.

"Oh, yes. He even had his chauffeur drive us home. I kept waiting for my mother to ask what had happened. But she never did."

"And she made you go back," I said, remembering what the saleswoman at Wanamaker's had said.

"Yes. About once a month we would go. My mother would sit downstairs and wait. No more party guests. I think he told her it was dancing lessons. There was a man who played the piano—I'd forgotten that."

"But it wasn't dancing lessons."

"No. The next time all I had to do was eat a cream cake while the men talked. A few times it was like that. Then they had me lie on a fur rug in front of the fire. Sometimes dressed, sometimes not. I usually fell asleep. It went on so long and it was so boring. At some point, they started to ask me to sit on their laps. 'Up you get . . .'"

Imitating the men, she strangled slightly. "Then one day, Mr. Charley said, 'You know one of those men—this is so silly, you won't believe it—but one of those men wants to see you drop your drawers again!' I laughed. He made it seem funny. I would, of course, get a cream cake."

Something I will have to call a smile passed over her face.

"Then he said, 'But just him this time. And in a special room.' Well, I went into that room and I ate the cake and a few hours later I woke up and there was blood all over the sheets. And it hurt. The next time my mother said it was time to go to Mr. Charley's house, I said I didn't want to. I screamed, actually. In the street."

She exhaled, folded her arms. "That's when it was explained to me that Mr. Charley was being very kind to us. That we had nice things because of him, and that later, I might be sent to a lovely, fancy school. A school every bit as good as Robert Newsome's own daughter went to. Didn't I want that? I think I said no, but what I wanted was hardly the point."

"You must be very angry with your mother."

"I think she told herself something else was happening. That it wasn't . . . that. She was sick. And Mr. Charley promised her he would provide for me."

She laughed briefly. "All that time, sitting, I would go off in my head. Somewhere else. I used to think about Schuylkill. Those children. My hands would be dangling or tucked in my lap and I'd play little finger games. 'Where is Thumbkin? Here I am . . .'" As she sang, her fingers began to pull on one another.

I said carefully, "But that's not how you met Mr. Newsome."

"No. But he has the same eyes."

The question came before I could stop myself. "How can you live with him?"

She looked amazed. "How could I *not*? I earned it. My father earned it. You have to understand: in our house, the Newsomes were *everything*. I think my father worshiped Robert Newsome more than God. At the very least he had them confused. I certainly did. As a child, I imagined God as a businessman in a dark suit and beaver hat. When the Newsomes blamed my father for the cave-in, he wasn't even angry. He said if his taking the blame helped the company, then he was happy to do it. Of course, stupidly, he expected to be rewarded for his loyalty. When that didn't happen, he was broken."

"And you wanted revenge."

"No, I wanted to be one of them. Not that stupid girl in the dirt—one of *them*." The hands started to twist again. "I thought a lot about Robert Newsome during all that jiggity-jog. You see, some of those men had daughters themselves. I knew because they would talk about them. They'd stop off to see them at school, then they'd come to Mr. Charley's. And of course, what do men also love to do? Brag. About what they're doing, who they know. 'You'll never guess who I saw at Phipps. Old Bob Newsome visiting his gal.' That's what I wanted to be, one of those daughters, safe in her nice school, waiting for Daddy's next visit.

"So when Mr. Charley said, 'Well, my poppet, you're getting a tad big for my clients. What should we do with you?' I told him straight off, 'I want to go to Phipps.' In some ways, he wasn't such a terrible man, Mr. Charley. He saw the joke right away. He did like a good joke . . ."

"How did he manage it?" I asked, thinking you couldn't send *any* girl to Phipps, no matter how much money was spent.

"Oh, he had a friend on the board. A man who attended his parties. He was quite willing to do him the favor. He said, 'Now, you'll be able to meet a nice man who'll take good care of you.'"

"And you did. Was it always your plan to . . . ?"

"Plan? When I left Mr. Charley's, I wasn't in any state to plan. Mr. Charley told me I should forget the past. Become someone else. Well, it's not so easy to 'become someone else.' I was empty. Blank. Teachers asked me questions, and I didn't know how to answer. One teacher asked if I had hearing difficulties; another thought I had been dropped on my head. The other girls didn't care why. They just knew I was wrong. I thought if I got to Phipps, the place *they* were, I'd be safe. But it felt all wrong. As if I'd died and was stupidly pretending to be alive.

"Then one day, Lucinda Newsome sat down next to me in class and began asking me questions in that blunt way of hers. Where was I from? Did I know how to read? What did I think of . . . I don't even remember what. When I saw her, it was like waking up. Suddenly I knew just what I had to do. I started making up that new girl then and there, before her eyes. Shy, eager to please. A girl embarrassed by her looks; *oh, people make such a fuss.* What she admired, I admired. What she despised, I certainly didn't care for. And when she asked, would I meet her father, she never knew what to say to him and it'd be easier for her to have a friend close by . . ."

Rose Briggs smiled. "I saw Robert Newsome, saw how he looked at me, and thought, *This will all work out just fine.*"

"He doesn't know who you are."

"Of course he does. I'm Mrs. Robert Newsome."

With everything her family was denied, I thought, the protection and largesse of the Newsome family. But not protected enough, it seemed.

"And Mr. Charley?"

At this question, Rose Newsome's expression changed. Became empty somehow, as if she had been daydreaming during a particularly boring tea party and had been asked a question she had not quite heard and was trying to think of an answer.

I said, "His face was destroyed, too."

"Only the eyes. I don't like the eyes. You get so tired, don't you? Of being looked at. Maybe some women feel flattered, but I've always felt the moment a man's eyes settle on me, he's halfway to feeling he can do anything."

Then she shook herself out of vagueness. "When Mr. Charley heard from his friends at the school who I was going to marry, he asked me back to his house to discuss what he called 'the financials.' He felt he deserved a reward—monthly and for the rest of his life. When I saw him, standing in front of that fireplace, when I thought about everything that had happened in that house, the way they laughed, pulled at me, left mess on me—I couldn't breathe. As if he were standing on my chest, crushing my heart."

Her hands had begun to stir; now she settled them, said simply, "He had to go away."

"And then Norrie." I looked back at her empty glass, filmy with the residue of egg white. "That wasn't done in a flash of rage, was it? You knew you were going to kill him. That's why you drugged him. His father had kept him short on liquor that night—was that your suggestion?"

She nodded.

"And when you met him in the library, you offered him your own drink."

"He was rude about it, sniffing at a silly girls' drink. But I told him, 'Oh, you'd be surprised.' I think he was, right before he passed out. I think . . . he knew." Her mouth quirked in satisfaction. "I like to think he was frightened. For the first time in his life."

"Why?"

". . . Did I do it?" she asked. "When I heard of Norrie's sudden interest in Philadelphia, I knew he wasn't concerned with business. So I asked one of the family . . . let's call them associates . . . to keep an eye on him. Norrie's behavior was so wild, nobody questioned it. The associate reported his journey to Phipps Academy and his overnight stay with a lady I guessed was Beatrice Tyler. That shocked me a little." Half joking, she widened her eyes at me. "Weren't you shocked? Such a fine young lady."

"And when Norrie came back?"

"When Norrie came back, he told me that unless I got his father to change his views on his allowance, he would make a very different announcement at the ball."

"Did he go to Schuylkill?" I asked.

"No. And he never made the connection with Coogan. That's how clever he was. Still, talking to Mayles and Gilfoyle, he'd found out enough about Mr. Charley to guess that he wasn't interested in my mother. I told him I needed time to think. But I knew Norrie would never keep his mouth shut—no matter how much money we gave him. When my husband decided to hire extra security for the party because of the death threats, I thought, *Oh. Yes.*

"I put Norrie off until the night of the party. So many people, anyone could get in. That night—you saw us arguing—I said I would meet him in the library and give my answer. And I did.

"While the drug took effect, he told me everything he thought he knew about me. As if he were important, so very important. And I thought, *You—you're absurd. You haven't done anything. You don't know anything. You don't know what it feels like. What old hands feel like. Slack, dry lips. Swollen, arthritic fingers pulling at you. You feel all that, then tell me how important you are. You feel it . . .*"

I had a vision of her bringing the fire iron down on Norrie's head, jabbing the eyes with the curved hook. To clear my head, I said, "You were still in the room, weren't you? When I found him."

"I was. It took Norrie longer to pass out than I had thought. But then, thankfully, you left, and I could take my place beside him, having made the dreadful discovery . . ."

"That's why no one noticed the blood on your dress."

"That's right."

"Where did you hide the poker? It wasn't there when I found the body."

"Behind the bookcase. The police were so convinced the anarchist had taken the weapon with him, they didn't look very carefully. And no one in this house reads books."

"But of course you had to put it back. Any scullery maid would have noticed it missing when she went to clean out the ash the next morning."

"That's right. It was a little tricky—the police took so long to leave. But around four in the morning, I was able to find Charlotte's dress, clean off the poker, and put it back in place."

"And you spilled the pills on the floor. To incriminate Charlotte."

"Or you."

Remembering how she had deliberately sent me off with Norrie, I felt chilled.

She explained, "I knew that death by beating wasn't really like anarchists. I thought about a bomb in one of the cars."

My surprise must have shown, because she smiled. "I grew up in a mining town. I know about dynamite. But I could never get the timing to work. So I wanted to make sure the evidence pointed elsewhere. I, of course, had not forgotten my gloves, so my fingerprints weren't on the bottle."

"Did you send the notes?" I asked her.

"No." She looked at me quizzically. "Can't you guess who did?"

I shook my head.

"Norrie. He kept telling his father the notes were a joke, and they were—*his* joke." Her face darkened. "I told him I knew it was him. But of course he wouldn't admit it."

"And your husband's medicine? Was that an accident?"

She twisted the middle finger of her glove. "When you went to Philadelphia, I panicked a little. I didn't know what you'd find out. I may have told the new nurse to be sure Mr. Newsome took his sedatives. And I may have told Lucinda she must do the same. It was a very difficult time. I can't be sure whom I spoke to. Thankfully, the mistake was discovered. And then, of course, the anarchist was arrested, so . . ."

So Mr. Newsome was safe—for the time being. "Are you sure you're thankful?"

"This might surprise you, but I don't wish Mr. Newsome harm. The current arrangement is very livable." She smiled. "Sometimes when he's sleeping, I go in and lie beside him. I put a hand over his mouth, just under his nose. I see how long it takes before he struggles. But I always take my hand away."

Then she took a step toward me. "Jane, I want you to know I'm very glad I didn't have to point the finger at you. I . . . I know that wouldn't have been fair."

Fair. Her tone was earnest and simple, as if the worst thing she had done was to think of incriminating me. She hoped that having heard her story, I would understand and not punish her. And the terrible thing was, I did understand. But it wasn't enough to understand.

"You didn't have to kill Norrie," I said. "You could have left. Taken the jewelry, sold it, gone to live in Europe. I can't speak to Mr. Charley. But Norrie, there was a choice. You didn't have to take that life."

"Oh, such a worthy life," she jeered. "Who misses him?"

"His sister. Who was kind to you."

"Not recently. Anyway, it doesn't matter now. It's done."

"It matters because there's a third life—one you can save." I saw from her expression she had no comprehension as to whom I meant. "Josef Pawlicec."

"The anarchist? But he confessed."

"But he's not guilty. You know he's not. He lost his nephew. Don't let him suffer any more."

Her eyes hardened, and I saw I had made a mistake. In mentioning Josef Pawlicec's nephew, I had reminded her of the children in Schuylkill. Now she had her stone, heavy and lethal, to throw right back at them.

"I won't ask you to confess," I told her. "Just one call from you to the governor, asking for clemency. The Newsomes asking for mercy for a man many would say was harmed by the family? It would be very admirable."

"Too admirable," she said. "The kind of admirable no one believes, so they pick at it. Find the hidden selfish motive."

"Then tell them the truth. Tell people what they did to you. Let the right people be punished this time."

She laughed. "Oh, yes. That's just what happened when Evelyn Nesbit told the world what Stanford White did to her when she was sixteen. I'd be the depraved slut who robbed the nation of a fine, upstanding young man."

That was impossible to argue. Still, I picked up the soiled dress. "If you don't call the governor and save Josef Pawlicec's life, I will go to the police."

"With *that*?"

"The stains look as if someone wiped off the poker. Would an anarchist do that?"

"There's no proof as to who did the wiping."

"I have Norrie's jacket from that night. There's a stain on the lapel."

She waved a hand. "Oh, well, you'd better clean it, then."

"Traces of opiate were found on his clothes. Also albumen, a protein found in egg white. Which, of course, gives the Rose Blush its unique froth."

"Norrie drank out of several glasses that night. Hardly surprising he chose mine as well."

"But yours was the only one he spilled on himself. Maybe the opiates and the egg white aren't enough to convict you. But it would make people ask questions, questions you don't want asked."

Something flared in her eyes as I said that, and I was reminded this woman had taken two lives. Both times when she felt cornered and helpless.

I said quickly, "I don't want to cause you any more pain. I swear to you, I won't tell a living soul what I know. But I won't let Josef Pawlicec die. Just call the governor. Please, Mrs. Newsome. Rose."

For the briefest moment, there was a look of uncertain hope in her eyes; she was a child who has been found out, but senses that this time, there might be no beating. This time, perhaps, someone will understand that it is not her fault.

But the hard lessons of the past had taught her otherwise, and I watched as the child Rose Coogan faded from view, to be replaced by an altogether different creature.

Drawing herself up, she said, "My husband expects the murderer of his only son to be punished, and my husband's wishes come first."

I knew it was the time to be hard, to make threats. But I found myself still wanting to reach her. "Hasn't that been the problem? That the wants of men like your husband always come first?"

She went to the mirror. As she checked her appearance, she said, "Have you heard of this theory, social Darwinism? My husband explained it to me several months ago. The theory states that the rich are rich because they are better, smarter, more hardworking, and so more able to survive. The poor, unendowed with such fine qualities, perish. And the strong feel nothing." She glanced at me in the reflection. "Because no matter how much we have, we hold on to every last bit of it. And we treat any threat of diminishment as a threat to our existence."

Turning, she said, "We are not talking about lives of great value. So perhaps we might call this survival of the fittest?"

I asked, "Did the miners at Shickshinny have value? Did your father?"

Gathering her skirts, she said, "I must get back to my guests. I'd be grateful if you left."

"I think they did. Josef Pawlicec's life has value. If you won't speak for them, I will."

She looked up, and for a moment I was able to look fully and clearly at this young woman who was the ninth child victim of the Shickshinny Mine disaster. The child who had held her father's hand as he stumbled in the dirt only to see him fall from her world completely, leaving her to the gleeful vengeance and savage use of others. Some might say she was the luckiest; once abandoned and abused, she was now resplendent. But she had brought the taste for blood with her.

My uncle had said it: someone must speak for the dead.

I said to Rose Newsome, "And I will speak for you."

23

That night, in my room, I wrote. Page after page of what I knew about the murders of Charles Farragut and Robert Norris Newsome Jr., and the person who had killed them. When I was done with the first letter, I made a copy. One I would give to Michael Behan, the other to my uncle. In case. I didn't know what Rose Newsome would do, and I thought it wise to write everything down.

I would give her a week, I decided. If in seven days I did not see headlines announcing that the Newsomes had called for mercy, I would find a way to the police.

I was in a strange, raw state, torn between feeling that I should act *now*, point the finger *now*, and a sense of despair when I imagined the outcome. Josef Pawlicec saved or Josef Pawlicec denied his role as righteous avenger. Rose Newsome exposed or Rose Coogan destroyed for the sins of others. When I saw a man give a girl an approving look on the street, I thought of Rose's blank look when she spoke of the stares of those men as she stood on the table. I thought of what was left of Norrie's skull when she had finished with him.

Michael Behan called the house several times. I didn't take his calls. For the first time in my life, I did not trust myself to act correctly.

Toward the end of the week, I was taking a pair of Louise's shoes downstairs for cleaning when I overheard Mrs. Benchley say to Charlotte, "I expect the Newsomes are in Rhinebeck by now."

I paused outside the door.

"I hope they stay there," said Charlotte.

"Well, you know, they might. Mrs. Newsome did say at Lucinda's party that they were simply worn out with the attention of the trial. She's worried about Mr. Newsome's health. Lucinda's taking her grandmother back to Europe, so Mrs. Newsome thinks it will be better if they hide themselves away in the country."

The Newsomes did hide themselves away in Rhinebeck, rarely leaving the house except to see a few old friends of Mr. Newsome's who also had homes along the Hudson. They left for one such visit on an early Friday morning, the day before I intended to speak with the police. Mrs. Farrell later told the newspapers she was struck by the exceptional tenderness shown by Rose Newsome to her husband as they got into the car. "It was cold, so she asked for an extra blanket and tucked it around him herself. And she gave him a kiss on the top of his head."

Sometime that morning, a farmer in Hurley reported hearing an explosion. He ran to see a car at the edge of a field, engulfed in flames. There was only one road that ran through the town, so it took some time for firemen to reach the doomed vehicle. It didn't matter. The blast had been so strong, the Newsomes had died instantly, as had the chauffeur, whose name was Harold Greider.

Naturally, suspicion fell upon Mr. Greider, who had started work with the Newsomes earlier that month. There were rumors that he had once belonged to a socialist organization, that his name was Galleani or Greenberg, not Greider at all. The police felt certain he had obtained the dynamite from the Newsome estate itself, where it was being used to blast through old tree stumps. One newspaper noted that this was a popular method of removal, especially for larger trees with entrenched roots that could resist less-explosive techniques. (DuPont also touted dynamite as an excellent additive to soil; its volatile, destructive properties were said to promote rapid growth.)

There was no public funeral. Fearing for their safety, Lucinda Newsome and her grandmother remained in Europe. But the public was not as eager as it might have been to assign individual blame to Mr. Greider. The man was dead. Rather than focus on the killer who could no longer be punished, the hunger for vengeance was directed at the one who still lived: Josef Pawlicec. Calls for his speedy trial and execution were numerous and shrill.

The day we heard about the most recent Newsome murder, Michael Behan called. And this time, I answered.

We met in Central Park a few days later on a damp, unseasonably warm February afternoon. As I walked down the path I saw him standing by a bench. He had his hands in the pockets of the same dark overcoat he had shared with me on the train. His derby was tipped slightly back. I was reminded of the time I had seen him outside the Benchley house when he sent the newsboy to draw me out. I tried to remember how I had seen him as an obnoxious, cheap tabloid reporter. I couldn't match that memory to the man standing in front of me. But there was a shadow of him when he said, "She lives. I was worried Rose Newsome had taken a fire iron to you. I had to call my friends down at the morgue to make sure you hadn't turned up."

I smiled an apology, and we sat down on a bench.

"So," he said. "They got her."

"Do you think so?"

I told him about my conversation with Rose Newsome,

including her comments on dynamite. When I had finished, he said, "Jesus." After a moment, he said it again. Then nothing for a time.

Finally he asked, "You really think she killed herself? Rather than save the anarchist?"

"I do."

"But you said you wouldn't turn her in. All she had to do was make a mercy plea."

"The truth was known. No matter what I promised, it could be told to someone someday. At any moment, she could be helpless again. It would have meant being that girl on the ground throwing dust against rocks. I think if she was going to be destroyed, she wanted to be the one to do it."

He sighed. "Well, there goes Josef Pawlicec's last best hope."

"Not necessarily. I want to write to Lucinda Newsome."

"Oh, yes, Mrs. James Newsome is going to admit her son married a soiled harpy who then murdered him and her grandson." He shook his head. "She'd let a hundred Josef Pawlicecs die to keep that secret."

"Lucinda cares about justice."

"Maybe. But the girl's lost her whole family. You think she's in any state to take this in? You've got no real proof. She'll think you're mad. Or out for money."

"We've got the scrap of fabric with the sedative."

"You can't prove the sedative came from her."

"Charles Farragut."

"A swine who got his head bashed in. So the eyes are the same. It's not enough to prove anything."

"We don't have to prove anything. If we can create doubt, wouldn't that be enough to get her to think about saving Pawlicec's life?"

He thought. And shook his head. "People don't like doubt. She won't thank you for creating it. And there's no way Inspector

Blackburn's giving up his moment as the anarchist slayer. He's already planning his run for Congress."

I sat, trying to think of a way around the obstacles. I couldn't see one. The Newsome household in New York was decimated. In the wake of the Shickshinny notes, any unfamiliar correspondence would be held and examined. There was a real chance Lucinda would never even see the letter, at least not in time.

I thought of Mr. Pawlicec, how he had asked for his nephew's picture so he wouldn't be scared to die. And I brought my fist down on my leg—hard.

Startled, Behan took hold of my arm.

"It's *wrong*," I said in a loud, foolish voice.

"I know it."

He still had my hand. I let him have it. He drew his thumb across the inside of my wrist. There was comfort there, and something else. I drew back.

And said, "At least get him his nephew's picture."

"The paper got hold of it. They'll want to use it, of course. Don't yell, they paid a lot of money. But they'll make sure it gets back to the prison in time."

"You're sure they'll give it to Mr. Pawlicec? Some might say he doesn't deserve it."

"They better give it to him; I already put it in my article. 'Killer Clutches Image of Dead . . .'" He raised a hand the way he did when sketching a story.

"You're going to the execution?" I asked, surprised.

"If it happens." He glanced at me. "I'll tell you about it. If you want."

"I don't know."

For a long time, we sat without speaking.

Then Behan said, "Now here's the funny thing in all of this."

In spite of myself, I laughed, a small explosion of feeling in place of tears. One of the things I would miss about Michael

Behan was the rueful pleasure he took in the strangeness of the world.

"When I first started on this story, I had the wrong murderer."

"You thought it was Charlotte Benchley."

"No, I thought it was you."

I stared at him to see if he was joking. He was not.

"When you came running out of that room hysterical, and then I heard the Newsome kid got bashed, my first thought was *That poor girl, the bastard made a grab for her and she beat his head in. Serves him right.*"

"'Millionaire Masher Mauls Maid, Is Murdered.'"

He nodded approvingly. "Remember when I came to the house? And I asked you if Charlotte Benchley could use a friend? I thought maybe you needed one."

"And when did you decide I was innocent? Or—did you?"

"When you snipped off that piece of cloth. At first I thought, *Aha, removing evidence, clever girl.* But you didn't take all of it. Which I figured you would have done if you were guilty. Also you turned down my offer of payment, which, if you were looking at legal bills, you wouldn't have been so quick to do."

"What would you have done if I had done it?"

"Oh, I had the whole thing planned. By the end of it, you'd have been a veritable St. Agnes, with Norrie as the lustful brute of a governor's son."

"Would it have made any difference?"

"Sure. I'm a good writer. And you're a lot prettier than Mr. Pawlicec."

Instinctively, I folded my arms against the compliment as I thought of how to say what needed saying.

"Please don't make those jokes with me. I know you only mean it to be funny, but . . ."

He shifted sharply away from me and looked over his shoulder.

For a long time, he stared into the distance. Then he said, "I don't think it's funny. And you're right, I shouldn't say it."

We were silent awhile. Then I got up to leave, and he followed. As we started out of the park, I felt him become agitated. I felt anxious, too. I knew why. But words like "last time" or "good-bye" seemed unwise given what had been said.

As we approached the street, he said, "You'll like this. Remember that Mrs. Farrell you were so fond of?"

"I remember the Mrs. Farrell I detested."

"She's been arrested for stealing Rose Newsome's jewelry. Seems quite a few pieces went missing, and the young mistress had been heard shouting at her the day before."

We had reached the end of the park and the point of separate ways. Inhaling sharply, Behan shoved his hands in his pockets and said, "Well, look, maybe I'll write you. Send you a clipping."

I knew I should say no. But knowing, feeling, and doing are different things, and I found myself unwilling to let go as completely as I should. Besides, there wouldn't be much danger in a clipping. "All right. You know my address."

"I do."

"Don't . . ."

"What?"

"I shouldn't tell you how to write."

"No, but go ahead." He grinned.

"Don't make it a *story*. You know, 'the poor brute' and things like that. Just tell me what happens. You don't have to tell me how awful it is. It will be awful enough."

He tipped his derby. "Good-bye, Miss Prescott."

Then, for no good reason, he held his hand out, turned slightly, palm up. This was not a handshake, but a request. I hesitated, unsure of what was being asked: forgiveness? Friendship? I didn't know. But for no good reason, I put my hand on his, and we stood there. After a moment, I thought, *He will let go now. Holding on becomes awkward, and that's what happens. People let go.* But he did not let go, seemingly content to stay as long as I was willing, his fingers under mine. Until they curled together and whatever had been asked for had been given.

★　★　★

The trial of Josef Pawlicec proceeded without further incident. As he had confessed, it was only left to decide whether his callousness and refusal to name his associates merited the death penalty. In the wake of the latest murders, many felt the answer was obvious, and most were confident of the outcome, especially Inspector Blackburn, who professed his deep faith in the American judicial system.

The trial was not spoken of in the Benchley household. Occasionally, when riding the bus or el, I caught sight of a copy of *Town Topics*. An illustration of Josef Pawlicec at the defendant's table depicted him as rough and sullen looking. At no time did he deviate from his story that he had murdered Robert Norris Newsome Jr. to avenge his nephew's death. His lawyer called upon his sister to testify. Tearfully, she insisted that her brother could never have killed anyone. But this was dismissed out of hand as the words of a heartbroken woman. His lawyer then produced a handwriting expert who said that the notes did not match Mr. Pawlicec's hand or linguistic patterns. This was also dismissed, as it was assumed the notes had been written by an accomplice whom Mr. Pawlicec refused to name.

Mr. Pawlicec's boss's testimony proved that the murder had been premeditated. The absence of the ice tongs, supposed to be the murder weapon, showed an attempt to evade justice. As promised, Michael Behan sent me clippings. One with a note: *Doesn't look good.*

I was very fond of elephants as a child. I do not know why.

Something about their improbability; what grand design had chosen such large, flapping ears, the sparse tail, the sensitive probing trunk, the stocky, wrinkled legs for a creature of such massive size. On a few occasions, my uncle indulged me by taking me to the Central Park Zoo. I can remember seeing a young elephant reaching with its trunk to grasp its parent's tail, trotting along behind in perfect security.

I had an illustration, cut from the newspaper, of Tip, the zoo's most famous attraction. He had once belonged to a circus owner named Adam Forepaugh, a great rival of P. T. Barnum's. In the Forepaugh Circus, elephants were made to ride tricycles and do other tricks. When Tip killed his keeper, he was donated to the Central Park Zoo. He arrived from Philadelphia, weighing five tons, and chained to an older, more sedate elephant named Old Jennie. They were met by a crowd of a thousand people, which grew steadily as the elephants were marched from the docks at Twenty-third Street, past the West Side tenements, and finally on to Fifth Avenue, where their presence caused great consternation among the city's wealthier residents. As *The New York Times* reported, "The masses have no respect for the classes, and in this case, the masses were all moving in one direction and moving rapidly to keep abreast of the steady-going elephants."

It may have been Tip's happiest day in New York. At the zoo, he was given into the care of William Snyder, who kept him confined for long periods in a martingale bridle that did not allow the elephant to lift his head. Snyder looked the other way when children fed Tip apples laced with pepper, and beat him. He taunted him and beat him himself. He then reported the elephant had tried to kill him with a swat of his trunk. As punishment, Snyder sawed off twelve inches from each of his tusks.

Tip was kept so confined for five years. He tried to escape, once breaking through the bars of his cage and pulling up the bolts of his chains. Snyder insisted the beast must be put down. Others

argued, saying Tip simply needed more exercise and that if he mis-
behaved, the correct treatment was to chain him and beat him
"until he squealed." Snyder may have taken this advice, because a
few years later, Tip again tried to kill him. He had already killed
four men in the Forepaugh Circus and gone after four more in
Central Park. The *Times* announced, TIP MUST REFORM OR DIE!

A plan of execution was devised. The other elephants in the
Elephant House, Juno and Little Tom, were moved out of
harm's way. Thousands of spectators were kept at a distance.
Tip would be given three servings of carrots and apples. The first
two would be safe, the third filled with prussic acid.

Tip did not like the carrots and apples, and rejected them. He
was given a bowl of bran laced with cyanide. This, he ate. And
spent the next nine hours dying in agony.

He writhed, throwing himself against the bars of his cage,
nearly breaking them. He snapped his chains, swung his blunted
tusks at the walls. He trumpeted, spraying blood. At one point, he
managed to break through the wall, and seemed on the verge of
freedom, but then he fell to the ground. With a last wail, he died.
His hide and bones were donated to the American Museum of
Natural History.

My illustration of Tip is an elephant form hastily scratched in
ink; in some ways, it is not an accomplished work. But it shows a
beast in chains, his great head lowered, his ears slack, long tusks
nearly touching the ground. There is no ferocity in his expression;
only exhaustion and sadness. The caption reads: THE ELEPHANT
"TIP" WHO IS ALWAYS READY FOR A BRUSH.

On the day they announced that Josef Pawlicec would die in
the electric chair, I took it out and set it in the corner of my mirror,
where I saw it each morning and then again before I went to bed.

Josef Pawlicec was executed at Sing Sing Prison on March 18.
Asked if he would like to say anything to the Newsome family,
he said, "I'm not sorry for what I done. Maybe it wasn't right, what

they done to the Newsome fellow. But it was worse what they done to those kids." The words were taken as the final proof of this remorseless killer's cruelty. Nobody noted the poor grammar.

The report in *Town Topics* clearly stated that Josef Pawlicec had been holding his nephew's photograph as he made the walk from his cell to the electric chair. After the execution, the picture disappeared. It was presumed stolen and sold to a collector of morbid mementoes.

At the table the next morning, Mr. Benchley read the report of the execution. Folding his newspaper, he put it on the table and said, "Well, that's settled."

24

A *week after the* execution, William Tyler arrived at the Benchley home and was given tea. He had been home for the spring holidays but would be returning to Yale. Charlotte was not present—the ugliness between her and Beatrice was still too fresh for ease of association. But Louise smiled, passed shortbread, and shyly answered William's questions about her stay in Philadelphia.

Mrs. Benchley, I am proud to say, managed to stay silent through the entire event.

When it was time for William to leave, Louise rose. For a moment, her head drooped and her shoulders slumped. I felt Mrs. Benchley's happiness become anxiety, and braced myself for intervention.

But then Louise straightened herself, lifted her head, and in a clear voice wished William a good trip back to New Haven.

At the door, I handed William his hat and coat. He said formally, "Thank you, Jane."

I smiled and stepped back, as was appropriate.

Then I heard him say, "Shame about that fellow. I meant to . . ."

I nodded, understanding that William was apologizing for letting down Mr. Pawlicec. Or himself. At some point, maybe it had been made clear to him that people thought his newborn ideals faintly ridiculous. Unable to withstand that scorn, he had fallen back into tagging along. I could hardly be angry. For all intents and purposes, I had done the same.

"Have a safe journey, Mr. William."

★ ★ ★

On one of my afternoons off, I found time to visit Mr. Rosenfeld and thank him again for his efforts. He seemed embarrassed by the thank-you and, nervously polishing his glasses, he asked, "Did you solve your mystery of the egg whites?"

"I did."

He put his glasses back on. "Satisfactorily?"

"No."

"I read about Mr. Pawlicec's nephew. It's hard not to feel he had some cause."

"If not a taste for egg whites and opiates."

He glanced up. "But no one was interested in that curious detail?"

"None of the right people, I'm afraid." I paused. "Especially after the deaths of Mr. and Mrs. Newsome."

"Yes, that was terrible. Do you think that was also the work of"—he paused—"the egg-white expert?"

"Yes. But I don't think we have to worry about them harming anyone else."

"Well, that's something."

The bell over the door rang as a customer came in. "Thank you again, Mr. Rosenfeld."

"You're very welcome, Miss Prescott."

★ ★ ★

On a day in late March, Mrs. Benchley and her daughters traveled downtown to take tea with a Mrs. Baiman. Mrs. Baiman was
from an old family, and she still lived near Washington Square
Park in one of the town houses that once formed the epicenter of
the city's old aristocracy. The park had served as the city's potter's
field. In 1889, when they built the arch to commemorate the cen-
tennial of George Washington's inauguration, they had uncovered
human remains and gravestones. (The arch itself was designed
by Stanford White.) As we passed under the arch, I thought how
odd it was to see the couples strolling, the children running, and
the nannies pushing carriages over the bodies of the unknown
dead.

Charlotte had had some dresses altered at a nearby seamstress,
and I was to collect them and drive them back to the house with
O'Hara, who would return later to pick up the Benchley ladies. It
was a Saturday in early spring, and as I walked to the seamstress,
I tried to feel the freshness of the afternoon and not brood on what
was past. In many ways, I was fortunate. I was healthy, relatively
young, and employed. Perhaps, I thought, this summer I would get
up the nerve to ask for a raise. Or even a promotion to housekeeper,
as Mrs. Benchley had still not found one who suited her. Although
no one could pretend that serving as a housekeeper was a tempo-
rary position. That was a position you held for life. An older
woman's place. Older and usually unmarried.

The dresses that Charlotte had had altered were not black. Or
even gray or mauve. The previous week, without explanation, she
had instructed me to put her mourning dresses into storage. She
was still avoiding public appearances, but the envelopes had
started to gather on the front table, and the phone had started to
ring. One of the dresses I was picking up today was an extravagant
confection of blue and gold silk. There was talk of a European trip.

And I had the feeling Charlotte would be yawning through the opera and peeking over her fan come the fall.

It was late afternoon by the time I was walking back to the car with the dresses. In my memory, the sound is much louder than perhaps it was in reality. It was a great gust, an explosion of air, then the sound of glass shattering. I looked up and saw black smoke churning in the sky over Washington Place. The smoke writhed, almost muscular, as if it were gathering itself into a great fist. People began to run. So did I, without quite knowing why.

A crowd had already gathered at the Asch Building by the time I got there. A policeman shouted at us to keep our distance, but the heat of the flames was a more effective deterrent. Everyone was looking up. I followed their collective gaze up to the ninth floor and saw two women crawling out onto the window ledge. The smoke billowed around them. Flames broke through the shattered window, catching their hair. Clasping hands, they jumped. The crowd shrieked as one, and I did not hear the women land. I did not hear it.

More women came, screaming at the windows, hanging from the ledge. Their skirts on fire, they tumbled out. Some held their arms out as they fell, as if they hoped to fly. People grabbed the blankets from horses, sheets and curtains from nearby houses. Men held them stretched taut, but the force of the fall was too great, and the bodies wrenched the blankets from their hands as they slammed into the pavement. In some places, they crashed through the cellar deadlights, leaving gaping holes in the street. The firemen poured water onto the building; it flooded out again through the windows, cascading down the sides of the building, past the banner signs for Blum's Clothing Specialists and Harris Brothers Men's Clothing, finally streaming into the gutters red with blood.

One hundred and forty-six people died at the Triangle Shirt-waist Factory that day, one hundred and twenty-three of them women, including Ruth Solomon, twenty. They might have escaped, but the factory doors had been locked to prevent workers from taking unauthorized work breaks. The cause of the fire was thought to be a cigarette, an ember that burst into flame as it fed on the brittle, flimsy fabric used for the shirtwaist.

The bodies were laid out on the sidewalk before being taken to a makeshift morgue at the pier at East Twenty-sixth Street. The police called for a hundred coffins, but the city did not have enough. If the bodies were not too badly burned, they were wrapped in shrouds. As one newspaper wrote, "Men and women, boys and girls were of the dead that littered the street: That is actually the condition—the streets were littered with bodies."

The precinct at Mercer Street was overwhelmed. A search was made of every body for some kind of identification. When a name was found, it was written on a scrap of cloth and pinned to the body. Six bodies were never identified.

For that day and a few days after, all the city's energies were concentrated on the victims of the Triangle Fire. Everyone, it seemed, from the grand dames of Fifth Avenue to saloon denizens wanted to do "something." The next day, I went down to the refuge. The Benchleys did not question my request, apparently feeling it was their contribution to the relief effort. But the refuge was empty. All the women had gone to help. I went, too, although I was among the many who had nothing to offer but a pair of hands. Some of the women from the refuge could translate for the mostly Jewish and Italian families searching for daughters, wives, and sisters—or those who needed assistance in burying them. As I neared the crowds by the pier, I heard street vendors shouting, "Get 'em while they last! Souvenirs of the big fire! Get a ring from the finger of a dead girl!"

I found Anna quite by accident. She was talking to a man in Italian, her voice gentle and firm. From his age and his expression, I guessed his daughter had been found. I waited until she was finished, then said, "Anna?"

That evening, we sat on a bench by the East River and ate sandwiches and ginger ale someone had donated to volunteers. Anna had spent the day talking in two languages, and I thought maybe she would prefer silence. But she said, "You know who sent the sandwiches? Andrew Carnegie."

"You're joking."

She shook her head, biting into one. "They're all making donations now. All scared."

"People are calling for the factory owners to be charged with murder."

Anna shrugged. "They won't be found guilty. Not by a trial jury."

"It's too big this time, Anna. People will want to see someone punished."

"Someone," she conceded. "Not necessarily the right someone. In the end, they'll make excuses, find perfectly good reasons one hundred and forty-six people died." She looked at me. "Whatever happened to that other someone? Your scrap of cloth?"

I looked down at my sandwich in its paper. "We haven't talked about the car bombing that killed the Newsomes."

"No." She smiled, puzzled. "Do you want to ask me about that?"

"No."

"Because you don't want to know."

"Because I do know. I know you had nothing to do with it."

Anna gave me a look of mocking admiration. "But you know who did."

"Yes, I do. And I think for the murderer of Norrie Newsome, there was some justice."

Anna looked at me quizzically. I stared out at the river, saw a small boat steaming toward the Bronx. So close to the Atlantic Ocean, the river had the smell of sea, and for a moment, I thought of the father who had brought me to this island, then left me as if, having done his duty and gotten me here, America would now take care of me.

"Did you write the notes?" I heard myself ask.

It was a long time before Anna answered. "Not myself."

So I was right and Rose Coogan wrong. The notes would have been too great an act of imagination for Norrie; he would have had to put himself in another person's shoes, something that completely self-centered young man was incapable of doing.

I asked, "Was there a plan?"

"There was."

A plan. A plan to kill. To end a life—to what end? I glanced at Anna, wondering what she imagined the death of Robert Newsome Sr. would have achieved. Had McKinley's murder achieved anything? The *L.A. Times* bombing? I thought of the cheers that had greeted the news of Josef Pawlicec's death. *That will show them. They can't get away with it.* But no one ever seemed to see it, even if they were shown with great brutality, and they often tried again. I remembered Rose Coogan's words: *They just liked throwing rocks.*

I heard Anna say, "We would have been careful. Made sure—"

You were not hurt. I waved my hand, not wanting to hear more. I did not want to ask if the plan had a date, if that date was before or after Norrie's marriage to Charlotte. I did not want to ask what the method was to have been, if the casualties could have been limited or if they would have been difficult to calculate. I did not need to ask her if my life had any value to her. Because hers had value to me; she was my friend, however ridiculous she might find that word. I refused to give that up.

Instead I raised my bottle and said, "To Josef."

Anna smiled, raised hers. "To Josef. And to Janusz."

"Janusz."

I thought of Ruth Solomon, laughing that she was to be a seamstress after all. "To Ruth Solomon."

Anna echoed the name.

Almost to myself, I said, "To Rose Coogan."

Then I looked back at the pier where so many people were still searching for the people who belonged to them.

25

This week, the newspapers announced with great sorrow the death of Lucinda Newsome. *Town Topics* has long since ceased publication, but the *Times, The Wall Street Journal,* and the *Daily News,* as well as radio and television broadcasts, paid tribute to New York's leading philanthropist. Her image—still homely yet compelling at the age of ninety-two—was everywhere. Flags were lowered at the Metropolitan Museum of Art. Lights were dimmed at the opera and on Broadway. The carriage horses of Central Park wore black plumes. Mourning wreaths were placed around the necks of the stone lions, Patience and Fortitude, at the New York Public Library.

The mayor offered the predictable obsequies. Society writers fell over themselves to capture the quintessential moments of Lucinda Newsome's life and career. She had married, but once widowed had gone back to her maiden name in honor of her slain family. The newspapers had never called her anything else. The funeral service was held at St. Thomas's Episcopal Church on Fifth Avenue. There was fevered speculation as to who would be invited, who would not, and why. The public was invited to view during certain limited hours.

I did not attend. Although a representative of the Gorman Refuge for Women was sent in recognition of Lucinda Newsome's extraordinary generosity to the organization.

Many years ago, many, many years, I met with Lucinda Newsome. Strangely, we met in the very same house where her brother had been murdered, but we spoke in her office, not the library. I told her what I knew and what I suspected. I told her one other person knew it as well, but neither he nor I had any interest in making it public; that would be for her to decide. Although a public figure, Lucinda Newsome remained a very private person, and I was not surprised that she did not choose to do so. Nor was I surprised when she began contributing some of her vast wealth to the Women's Trade Union League, Hull House, and the Gorman Refuge for Women.

But now that she has died, I can tell the full truth of what happened that Christmas Eve of 1910. Of course, not many people remember the Newsome murder now. It has been followed by so much slaughter, both intimate and global. (The Newsome murder was my first encounter with violent death, but far from the last. However, those are stories for another time.) By telling what I know, I hope to redeem the reputation of Ida Pawlicec, who insisted on her brother's innocence to the day she died in 1956. And, of course, the reputation of Josef Pawlicec.

Will it matter to people today? If she were still alive, Anna would point out that society makes its own judgments as to which deaths matter and which do not. The death of what she called "one stupid, worthless, rich boy" mobilized the city's full resources in the capture and punishment of his killer. In contrast, the owners of the Triangle Factory, Max Blanck and Isaac Harris, were found not guilty of manslaughter. A civil suit later earned the victims' families $75 per victim. However, the insurance company paid

Blanck and Harris $60,000—or $400 per victim. So they came out of it not too badly.

And yet, whether out of guilt or a sense that the center could not hold without some shift in the balance, change did come in the wake of the Triangle Fire. New laws mandated the presence of fire extinguishers, alarms, and sprinkler systems. The working hours for women and children were shortened. What Josef Pawlicec's lonely death—or Norrie Newsome's, if you prefer to see it that way—failed to achieve, one hundred and forty-six sacrifices did.

Shortly after Lucinda Newsome's funeral, I received a letter. It was in an oddly shaped envelope, and the stamp was foreign, although I could not tell from which country. There was no return address, and at first, I hesitated to open it. But something about the beauty of the handwriting, the richness of the blue ink, the use of my maiden name, intrigued me and I read.

> *Dear Jane,*
> *It's strange to be old, isn't it? Especially when you've*
> *been dead for seventy years. I was sorry not to see you*
> *at Lucinda's funeral. I had hoped we could talk. You*
> *see, I never properly thanked you. You've protected my*
> *privacy all these years. You could have sold my*
> *story—perhaps to that handsome reporter. You didn't.*
> *You kept your promise and that's a rare thing.*
>
> *(I also thank you for the kind suggestion that I*
> *take the jewels and disappear.*
>
> *Don't worry too much about Greider. I hired him*
> *personally and he was deserving of the honor.)*
>
> *But I release you from your promise. I don't have*
> *a lot of time left.*
>
> *You may now speak ill of the dead.*
> *With affection and respect,*
> *Rose*

If Anna were here, or Michael Behan, or Louise Benchley, or Norrie Newsome himself, I'm sure they would say, "No, Jane, it wasn't like that." They would remind me of things I've forgotten, insist that so-and-so said this and not that. They would tell me that I have portrayed one person too kindly, another too harshly. They would be aware of things I am not, because I never witnessed them.

But this is the truth as I know it. As I lived it and saw it lived. Make of it what you will.